Beneath His Wings:
The Plot to Murder Lindbergh

A Novel by

F. Mark Granato

Beneath His Wings:
The Plot to Murder Lindbergh

By

F. Mark Granato

Edited by Gail A. Donahue

F. Mark Granato
fmgranato@aol.com

Published in the United States of America, August 2011

To Bobbie, my wife...

You were <u>so</u> worth the chase.

Author's Statement

Beneath His Wings: The Plot to Murder Lindbergh is a story that combines historical facts concerning Charles Lindbergh's epic transatlantic flight with both real and imagined characters, places and events. The supposed plot to ambush the great aviator is entirely fiction, although this tale includes actual persons of the post-WWI German military, all of whom have long since passed. The story, however, is largely a product of my imagination and the "What if?" game I played as a young boy with my beloved Irish grandfather, William J. McGrath. After fleeing the potato famine in Ireland, he came to the United States only to be recruited to serve with the Allied Expeditionary Forces in France in exchange for American citizenship. The gentle old man would often share with me fantastic stories of the Great War, and we would also talk for hours about the *Titanic* tragedy, Lindbergh's epic flight and other profound historical events of the early 20th century that captivated him. In the many days and hours we spent together, my grandfather fueled my imagination with his vivid stories — some fact, some fiction — and instilled in me a love of history and what might have been.

F. Mark Granato
August 2011

Dingle Bay, Ireland
May, 1927

The pre-dawn stillness of the waterfront was broken by the clipped gait of a wooden leg being dragged across the dock with the crutch of a homemade hickory cane. The noise reverberated over the harbor as it approached, much like the sound of a lame, shoeless horse. It was a familiar echo to those who worked the waterfront and recognized its source immediately.

Seamus McGill's ears perked up. His fishing trawler was tied off at the end of the long, salt-licked timber pier, and he listened carefully for the direction of the pace as it drew near. McGill was well acquainted with the crippled gait that belonged to old Paddy Griffin, the one-legged fixture of the squat but crowded village docks of Dingle Bay in County Kerry in southwestern Ireland. He supposed that the old man, more than likely in the company of at least the day's second pint of cheap whiskey, was perhaps eighty yards away. There'd be just time enough to bring aboard the two unmarked wooden crates that were piled on the dock before the old man arrived. The unusual freight was sure to attract his attention. McGill sighed at the interruption. He should have known better than to think he'd escape Paddy's smell for the unusual even this early into the dawn, when the day was still cloudy and full of cool, moist fog.

It wasn't that he didn't have a bit of patience or pity for the old fisherman. A homeless, grizzly character with skin leathered the color of tanned riding boots by years of tending his nets in deep water, Paddy Griffin's left leg was missing just below the knee, victim of a fouled winch decades before. While he might not have had a good bath and a shave in a month, Paddy's stomach was always full from the handouts of the locals. The trouble was, he'd trade a meal and some whiskey for the gossip he collected in his endless wanderings along the harbor village of Dingle Bay. From time to time, that was a problem.

Dingle Bay was located on the tip of a peninsula, which ran some twenty-five miles from northeast to southwest into the Atlantic Ocean. Its eight hundred inhabitants, nearly all of who survived off the bounty of the sea, found little joy in life other than sharing gossip over a pint of dark ale at Kerry's Ring, the local pub. An hour before dawn, and Paddy was already on the prowl for fodder to trade, despite the chilling fog that hung heavily on the docks.

"Who's that getting ready to break water?" Paddy yelled, sure that someone was preparing to cast off his lines, but not of his identity. "I'd be thinking 'tis a tad early for even the hungriest mackerel man this far southwest on the shoals to be shoving off."

With the loading of supplies still to be done and no escape from the intruder, McGill responded.

"There, there now, Paddy, 'tis just yer old friend, Seamus McGill," he shouted back through the fog while quickly wrestling the two heavy wooden crates aboard. He tossed a soiled canvas tarp over them.

"With the beloved Mrs. McGill gone to be with her favorite saints ... the night 'tis no longer a friend," McGill paused, the words sticking in his throat. "You'll be finding me dragging my nets near Baileybunnion for a few days to keep me busy. I hear the herring are running strong, they are," said the heavy-hearted fisherman.

Paddy finally came into view, dragging his wooden leg beneath him. "'Tis true, dear Seamus. God tests a man's strength to share a roof with a woman, but even more so if he calls her home before ye."

McGill muffled a laugh at the thought of the old man talking on as if he were an expert at marriage. No sane woman had ever considered him as a potential husband, he was sure. His own prospects weren't looking very good either, McGill thought, although he certainly wasn't in the market for a new bride. He had buried his one and only true love, Mary Elizabeth Devereaux McGill, just more than a year ago, their three grown children at his side. The cancer had taken her quickly, for which he both thanked God and cursed him daily. He would trade his soul for one more day with her.

Seamus McGill, a fisherman all his life, had been captain of his own thirty-five-foot fishing trawler, *The Lovely Mary*, for nearly forty years. He had built the boat with his own two hands. The ocean was all he knew, and now in his early sixties, he wasn't looking for new adventure — or companionship.

Once, it hadn't been unusual for him to put out to sea for a week or more, about as long as he could endure being without his Mary; but lately, he'd had no reason to hurry home to Dingle Bay. On this late April morning, he was busy loading provisions that would last him much more than a month, if necessary. There was no Mrs. McGill waiting for him; and truth be told, he had more than fishing to do on this voyage.

As dawn broke over the fishing village, McGill stored away the last of his provisions, filled his tanks with diesel; and without so much as a look over his shoulder at his hometown or a word of goodbye to his children, slowly motored his way out of Dingle Harbor. He took in a long breath to fill his lungs with crisp, salt air, then pointed the nose of *The Lovely Mary* on a northerly path toward the Killarney coast, about eighty miles away. There he would turn west for deeper waters a hundred miles or more off the coast of Ireland.

McGill had made the journey countless times in his lifetime, his soul at peace and his mind at ease. He felt no such well being this morning, in fact, quite the opposite.

Steering his boat through the breakwater at the harbor's mouth, he reflected on the encounter he'd had with a stranger last night at Kerry's Ring. The man had been wearing a suit and tie that made him stand out in the crowd. McGill thought he was a teacher, or perhaps a salesman. He'd been wrong. The tall, thin, middle-aged man, who introduced himself as Matthew, said he was a scientist.

He man bought another round and explained that he was conducting a "scientific experiment" and needed the help of a trawler captain planning to make water. The work was simple and would pay McGill handsomely, two hundred pounds for a few days work. All he had to do was position *The Lovely Mary* at a spot near where the fisherman had intended to cast his nets anyway, then wait and watch. The radio equipment McGill had hauled on board would help him report what he saw.

He scratched the rough stubble of beard on his chin and wondered again about the stranger who had given him so much money for so little work. It didn't really matter who or what he was, McGill thought. The offer was just too good to pass up in such hard times. But something nagged at him. Why had the man singled him out? There must have been two dozen or more fishermen crowded around the bar last night, many of whom sailed their own boats. Perhaps it was because he had been sitting alone, as he usually did, deep in his thoughts as he stared into the head of his ale.

Shaking off the irritation, he brought his attention back to the sea. The fisherman swung the bow of *The Lovely Mary* hard to port and braced for the white-capped chop that would signal the flow of the River Maine as it entered the bay of the Dingle Peninsula. Then he sat back in his worn captain's chair and put a match to his well-seasoned corn pipe. Already he could feel his tensions begin to ease at home on the water.

While his thoughts turned quickly once more to his Mary Elizabeth, a solitary figure dressed in a dark suit and tie stood out of view on the docks and took note of McGill's departure. The report he would pass on later in the morning would please some people who cared for such information. They would also be especially satisfied to know that Seamus McGill, a man of fierce pride and loyalty, appeared to be completely unsuspicious that he unwittingly had become a sad pawn in a saga that had taken roots nearly a decade before.

One

Nearly a decade after the Armistice brought a cessation to the fierce aerial combat that had marked the Great World War, American fighter pilot Eddie Rickenbacker remained a hero of the surviving French and American pilots who had joined him as members of the 94th Aero Squadron. For his leadership and bravery in commanding the squadron which had defeated Germany's vaunted air force, the Luftstreitkräfte, and ultimately seized control of the skies over Europe's Western Front, Captain Rickenbacker had been awarded the Medal of Honor.

When the fighting ended, the war hero returned to the United States not only convinced of the importance of the role of the airplane in future hostilities, but also with a vision of its commercial possibilities. Unfortunately, without conflict to motivate more rapid development, he was sadly disappointed to watch the evolution of modern aviation slow to a crawl.

Rickenbacker was befriended by Raymond Orteig, a New York City hotelier and self-made millionaire who had been gripped by a lifelong fascination with aviation. The Frenchman's allure to flying was spurred by the Captain's remarkable stories of savage "dogfights", the aerial battles which undoubtedly became more romanticized as the real horrors of war faded. Orteig saw Rickenbacker and his comrades as young men who had literally danced with death high above the blood-soaked trenches and battlefields. Through his piercing black eyes, Orteig saw them as heroes akin to the Knights of the Round Table.

Although he was short, balding, and sported a waxed vaudevillian mustache, the Frenchman's somewhat comical appearance was deceiving and caused many to underestimate him. He had a brilliant mind for all things financial, and by the age of thirty-five had indeed become very wealthy. He could afford to rub elbows with those bigger than life personalities he chose and to probe their imaginations and dreams. Eddie Rickenbacker was Orteig's mind's eye to the azure blue skies he dreamt of above the clouds.

The millionaire stunned Rickenbacker with a question one evening as they dined privately at his Brevoort Hotel. The pair had been locked in a discussion over the potential for stronger Franco-American ties in the post war period.

"My dear Eddie, I have a question to pose to you," Orteig said while savoring an after dinner cigar and a rare, aged port which he had opened especially for this occasion. It was a Garrafeira Vinho do Portois, made from the grapes of a single harvest in the Douro Valley in the northern provinces of Portugal. The bottle was worth six months of their waiter's wages.

Rickenbacker sipped slowly, luxuriating in the bouquet of the prized port, but was puzzled over the sudden, more serious tone of his host. He carefully placed his crystal snifter down on the starched, white linen tablecloth and gave Raymond Orteig his full attention.

"Eddie… or should I say 'Captain' Rickenbacker?" the Frenchman began. "I ask you to indulge me for a moment with your vivid imagination and to wrap your flying scarf around your neck once again."

"Raymond, whatever…" the pilot began to protest, somewhat embarrassed.

"Please, Eddie, do as I ask."

Rickenbacker frowned, feeling adolescent, but honored his host by closing his eyes and letting his mind drift back into the cockpit of the rickety SPAD XIII he had flown into battle over France. He imagined again the smoothness of the white silk against his skin as he tucked it into the collar of his leather flying jacket. At once he was climbing through the clouds through ten thousand feet. It was not difficult for his imagination to take him there. He had used the same romantic description on more than one beautiful redhead who inevitably succumbed to his charms.

"And now my question to you," Orteig said with a seriousness that brought Rickenbacker back to earth.

"Why, Raymond," the Captain laughed softly. "I fear that you are in a particularly passionate mood this evening. Something tells me we should find you some suitable company for the night. I will hardly do, dear friend."

Orteig did not smile.

"Well then, what is the question, my friend?" the pilot asked.

Orteig took careful aim and fired.

"Captain Rickenbacker, my question is the following." The hotelier hesitated, making sure he had finally had the pilot's full attention.

"Would it be possible to fly an airplane nonstop, a so-called transatlantic flight, between New York and Paris?"

The former fighter pilot didn't blink. The question was not new to him, but he sat in silence for a moment before responding, as if newly contemplating the possibilities.

"That would depend on many things, Raymond. If you mean, can we gas up a surplus Army 'Jenny' tonight and go and give the old girl a whirl in time for espresso on the patio of La Crillion by the Place du la Concorde, I'd say there are a few things we might want to consider first." He laughed at his own humor, still underestimating Orteig's sincerity.

"The first problem is traffic, of course," Rickenbacker continued jokingly. "The Champs Elysees can be so difficult early in the morning. We must time our arrival just right."

It was only after Orteig did not respond that Rickenbacker finally realized his French friend was deadly serious.

"Eddie, there are times you try my patience. Please answer the question."

The pilot was startled by his friend's determination.

"Why yes...yes, of course, Raymond. The answer is: no, it is not possible now, but yes, it may be possible in the future."

Orteig pondered the response. "I see. How long do you foresee before such an attempt could be reasonably attempted?" he probed.

"Raymond..." Rickenbacker finally saw where his friend was headed and hesitated before responding impolitely to his ignorance.

"It is at least a thirty-six-hundred-mile journey on the Great Arctic Circle route, which of course would be the shortest path between New York and Paris. At the moment, we do not possess the ability, or rather, the mechanics and equipment to fly an airplane nonstop between New York and Washington, D.C. That is less than two hundred fifty miles. There are many things that must improve before a flight could be attempted that is …" he thought for a moment, "fifteen times that length, in the harshest conditions, I might add, with any chance at all for success."

"Such as?" Orteig pressed immediately.

"Fuel burn, for one," Rickenbacker responded without hesitation, obviously having given the idea some previous thought. "I envision an aircraft with at least three motors for such an expedition. They would require more than two thousand pounds of fuel, an enormous weight to lift off the ground. Another concern would be navigation which poses its own set of problems. Such a course has never been charted before, and one would have to be a genius to plot a crossing by the stars."

Orteig did not blink.

"Design of the aircraft would be another huge consideration," Rickenbacker continued. "There have been few advances since the War and an open cockpit biplane would hardly be up to the task. You have no idea how flimsy such a craft would be, and a pilot could not survive across thirty-six hundred miles exposed to the frightful elements."

Orteig looked puzzled. Rickenbacker paused, searching for an analogy.

"My friend, do you recall sailing the North Atlantic as a young boy when you came here from France? Did the frigid cold, the ice and heavy seas frighten you? Well, I can assure you, the only thing more dreadful or terrorizing than sailing over such a mass of water would be to fly over it. The cold would be intense. A pilot would have to deal with constant squalls and high cross winds, and there would be the continuous and terrifying problem of icing on the wings to contend with. Too much ice and the weight of it would simply make the airplane fall from the sky -- that is if the wings didn't break off first. Frankly, a pilot could not close his eyes for the entire journey."

Rickenbacker drained his port and took a deep drag from his cigar. "Having said all that, I suggest that there is one final ingredient, but perhaps the most important one of all."

Now it was Orteig's turn to raise an eye.

"Yes?"

"The pilot must have the biggest pair of balls on the planet," Rickenbacker concluded.

The two laughed aloud and exchanged a toast. "Then I am dining with our candidate," Orteig said.

"Hardly, " Rickenbacker replied, both complimented and amused. "I'm afraid I'm a few years beyond my prime for such adventure. But tell me, please, what is it you have in mind? I know you are thinking of something wicked."

Orteig laughed again, but his mind was whirling. Despite the pessimistic outlook of his dinner guest, Rickenbacker had actually convinced Orteig of two things. First, that a transatlantic flight could eventually be achieved; and second, that it would fuel a race for aircraft development that would spur an investment in commercial aviation. It was only a matter of time.

The following day, May 22, 1919, the hotel magnate wrote to the President of the Aero Club of America:

Gentlemen:

As a stimulus to the courageous aviators, I desire to offer, through the auspices and regulations of the Aero Club of America, a prize of twenty-five thousand dollars to the first aviator crossing the Atlantic in one flight, from Paris to New York or New York to Paris, all other details in your care.

Yours very sincerely,
Raymond Orteig

Although Orteig's cash reward was a handsome sum and quickly caught the attention of the world's aviation community, there were no takers. While there were quite a few pilots who had the nerve to attempt such a feat, there simply was no airplane flying or even on the drawing boards that could come close to the requirements of the attempt.

Five years later, the Orteig Prize remained unclaimed. However, several major advances in aviation design began to encourage the attempt at a transatlantic crossing. Aircraft design and performance was quickly being revolutionized by two advances: the monoplane, which used only a single wing, and aircraft motors that produced several times more power with greater efficiencies than even Eddie Rickenbacker had envisioned. Suddenly, a flight of thirty-six hundred miles between New York and Paris did not seem so formidable. The vision was grand, and the fame and reward was even more seductive. The renewed Orteig Prize captured the attention of every pilot in the world who had an ounce of adventure in his soul.

Nations, too, coveted the Orteig Prize, but some with far less quixotic motivation. Where the grievous wounds of defeat continued to fester in those countries defeated in the Great War, the opportunity for renewed national pride and prestige posed by the transatlantic challenge was equally compelling -- yet hardly as noble.

Two

Orteig had been right about his contest prompting renewed enthusiasm for engineering innovation that would provide more power, speed and efficiency for a new generation of aircraft. Combined, the improvements meant the ability to fly farther, faster and safer. But the act of lifting a heavier than air machine took some doing itself, and the performance leaps that both he and Rickenbacker had envisioned came more in the form of baby steps.

Simply put, the challenges that a pilot would have to confront in order to cross the typically foul-weathered Atlantic were enormous. Although there were many pilots who investigated an attempt, an airplane capable of making the journey simply did not yet exist by 1924. Additionally, the reality was that the cost of a conventional approach to the challenge — a fully equipped, state-of-the-art, three-engine, multi-passenger commercial transport — was far in excess of the Orteig Prize money.

Nonetheless, few pilots thought of little else than the Orteig Prize. It was not until 1926, a full seven years after Orteig had originally announced his competition, that serious challenges to win the Prize began to take shape.

By then, aircraft design and technology improvements had put the Orteig Prize within reach. In particular, improvements in aircraft engine design by the Wright Aeronautical Corporation of Paterson, New Jersey, made feasible the lifting of enough gasoline, at some six pounds per gallon, to enable a transatlantic flight on the Great

Arctic Circle route. Indeed, from a power and fuel efficiency perspective, a New York-to-Paris transatlantic crossing was now possible, but there would be little margin of error for a challenger.

Several teams in Europe and the United States, all with the backing of financial syndicates, announced plans to attempt the flight. It seemed all but certain that the Orteig Prize would be claimed within the year. Excitement built in the U.S., and particularly in France, as war heroes, adventurers and explorers stepped up to the contest, most with strong financial support and deep pockets as they announced their planned attempts one by one.

The very reputations of those announcing participation in the race kindled daily news coverage. Commander Richard E. Byrd, having just returned from his claimed successful flight over the North Pole and with the financing of his department store magnate friend, Rodman Wanamaker, was one of the first to enter the Orteig competition.

French war hero and ace René Paul Fonck quickly followed suit, as did fellow Frenchmen Charles Nungesser and François Coli, who would instead attempt a Paris-to-New York crossing together. Keystone Corporation, a Pennsylvania airplane manufacturer that built bomber aircraft for the U.S Army, announced its intention to seek the Prize using a specially designed aircraft to be flown by U.S. Navy pilots. Countless other individual pilots, who lacked the resources even to dream of an attempt to make the crossing, still found themselves mulling over the requirements, should some eccentric millionaire call and offer them the job.

While the world's headlines continued to trumpet the excitement building for the Orteig Prize competition, at least one capital of Europe was conspicuously silent.

In Berlin, the conditions of the Treaty of Versailles, which had been signed seven years earlier and officially ended the Great War, essentially disallowed Germany to compete in such competitions. Among other, far more punitive terms of the Treaty, the country was forbidden to design, develop, manufacture, import or export military aircraft, ships, tanks or other weapons of war.

It wasn't as if there was no German interest. From a technology perspective, the Germans had led aviation development throughout the war. Its engineers had accounted for virtually every new advancement put into service during the war years, including the interrupter gear that allowed machine guns to be timed to fire through a whirling propeller. That one German innovation had changed the face of aerial fighting forever. The severely punitive requirements of the Treaty of Versailles, which constituted thinly veiled vengeance, all but eliminated any possibility of Germany rebuilding its aviation industry.

In addition, saddled with billions of dollars in reparations to be paid to the victorious European allies, Germany was suffocating under twenty-five percent unemployment, food shortages, and the lack of resources to renew its industry. Germany had been shattered by the war in many ways; but in the end, it was the innocents, the German people, who were bearing the weight of the tragedy and the fragile future of their beloved homeland. Understandably, a sense of anger and resentment rose as high among the defeated German people as the jubilation and satisfaction felt by the victors.

For the common man, there were far more important concerns in Berlin than the Orteig Prize. Food for the table, a lump of coal for the fireplace and keeping a roof over their heads fully preoccupied the imagination of the family breadwinner. But the Orteig Prize was very much on the minds of others in Germany for whom the scars of defeat had not yet healed.

A world away, among a large pack of American aviators who dreamt of attempting the flight, was a twenty-five-year-old U.S. Army Air Corps pilot born in Detroit, Michigan. He was far too young to be awed by the big name heroes and adventurers who had already announced attempts at the Prize and too much of a farm boy to be all that impressed with the high rollers staking their efforts. Nor did he have any sense or interest in the global politics involved. He was just a young man who thought he had a legitimate shot at making a successful flight across the Atlantic. It wasn't the fame, fanfare and money that motivated him. On the contrary. Despite the fact that he didn't usually have more than two bits to his name, the young pilot had the same vision of the future of commercial aviation as millionaire Raymond Orteig, the man who had started all the ruckus. Like the Frenchman, the American pilot knew that New York to Paris was just the beginning.

His name was Charles A. Lindbergh.

Three

"Aw, Ma, we've had this conversation a hundred times," Charles A. "Slim" Lindbergh shouted into the telephone receiver of a payphone inside a freezing cold hanger at Lambert-St. Louis Field on the outskirts of the Missouri city.

"I'm the chief pilot for the United States Mail Service, and I've got a job to do," he continued before listening to his mother inform him again that the weather over Peoria Field was horrible. She begged him not to fly on to Chicago, the next leg of his delivery, in the freezing weather. The three sacks of mail stowed in the forward passenger compartment of the war surplus silver and maroon DH-4 Jenny biplane could wait.

"Now, Ma, I know you have feelings about things like this; but I feel pretty strong about doing my job," young Lindbergh argued. He hated these arguments with her. "Listen, I'll be okay. I'll call you when I get to Chicago." He hung up without another word and walked across the hangar, a pang of guilt building in his gut for not being more patient with his aging mother. He considered calling her back and actually turned back to the phone, then thought better of it. *If I call her back, she'll think I'm weak,* he thought to himself. *That will only make matters worse.*

Frank Robertson, who together with his older brother Bill owned the U.S. Government Contract Air Mail Route between St. Louis and Chicago, wiped an oily wrench clean as he stepped back from the still-smoking engine of the four-hundred horsepower De Havilland biplane that

Lindbergh had ferried in less than twenty minutes ago. A spark plug was misfiring in its tired twelve-cylinder motor. Robertson looked up to see Lindbergh approaching, his head down, obviously deep in thought.

The night weather was miserable, and freezing sleet stung Lindbergh's face as he had dropped through the low-hanging clouds and landed on the grass of Lambert field almost by feel rather than sight. His wings had iced up badly. If the airfield had been much farther away, he would have had to put the airplane down in a farmer's field somewhere in the darkness or parachuted from the cockpit when the ancient Jenny finally got too heavy to stay in the air. Ice was just about the most dangerous enemy of the lightweight biplanes there could be.

Lindbergh had stuck with his airplane, nursing it through the dangerous storm, pushing down his fears like he'd always done since he'd been a boy growing up on his father's farm in Little Falls, Minnesota. C.A. Lindbergh, a country lawyer who had been elected to Congress in 1906, had trained his son well in the art of hiding pain and fear. The two were much alike. The elder Lindbergh could come across as a rather cold and reticent man, despite his highly visible public life. In truth, he longed for solitude. The apple hadn't fallen far from the tree.

Charles Lindbergh, now a tall, lanky, blond-haired young man, was an introverted figure with few friends or acquaintances outside of his job as chief pilot for the Robertson Aircraft Corporation, but that was hardly surprising. He liked to be alone, and he especially liked to be alone to tinker with machines.

By the time he was twenty, young Lindbergh's whole world revolved around machines. While a student at the University of Wisconsin, he made few friends outside a group who shared a passion for speed. They rode motorcycles across rough country roads without regard for life or limb, and in winters sailed motor-driven ice boats across frozen Lake Mendota in sub-zero temperatures with equal disregard for danger.

An undergraduate student majoring in mechanical engineering, he rebelled at the tedium and constant testing. "Why don't they treat us like students in a European university?" Lindbergh complained to his father. "There they leave you alone, just so you get the work done and pass stiff examinations when the term ends." Despite general recognition that he had an extraordinary aptitude for all things mechanical, he gave his professors little choice but to give him low marks for his poor academic efforts. Consequently, Lindbergh stayed only three semesters at the University before dropping out at the end of March, 1922.

His parents were hardly surprised by his academic failures. As a boy growing up on the family farm, he devoted himself to tearing apart the family's car and tractor, teaching himself how the contraptions operated. At fourteen, he took responsibility for driving his mother to Los Angeles, a long and challenging drive over unpaved roads, in an ancient automobile that tended to break down every hundred miles or so. By the time he was eighteen, the local gas station mechanics thought he was a mechanical genius. Machines were the only interest in his life and he never had a girlfriend.

Two days after leaving the University of Wisconsin, Lindbergh rode his motorcycle to Lincoln, Nebraska, where he enrolled as a flying student with the Nebraska Aircraft Corporation. His life would never be the same. After just one lesson, he found the wide open skies were the perfect home for the young man, where he could be free and alone and could tempt the hand of fate at his whim.

Lindbergh's instructors were in awe of his instinctive abilities at the controls of an airplane; and in less than ten hours of instruction, he was ready to solo. His prowess as a pilot appeared to be a natural gift, but there was more to it than that. His intuitive feel for any airplane he flew was supported by a complete understanding of how the machine worked and how it was built, because he spent months at Nebraska Aircraft's assembly plant studying how they were constructed.

Unfortunately, although he was more than ready to solo, company policy required him to post a bond to cover possible damages before he could take one of its planes up alone. He couldn't afford it. In typical style, never willing to admit defeat, Lindbergh immediately took a job with a flier who happened to be passing through Lincoln on a barnstorming tour through Nebraska, selling rides to anyone who could pay a dollar a minute. The young man became the pilot's chief mechanic but also quickly volunteered to be his stunt man. Crowds gasped as Lindbergh would fearlessly climb out of the cockpit and stand on the wing of the plane and wave as his employer flew aerobatic maneuvers through the sky.

Returning to Lincoln in the summer of 1922, he met up with a parachute maker by the name of Charles Hardin. To demonstrate his product, Hardin would jump from an airplane flying at several thousand feet and land with fair precision back on the airfield. Occasionally, he made a double drop, where he would jump from an airplane, open his first parachute, release it after several minutes and then freefall to earth hundreds of feet before pulling the ripcord of his second 'chute. Crowds at the airfield, fooled by the two parachute stunt, would watch in awe as Hardin fell unimpeded toward the ground for agonizingly long seconds to what seemed his certain death before opening his second parachute and landing safely.

Lindbergh was fascinated and immediately looked up Hardin. He convinced the parachute maker to let him do a double drop on his very first leap from an airplane.

He took off with Hardin at the controls of a borrowed airplane, and they quickly climbed to the correct altitude for the jump. Despite last-minute second thoughts about his own sanity, the twenty-year-old Lindbergh stepped out onto the wing then slid down the fabric surface until he was hanging beneath it with a precarious grip on the trailing edge. He looked down at the ground from five thousand feet. It was the only time he had ever felt cold fear in the air.

With a hard swallow and a silent prayer, he let go of the wing and was immediately blown clear of the airplane. He pulled the rip cord, jerking the knot so hard he thought he had torn it out of the packing. To his tremendous relief, the first parachute opened, billowing out over him in a split second. His fear evaporated almost instantaneously as he felt the reassuring tug of his harness against his shoulders. The earth below looked far more inviting now.

Full of confidence, he reached up with his pocket knife and cut the first parachute loose. He was not aware that Hardin, fearing for the young man's life, had rigged the second parachute to open simultaneously with the release of the first. Hardin gasped as the second parachute failed to deploy and watched helplessly as Lindbergh tumbled towards the earth in an uncontrolled free fall.

Unaware that anything was wrong, Lindbergh exulted in the moment, a rush of adrenalin coursing through him as he sped towards the ground. He felt like a bird in a steep dive. Suddenly, as the airfield below began looming up at him, he had the distinct feeling that something was wrong. At that exact moment, the parachute released from its packing and bloomed over his head. Lindbergh was jerked up hard in the harness but thought nothing of it, enjoying the last few minutes of unbridled freedom as he hung from the parachute. He landed hard, falling to the ground face first; but he quickly jumped to his feet and brushed off the dust from his flying suit.

Hardin landed the plane and rushed to him, tremendously relieved to see the young man walking towards him. Anxiously, he told Lindbergh that he thought his second parachute would never open.

"Wasn't that the way it was supposed to work?" Lindbergh asked, unaware that there had been a problem.

Hardin shook his head in disbelief. "Son," he said, "I've never had one of my 'chutes take so long to open before."

Lindbergh shook off the close call with his cold, hard logic as just another experience. In fact, it would serve him well, as over the next several years he would be forced to parachute to safety on four different occasions. His luck held each time.

It seemed that Lindbergh's luck was almost supernatural. After buying a war surplus Curtiss Jenny at auction in Americus, Georgia, in the spring of 1923, the pilot embarked on a long barnstorming tour of his own through Mississippi, Texas and parts of the Middle West. It seemed that he had one close call after another during that hot summer and into the fall.

He crash landed his Jenny into a ditch in Mississippi shortly after starting his tour, breaking a propeller. In Kansas, he hit a large rock when he was forced to land on a steep hillside and buried the nose of his airplane in the ground. In Minnesota, he was forced to land in a swamp. In Florida, he had to land on a sandy beach and smashed his landing gear and another propeller. In Texas, he was forced to land in a town square. After making repairs, he decided he could take off from the street, even though his plane had a forty-foot wingspan, and the telephone poles lining it were only forty-six feet apart. On his take-off run, a wing caught a pole, and he careened through the plate glass window of a store. A newspaper reporter covering the story nicknamed the young pilot "Lucky Lindy." The tag stuck.

In a rare moment of self-doubt however, Lindbergh began to think it was only a matter of time before his luck ran out. He was often flying on sheer nerve rather than skill. His natural agility had saved him countless times; but inside, he knew that he had to become a better pilot with honed skills if he was going to live to see twenty-five. Soon after, on the advice of an acquaintance who had just graduated from the U.S. Army Air Service Training School, he enlisted as an Air Service cadet in March of 1924.

Stationed at Brooks Field in San Antonio, Texas, Lindbergh trained for the next twelve months in the powerful, four hundred horsepower DeHaviland DH-4, interrupted only by the sudden death of his revered father in May. C.A.'s passing was a heavy blow to the young man, and he withdrew into solitude even more than he had as a child. Somehow, he collected himself and became a model cadet throughout his training, staying to himself but applying himself as he had never done before.

The experience was one of the most rigorous and exhausting he had ever known and not without a certain amount of danger. The young man survived yet another miraculous crash when a DH-4 he was flying in close formation locked wings with another, forcing him to parachute to safety for the first time. He landed with a grin on his face, and his instructors took note of the fact that the pilot almost seemed to revel in high risk situations.

In March 1925, of the one-hundred-four cadets who had entered the class at Brooks Field with him, Lindbergh was one of only eighteen pilots to earn their wings. He was commissioned a Second Lieutenant in the Air Service Reserve Corps.

Following graduation, Lindbergh looked up the Robertson Aircraft Corporation at St. Louis' Lambert Field. The company had just landed the airmail contract for the St. Louis-to-Chicago route. He applied for a position, and with his Army Air Corp credentials, he was quickly hired as its chief pilot.

While waiting for the inauguration of the airmail service, Lindbergh agreed to run some tests on a new, four-passenger commercial airplane that had just been constructed at the field. It was dubbed the OXX-6 Plywood Special.

On his first flight in the airplane, he found that it handled strangely; and when he purposely put it into a tailspin, he was alarmed to find he could not pull out of the dive. The airplane fell more than fifteen hundred feet; but Lindbergh, dreading the thought of losing his customer's custom-built airplane, stubbornly and furiously worked the controls in an attempt to pull out. Bitterly, he finally gave in, and at the very last minute managed to save himself by rolling out of the cockpit on the right side and jumping, a mere four hundred feet from a crash and certain death. His parachute opened immediately but so low that it only partially broke his landing. Worse, the falling aircraft nearly cut him in half, missing the pilot by a scant twenty-five feet. Lucky Lindy had dodged death once again.

Finally, on April 15, 1926, at four o'clock in the afternoon, Lindbergh took off from Lambert Field in one of Robertson's Army salvage DeHavilland observation planes and headed for Springfield, Missouri, to pick up fifteen thousand letters which had to be flown to St. Louis. A crowd of two hundred people watched the flier take off, inaugurating the Robertson Aircraft Corporation's St. Louis-to-Chicago airmail route.

Included in the spectators were executives from each of the St. Louis banks that were investing in the company, agreeing to pick up its losses as it struggled to launch service.

And a struggle it was, especially for the pilots. Their tired airplanes were a constant headache, routinely breaking down. The only navigation Lindbergh had was a small compass taped to the top of his joystick. The planes had no lights other than the flashlight he carried. During the summer months, he flew his route mostly in daylight; but as fall and winter descended, he found himself flying blind more often than not in freezing cold weather.

On September 16, as he was about to make his final landing approach into Chicago Airport from Peoria, he encountered fog so thick he could not fly above it and he was unable to see the field. Landing there was virtually impossible, and the fog spread out farther than his fuel would allow him to fly.

After circling what he believed to be the airfield right up to the moment his engine ran out of gas and died, he finally faced reality and rolled out of the cockpit into the thick fog. He allowed himself to fall several hundred feet before pulling the rip cord of his parachute, trying to avoid his airplane, which to his surprise had restarted as the nose dipped down and a small amount of fuel on the bottom of the gas tank fed into the carburetor. He had forgotten to cut his switches, and the airplane began to fly in circles. As he hung helplessly in his parachute harness, slowly falling almost a mile to the earth below, the plane came at him, missing him by no more than a few yards. He waited for a second pass, which never came, to his great relief; and the airplane crashed into a field several miles away. The fortunate pilot walked away again, landing safely in a cornfield.

Only six weeks later, on November 3rd, fate reached up and grabbed him again. He was only a few miles outside of Springfield, bound for Peoria, when he found himself completely socked in by darkness, fog, rain and snow despite good weather forecasts. With no hope of flying above or below the storm, he was forced to jump one more time. Waiting until the last possible moment, he remembered to cut his switches and then bailed out from fourteen thousand feet. On the way down, the young flier began to have second thoughts about his airmail career.

In late August, he happened to read a newspaper account of Raymond Orteig's challenge and the fact that his prize of twenty-five thousand dollars still had not been claimed. In fact, no flier had even attempted the nonstop transatlantic crossing between New York and Paris. Intrigued, Lindbergh had to admit that a New York-to-Paris flight was not without its risks, but he was not particularly put off by the danger, considering his flying experiences of the last several years. He began thinking through the puzzle with his cold, analytical approach to problem solving, coming to some surprising conclusions.

The events of the early morning of September 15, 1926, caused him to finally consider the transatlantic challenge seriously. A disaster in Long Island crystallized his thoughts, and a plan began to form in his mind.

After a long day of flying the mail, Lindbergh had nursed his rickety DeHavilland back to Lambert Field. He was bone tired but decided to ride his motorcycle into the city for a late dinner, stopping first to pick up the afternoon edition of the St. Louis Post Dispatch at a newsstand. His jaw dropped when he saw the paper's screaming headline: "*Two Die In Fonck Crash; French Ace Survives.*"

René Paul Fonck, age thirty-one, a celebrated French ace of the Great War and the most victorious of the Allied pilots with seventy-five confirmed kills, had somehow survived the fiery wreck of his three-engine S-35 sesquiplane, a biplane with asymmetrical wings, on takeoff from Long Island's Roosevelt field earlier that morning. Designed by famed émigré Russian aviation designer Igor Sikorsky, the plane carried four crew members: a pilot, co-pilot, navigator-engineer and radio operator.

Fonck, well backed financially by the French government and an American syndicate, had planned to fly eastbound from New York in Sikorsky's untested airplane, but the heavily modified transport never got off the ground, as it was grossly overloaded.

Sikorsky's design was rated for sixteen thousand pounds. He had envisioned that most of the airplane's weight would be accounted for by fuel, but Fonck had overloaded the plane to twenty-eight thousand pounds with unnecessary accoutrements, including an oven containing a hot celebration dinner prepared by chefs at the Hotel McAlpin in Manhattan, gifts for French government officials and other VIP's, a thick, full-sized bed, red leather upholstery, extra radio sets, and a huge load of baggage for the crew members. Sikorsky objected strenuously to the overload and wanted to delay the takeoff until he could perform more tests, but the brash, chunky Frenchman would not listen, spurred on by his own bravado and heroic reputation.

On takeoff just before dawn, Fonck, at the controls, revved his three five-hundred-eighty horsepower, nine-cylinder Gnome-Rhône Jupiter engines to their maximum rpm's, but the plane barely moved. With a running shove from his mechanics, the behemoth began to lumber down the muddy runway with its motors running wide open, but the S-35 failed to gain the speed the pilot had anticipated. Halfway down the field, the airplane's auxiliary landing gear, which Sikorsky had added to accommodate the excessive weight, ripped off at the tail, which fell to the ground and dragged up a huge cloud of dust. Spectators screamed for Fonck to abort the takeoff, but the Frenchman either would not or could not. At the last minute, the hundred-thousand-dollar airplane rose slightly off the ground but settled back heavily and shot over the end of the runway into a steep gully.

The large crowd on hand gasped and shrieked. Then there was a moment of ghastly silence as the wreckage settled into the lowland, followed by the massive explosion of nearly three thousand gallons of aviation fuel and fifteen hundred pounds of motor oil on board. In the ensuing fireball, Fonck and his co-pilot, U.S. Navy Lieutenant Lawrence Curtin escaped. The other two crewmen, Charles Clavier, navigator-engineer, and Jacob Islaroff, radio operator, were buried under a mountain of baggage in the tail section and were unable to escape the wreck. The two were cremated in the shattered remains of the S-35, which burned for hours, the blaze fed by the massive load of fuel.

The disaster rocked the news media, which until that moment had half-heartedly covered the Orteig Prize story. Suddenly, millions of people were enticed via newspapers and newsreels to follow the exploits of the remaining and mostly well-known challengers.

As Lindbergh digested the shocking news, his hands shook with fury. *What a waste,* he thought. *What was Fonck thinking? A roast duck dinner? A bed? Why did he need three other crewmen? And why did he believe he needed a three engine airplane to cross the Atlantic? The Frenchman was a fool,* Lindbergh concluded.

If he had the chance to make the crossing, it would be different. For one thing, if he were to attempt the flight fittingly, he would do it alone in a single-seat aircraft of his design. Weight would be his mortal enemy. He wouldn't even carry a change of underwear. The real challenge would be fuel. Could he carry enough to make the crossing, yet still be able to get airborne? Would he be physically able to manage the flight, to stay awake for more than thirty hours at the controls? And where would he get the money he needed?

He wasn't sure of the answers to any of his questions, but the more he thought about it, the more convinced he was that he was right. One man in a single-engine airplane would be lonely, but he was certain that the combination had the best chance of success. He began to dream about the attempt, putting himself in a cockpit, alone over the vast and forbidding North Atlantic Ocean, listening intently to the sound of his engine, wary of any change in its endless hum, checking his fuel gauge every few minutes, letting his eyes wander over the horizon, worrying about storms, lightening, ice on his wings.

He played out the worst scenarios he could think of but realized there was almost nothing that could happen that he hadn't already experienced. The only difference would be that the bulk of his flight time would be spent over water instead of land.

Intuitively he knew that he was superior to the average pilot, and his confidence had grown immensely as a result of his Army Air Corp training and harrowing ordeals flying the mail. In the few years he had been flying, he'd managed to squeeze in a lifetime's worth of aviation experiences and had lived to talk about it. Could the New York-to-Paris flight be any more dangerous than what he'd already encountered? He thought not.

His soul-searching, self-analysis and assessment of what he needed to do complete, he made up his mind, and that was that. Like generations of his family before him, when Lindbergh made a decision, there was no turning back, no second guessing. Somehow, someway, Charles Lindbergh was going to be the first man to fly nonstop from New York to Paris.

So it was that on a cold December afternoon in 1926, the young man from Little Falls, Minnesota, just two months prior to his twenty-fifth birthday, came to the decision to compete for the Orteig Prize. His confidence was high; and he felt there was no challenge he could not overcome, save one—assuaging his mother's constant fears for his safety.

Wearing his heavy, fur-lined flight suit, Lindbergh was still shaking his head as he approached Bob Robertson. It was the mechanic who had dubbed the skinny flier "Slim". Bob felt like a father to the boy, who was young enough to be his son. Lindbergh was furious. "You know, someday that woman's going to recognize that I'm no longer a …"

Robertson laughed out loud, a cigarette hanging from his bottom lip as he spoke. "A what, Slim? Why you're going to be her baby boy till the day you die, which won't be long from now, if you keep making these crazy runs in this weather. Seems like we should have taken a better look at the meteorological patterns in these parts before we bid this job. Hell."

"'Hell, nothing," Lindbergh shot back. "Bob, if we can't deal with the weather, then there's no point to airmail. How long before you can get me back up?"

Robertson laughed again. "Twenty minutes tops. Seriously, Slim, much as I'd hate to lose you, when are you going to think about a real job? You know, something you can do that won't kill you?"

Now it was Lindbergh's turn to laugh. "Funny you ask, Bob. I've been meaning to ask you about something. I was wondering if I could get you to invest a bit in me."

Robertson stopped wiping the wrench, knowing that whatever it was the kid had to say was serious, or he wouldn't waste time saying it.

"I'm all ears, Slim," Robertson replied.

Lindbergh swallowed hard and looked Robertson straight in the eye, hesitating just for a moment. Whenever he got very serious, his face was a contradiction. His piercing blue eyes could bore holes through your head with the intensity of his stare, but just the slightest of smiles would cross his face. Robertson caught the look instantly.

"How'd you like to help me get to Paris, Boss?"

Four

German President Paul Ludwig Hans Anton von Beneckendorff und von Hindenburg shifted his three hundred pound frame uneasily in his favorite oversized arm chair, hand carved of black cherry by German artisans a century before. Defence Minister General Wilhelm Groener was just completing his briefing. The seventy-nine-year-old von Hindenburg was only half listening to the gray-haired advisor some twenty years his junior, and absentmindedly played with one end of his trademark enormous handlebar moustache.

The President's most intimate advisors sat closely by him as Groener spoke, but each was silent, awaiting his reaction. The German leader did not speak but drew long from his fat cigar, staring into the roaring fire contained inside the great marble fireplace of his sumptuous office in the Imperial Chancellery in the Radziwill Palace.

It was von Hindenburg's sanctuary; a serene place where the rapidly aging President could escape the troubling memories of a lifetime spent waging wars both on the battlefield and in politics. A veteran of the Austro-Prussian War of 1866, the Franco-Prussian War four years later, and finally the Great War, he preferred wrestling with the lingering ghosts of warriors on the battlefield. Unlike politics, in war one always knew who the enemy was.

The President, his ego intact despite his role in the terrible defeat of the Great War, also enjoyed his official sanctuary for the statement it made about him. One could almost sink into the lush sea of hand-woven, gold wool carpet which surrounded the German national coat of arms at the center of the room. A huge, single-headed black eagle, its head turned to the right, wings open and feathers closed, its beak, tongue and talons depicted in a brilliant, blood red shade, boldly proclaimed to visitors that this was the absolute seat of power of Germany. The black-red-gold theme had survived the ages; its roots lying in the coat of arms of the Holy Roman Empire of the German Nation.

Von Hindenburg reveled in his life as the supreme commander of the Fatherland, but his leadership was a pronounced contradiction in terms. On one hand, he felt a deep responsibility for the plight of the German people and for the future of his nation. On the other, he was one of the last of the German aristocracy. His lifestyle of excess and pompous demeanor caused him to be caricaturized as a tired and essentially useless figurehead of state by the very people he worried over.

Few Germans had ever actually entered the *Reichskanzlei,* or Imperial Chancellery, where von Hindenburg was located. It was a distinctive palace resembling the late French Renaissance buildings such as the Château de Fontainebleau and the Luxembourg Palace in Paris. In this building nearly all important decisions affecting the lives of the German people were made. Its flamboyance and sumptuous fittings however were almost blasphemous, given the state of the national economy and the plight of the common German. Unfortunately, few of the Chancellery's elite occupants felt the need to apologize.

Hindenburg was tired, physically near exhaustion, but even wearier from hearing bad news. "Is there no end?" he would often ask his son and closest advisor, forty-four-year-old Major Oskar von Hindenberg, who was never far from his side.

The war had ended more than eight years before, but the repercussions of Germany's defeat and the punishing Treaty of Versailles had created a new kind of war within the country. It was a battle for subsistence and pride.

Von Hindenberg exhaled a large cloud of blue smoke above him before he spoke and swirled his brandy in a large snifter, bringing the goblet to his nose to inhale the aroma before drinking from it. Each of his guests, sitting in similar antique chairs, enjoyed the same cigars and scarce cognac as rewards, perhaps more for their loyalty to von Hindenberg than to the German Republic and the Weimar Constitution that had replaced the Monarchy following the disastrous war.

They included Otto Meissner, Secretary of State and Chief of the Reich President, General Wilhelm Groener, Defence Minister, and General Kurt von Schleicher, who headed up the *Ministeranmt* or Office of the Ministerial Affairs, the primary liaison between the army and civilian government officials. Schleicher had a low-key presence among Germany's highest government officials, despite his rank. His unofficial responsibility was to poke his nose into the workings of other Reich departments through a network of carefully placed informants. As such, he was one of the President's most valued advisors and sat to von Hindenberg's immediate right.

To his left, as always, sat his son, Major Oskar von Hindenburg, who served as his father's aide-de-camp and keeper of the gate. It was Oskar who controlled access to his father, choosing those who would be allowed access to the President and those who would not.

Together, the members of this group were widely known as the Hindenburg "Kamarilla". In truth, in their official capacities and in spite of their inflated titles, each man had little power or authority. With the abdication of the Monarchy at the end of the war, the real power of the Reich had transferred from the Kaiser to the President;

but as unofficial advisors to the aging President and with their close proximity to him, they were giants of the Weimar Constitution-based government that von Hindenburg led.

The Weimar Constitution, the guiding document of the Reich so named because it was drafted by the German National Assembly following the end of the war in the small village of Weimar in January 1919, directed that Germany would be a Democratic Federal Republic governed by a president and a parliament elected on a proportional basis. At least in theory, gone were the days of the Kaiser and the Monarchy that put all the power to govern Germany into the hands of one man or one incestuous, nepotistic family.

The first article of the Constitution stated that "The power of the state emanates from the people." In theory, it was the bedrock of the Republic. In actuality, the German people were desperate for leadership and Paul von Hindenburg was a substitute emperor no matter how he performed.

Silence hung heavily over the smoke-filled room as the Defence Minister completed his briefing to the President and the Kamarilla in von Hindenburg's lavish office. The subject was the Orteig Prize, a seemingly inconsequential subject for the German people. In the immensity of their defeat, neither industry nor the military had given the announcement of the Orteig Prize much consideration. Abruptly, that had changed.

News had reached Berlin that very night that the first of the serious and famous challengers actually to attempt the flight from New York to Paris, the despised French fighter ace René Fonck, had failed disastrously.

The news took Berlin by surprise, but not because it was Fonck who had failed. The shock came from the acknowledgement that the French were pursuing the challenge, while the Germans had dismissed such an attempt.

"Once again, Germany, by its very lack of participation on the world stage, will hang its head in shame," Defence Minister Groener concluded his remarks with a personal observation unappreciated by von Hindenburg. Groener was deeply displeased that the German government had exhibited no interest in the competition, although he had raised the subject several times himself with the President.

Von Hindenburg did not welcome the tone of his subordinate's voice, and the stiff collar of his military uniform chafed as his neck swelled in anger. The look on his face escaped no one in the room.

"General Groener, I fail to share your emotions," von Hindenburg admonished him quickly and firmly, struggling to hide his anger. He motioned to a fully uniformed valet to refill his snifter. The officer caught von Hindenburg's slight nod to refill the glasses of the President's guests, as well.

"I would be lying were I to suggest that I am unhappy with Fonck's failure," the President continued. "Had we been successful in 1918, I would have enjoyed watching him hang for war crimes. The name Réne Fonck grows older and more forgettable with each passing day, and the Orteig Prize is a means of keeping daredevils employed. Consequently, I am simply not convinced that the German people would now rise up with enthusiasm for a national effort that amounts to a publicity stunt."

"Finally, General," von Hindenburg continued as if to put the matter to rest once and for all, "I suggest that the Reich, particularly the military, have far more important tasks to occupy their time and resources."

Groener was silent but seething inside. How could his President not share the sense of revenge that the military officer carried with him day and night? It seemed as if von Hindenburg's advancing age was mellowing his memories. Had he forgotten what it was like to write a letter to the parents of one of the young pilots Fonck had murdered?

Oskar von Hindenburg stared at Groener, silently sympathetic to his position. Although his love for his father knew no bounds, more than once lately he had struggled to align himself with the President's policies. Out of respect, he said nothing. Perhaps an opportunity would avail itself later in private.

"Of course, there is also the Treaty, General Groener," interrupted Otto Meissner in support of the President. As Secretary of State and Chief of the Reich President, it fell on him to convince the Allies that Germany was living up to the accord it was forced to sign in Versailles. For Meissner, the truth was not the issue. After all, it was just a game that would some day come to a shocking conclusion for the vengeful Allies. Germany may have appeared to be sedentary, but the truth was far from visible.

"No doubt, an entry into the Orteig competition would be seen as a direct violation of the Versailles accord," Meissner added. "It is hardly something we could do in secret. It is not as if we could pull an appropriate multi-engine airplane from an assembly line we do not possess. All our surviving aircraft, nearly three thousand assets, were destroyed per the agreement in May 1920. What remains of our fleet are training vehicles, and they are tired and hardly suitable for such an effort."

General Kurt von Schleicher took a drag from his cigarette and stamped it out into an ashtray. He leaned forward for effect.

"Gentlemen, gentlemen, let us not fool ourselves," he said, trying not to sound sarcastic. The Office of the Ministerial Affairs, of which he was responsible, gave him insight into virtually all dealings between the army and civilian government officials. He was quiet, subversive and effective behind the scenes, and he maintained an extraordinary network of both informers and operatives to make things happen—his way.

"We are all aware of Lipetsk and the capability we have hiding there," he said. "It is not as if we are without the resources necessary to take on Orteig's challenge if we so desired."

Von Schleicher, to von Hindenburg's unmistakable displeasure, had referred to the secret facilities that Germany had established in Lipetsk, a city located in the Central Federal District of Russia on the banks of the Voronezh River, some four hundred forty kilometers from Moscow. Disguised as a civil aviation school under Russian ownership and command, it was a source for secretly training German air force fighter and bomber pilots. The facility had been established before the ink was even dry on the Treaty of Versailles.

The Treaty allowed for training of civil aviation pilots; and initially, several commercial schools had been used to facilitate training in light aircraft for Lufthansa pilots. Germany turned to its new ally Russia for help in building a facade to provide German military pilots with adequate training. In return, Germany would provide aviation technology, design and engineering to the Russian military, which had fallen far behind the learning curve in this newest of war weapons. Consequently, a secret training airfield was established at Lipetsk in 1924 using Russian and Dutch combat aircraft. Here, hundreds of German pilots were trained in secret. Development and testing of new German military aircraft also continued under cover of the Russian airbase. Officially, it was known as the fourth squadron of the fortieth wing of the Red Army, a facade which made it appear to be a Russian operation.

"It is not as if the engineers, aircraft and pilots do not exist," von Schleicher said, the admission adding to the tension in the room. "Were we to decide to make the effort, this could be done without much preparation, I am sure. "Although," the propagandist in him added, "I would do Herr Orteig one better. I would consider making the nonstop flight from Berlin to New York, not Paris to New York, for obvious reasons. I doubt the added distance could not be overcome."

Oskar von Hindenburg said nothing, which the President erroneously took as a sign of agreement by his son.

"Perhaps I have had enough of useless propaganda which in truth does nothing to advance the well-being of the Reich," von Hindenberg said, "but it is pointless to argue the state of the German psyche. It is most obvious that our nation is depressed in many more ways than economically."

He looked into the bottom of his freshened cognac. "Although, having said that, a French or American conquest of the challenge to make a transatlantic crossing will do nothing to improve the mood of the country." Von Hindenburg fell silent again.

"Perhaps I underestimate the potential effect on German pride. The room fell silent again as each man was lost in thought. The risks involved in whatever it was they were considering were enormous, given the potential for failure; but the opposite was equally true.

At the same time, but unspoken on this evening, was an issue that was heavy on their minds. On other occasions in this very same room, the Kamarilla had conceptually agreed that Germany could not continue to survive by abiding by the Versailles Treaty. Eventually, they would have to make it known to the Allies that the German industrial and military complex was going to be jump-started. They worried over the predictable Allied reaction that might even trigger a military response that Germany was not ready to resist. The potential for making the situation worse was of grave concern.

While they spoke, von Hindenburg's intrigue with the Orteig Prize was piqued, despite the *laissez-faire* attitude he had previously displayed on the subject. What if Germany, seen by the Allies as the greatest aggressor and evil threat of the twentieth century, were to re-emerge in such a peaceful way that could not be criticized other than for the technicality of breaching non-military Treaty terms? A Berlin-to-New York commercial, transatlantic flight would help open the doors for greater free economic trade every bit as much as a New York-to-Paris trade route. *We come in peace,* he thought, a somewhat novel twist for a German leader; but the idea was growing on him.

Finally, the President politely cleared his throat, thereby giving the signal that the discussion was concluded. Von Hindenburg's guests were well aware that the President would want to further discuss their conversation in private with his son. Oskar's silence in such situations was always an indication that he had something to add or a differing opinion, but he would never challenge his father publicly. The Kamarilla understood the game and recognized Paul von Hindenburg's admiration of his son; but even more importantly, his respect for him. It was almost as important to stay on the good side of the young von Hindenburg as it was his father.

"The hour is late, my friends. I suggest we wait and see what the morning news brings regarding other challengers to the Orteig Prize." There was a nodding around the fire, and each man downed the last of his cognac with a salute to the President.

"In the meantime, Kurt" von Hindenburg said to General von Schleicher in a rare informal salutation to one of his staff, the formality of the moment no doubt eased by the cognac, "let us put our intelligence assets to use and gather a more comprehensive look at what the French, Americans and others are planning. Let us learn what we do not know."

He turned to General Groener. "I suggest you deploy your own considerable talents, General, to know if we do indeed have the assets you suggest at Lipetsk. I find too often that our convictions are stronger than our capabilities. Let us know for sure what we are capable of." Groener nodded understanding of his assignment. In fact, if von Hindenburg knew his man, the Defence Minister was already formulating the instructions he would issue following the conclusion of the meeting of the Kamarilla and would leave for Lipetsk immediately. The President was right on both counts.

Hours later, the lights would burn throughout the long, cold night in a concrete drawing room at Lipetsk as a handful of specially selected engineers began the arduous task of finding a way to stretch an already impossible transatlantic flight of more than thirty-six hundred miles to forty-five hundred miles – and then to double the distance to meet the caveat of General Groener who insisted on the capability of a return flight.

"Just think of the possibilities, gentlemen, if we were capable of landing safely in New York and returning to Germany on the same day," Groener had told the engineers. He spoke to them as if they were prized engineers and academics who had dedicated their lives to the Reich. In fact, most of them were slaves, prisoners of war who had not been allowed to return to their native countries even nearly ten years after the signing of the Treaty. They were hardly motivated.

A tall man, a young German engineer known as "Heinz" whose haggard appearance suggested that he was far older, elbowed a companion as they listened to the General's briefing. He was not a "prisoner" at Lipetsk, but his "voluntary" service had been required to ensure the safety of his family in a small village just outside Berlin.

The Swede jumped slightly, startled by the interruption. "What is it?" he whispered.

The German looked down on his co-worker with disdain. "This one is crazy," he whispered back. The Swede shrugged his shoulders. The thought had not entered his mind. The assignment was hardly of consequence to him.

"He thinks we do not understand what he is describing," the German whispered again. "This is no mere competition he speaks of."

"What do you mean?"

"What he wants is an airplane in which he can fly to their New York City, bomb the Americans and then fly back to Berlin," the German said with certainty. The Swede's eyes went wide.

Despite the dull look on his face, the German engineer's mind was roiling with scrutiny. A brilliant engineer, he had stayed alive with his cunning talent to appear to be cooperating while in fact offering little to the projects to which he was a slave. He had an innate ability to know when to shine and when to placate the swine whose family survived on his ability to appear useful. Most importantly, he had the instincts to know when he and his fellow prisoners were being fed a line of propaganda. At this moment, every nerve ending in his body was screaming in defiance at Groener's lies in describing the peaceful mission that had been proposed before the German President. He heard the General say that success would mean their freedom and knew that was the greatest blasphemy of all.

What the German volunteer knew intuitively was that it was all a charade and that what the German General actually intended was something quite different -- quite sinister, in fact.

He had long ago lost hope for vengeance. Perhaps the god who had forsaken him had presented an opportunity.

Five

It was one thing to plan a transatlantic flight, another thing to finance it. For a twenty-five-year-old air mail pilot with a few thousand dollars in the bank, raising the kind of money necessary to pull it off would take a miracle. Lindbergh's conviction that the crossing could be accomplished using a lightweight, single-engine airplane rather than the tri-motored behemoths his competitors were preparing meant that he could equip himself for less than fifteen thousand dollars. It still seemed an unreachable sum, but he was more determined than ever.

Even with his own savings and his constant efforts that brought home a thousand here, a thousand there, he was still short ten thousand dollars or so the day he knocked on the door of the St. Louis brokerage firm of Knight, Dysart & Gamble. He had been invited to pitch his plan to Harry Hall, an outspoken son of one of the firm's founding fathers. Hall also happened to be president of the St. Louis Flying Club, and he was more than impressed by the tall young man who looked as uncomfortable in his new suit as he felt.

"Goddamn it," were his first words to Lindbergh when the flier had finished describing his plan for the flight and the attention he felt it could bring to the city of St. Louis. "When the hell are boys like you going to leave the banking to fellas like me? Would I tell you how to fly a goddamned airplane, boy? Sit here for a minute while I make a phone call or two." Fifteen minutes later, they were joined by a vice president of the State National Bank of St. Louis, a private pilot himself who was also the president of the St. Louis Chamber of Commerce.

Together, the two financiers agreed to raise the fifteen thousand necessary for Lindbergh to attempt his transatlantic crossing.

The *"Spirit of St. Louis"*, an airplane to be named in honor of his financial backers in the Missouri city, was about to be born. Lindbergh finally had the financial backing he desperately needed. Now he had to find someone to build the airplane to his requirements, and he had little time to waste. The competitors he knew about were already finalizing their plans and testing their aircraft.

Commander Richard E. Byrd, a famous explorer who had recently flown over the North Pole, was preparing a huge Fokker for an attempt at the transatlantic crossing. Fonck had convinced Igor Sikorsky to build him another plane, and he was already testing it. Navy fliers Noel Davis and Stanton Wooster had just taken delivery of a Keystone Pathfinder biplane for their attempt. Charles Levine, a millionaire who had made his fortune buying and selling war surplus materials, was putting together a team to fly his new Bellanca.

Overseas, the Orteig Prize had captured the fancy of a bevy of European daredevils, particularly the French. Captain Charles Nungesser, who had also won fame in bloody dogfights over the French trenches, and his one-eyed co-pilot, Captain Francois Coli, another French ace, were readying an attempt from east to west in a Levasseur biplane. Maurice Drouhin, another Frenchman who held the world's flight endurance record of more than forty-five hours, was readying an attempt in a Farman biplane. Reports also surfaced that fliers in England, Italy and Poland were making preparations for a go at the Orteig Prize.

The competition was stiff, and Lindbergh scoured newspapers every day for news of their progress. Contrary to the decisions of most of the pilots who were intent on making the crossing, Lindbergh was adamant about making the crossing using a single-engine, single-passenger monoplane. Some of the manufacturers he approached were reluctant or even refused to deliver an aircraft of this design, either worried about their reputations, the pilot's safety or both. Lindbergh wouldn't budge on the design he had in his head.

Upon inquiry, Douglas, Curtiss, Boeing, Martin, Bellanca, Fokerghker, Wright, Travel Air, Columbia and Huff-Daland—all the major aviation design and manufacturing firms—turned him down or offered to build him a tri-motor airplane at more than double the cost Lindbergh had proposed to his small cadre of investors from St. Louis.

One, however, the fledgling and almost unknown Ryan Company of San Diego, took him seriously enough to agree to discuss the design the young pilot had in mind.

Down but never out, the determined Lindbergh headed west by train to San Diego to visit Ryan, a tiny, relatively obscure company and one of several small aircraft manufacturers that had sprung along the coast that had been a sixteenth century Spanish settlement. Fishing was still its number one industry, but San Diego's population had doubled to more than one hundred thousand over the last ten years, and industry was beginning to sprout along the waterfront.

A short taxi ride from Union Station brought him to the Ryan headquarters, a rented, vacant cannery which smelled more like fish than grease, oil and engines. Ryan had no hangar but was building high-wing, M-1 monoplanes as the aircraft that was used by Pacific Air Transport for airmail service between Los Angeles and Seattle.

Lindbergh was familiar with the M-1's capabilities; and as he toured Ryan's ramshackle, but purpose-driven facilities, he quickly grew confident of owner Benjamin Franklin Mahoney. Like Lindbergh, Mahoney had a no-nonsense, no-frills approach to building airplanes, and although he had his doubts about Lindbergh's proposed design, he focused their conversation on what could be done instead of what couldn't.

With Ryan's chief designer, Donald Hall, Lindbergh outlined his planned transatlantic route to Paris and his requirements for the airplane he needed. Nothing about Lindbergh's plans exceeded the envelope of current-day flight design experience. First, they would use a lightweight, air-cooled engine built by the Wright Aeronautical Corporation in Paterson, New Jersey. The J5 Whirlwind engine was the most advanced of its day in terms of power-to-weight ratio. Being air-cooled, it eliminated the weight of radiators, plumbing and pumps, and other peripheral components.

Then Lindbergh stunned Hall by informing him that he would be the only pilot to make the flight. Hall had great difficulty accepting the theory that one pilot could make it to Paris, estimated to take about forty hours on the Great Arctic Circle route. The idea became more palatable when Lindbergh pointed out that the second cockpit could be replaced with another fuel tank which alone would hold three hundred fifty pounds, or fifty gallons, of fuel. The one-pilot concept would actually allow the installation of five fuel tanks of soft steel: a small tank in the nose, the largest tank just behind it, and three others in the overhead wing. Altogether, they would hold four hundred fifty gallons of gasoline weighing approximately twenty-seven hundred fifty pounds, enough to travel some forty-two hundred miles at a cruising speed of over one hundred miles per hour.

Hall bought it, but the additional weight of the main fuel tank required a wingspan ten feet longer than anticipated at forty-six feet, and an increase of the fuselage by slightly more than two-and-a-half feet. The landing gear was widened, and the longer, fabric-covered wing was bolted to the fuselage by two steel struts. Also, by fitting the main tank at the plane's center of gravity, Hall had to move the cockpit farther back, with the consequence that Lindbergh would not be able to see directly ahead. Instead, he would have to use a small periscope to see forward, to which Lindbergh reluctantly agreed. To save weight, removable plastic windows would replace the cockpit's normally fixed glass.

Lindbergh was won over by Hall and Mahoney and convinced of Ryan's capability, despite the company's shoddy overall appearance. He signed a contract on February 27, 1927, calling for one Special Ryan monoplane with a Wright J-5 Whirlwind engine for delivery within sixty days. Further, the plane was to have a fuel capacity of more than four hundred gallons and a minimum cruising range of thirty-five hundred miles at fifteen hundred fifty rpm's with a ten percent reserve. Additionally, Ryan was to install a tachometer, an oil pressure gauge, temperature gauge, altimeter, air speed indicator, clock, compass and a relatively new instrument known as an earth inductor compass, for the sum of ten thousand, five hundred eighty dollars.

It sure as hell wasn't a Cadillac, Lindbergh thought, but it would get the job done. He was sure of it.

What more certainty could a pilot ask for?

Six

The report back to von Hindenburg regarding the Orteig Prize some several weeks later was nothing less than he expected. Perhaps he was just too old for this job. He was tired of war, tired of the weariness and depression that were always the outcome of another German attempt at greatness. He had found himself of late wondering why the German military always felt it necessary to wage war in order for them to be proud of the Fatherland.

Nonetheless, the young men, and even the not-so-young men under his command saw it differently. They would simply not be satisfied until Germany had completely risen from the ashes of its latest tragic failure and had become a power to be reckoned with once more. Von Hindenburg, softening in his late years, would often muse with his wife that he had come to believe that without love there was no life. It sometimes seemed to him that he was surrounded by those who felt that without power, there was shame, and therefore no life.

His beloved son, Oskar, still youthful at forty-four, did not share his father's growing distaste for confrontation, let alone war, but hid his true feelings well. He, like most of von Hindenburg's senior staff, had felt shame when Bismarck was forced to sign the Treaty of Versailles and longed for the day when Germany might once again exercise its might over Europe.

Oskar, in particular, had become a staunch war advocate; but he cleverly kept his true feelings from his father, opting instead to use his immense influence over the German President to exercise slowly the military high command's plan to openly breach the Treaty's requirements and once again rebuild its military to a position of might. The young von Hindenburg felt the blood boiling in his veins as he came to understand the amount of power he had over his father, and consequently the Reich.

Together, in the Imperial Chancellery office that he now rarely left, the President, with his son at his side, was receiving a briefing on the status of the Orteig Prize and the outline of a plan of German response from Minister General Groener and his most trusted military officers and advisors.

Now, in the winter, the odds of a transatlantic flight attempt were slim, Groener told von Hindenburg. However, with the advent of spring, any number of efforts, by teams and individuals from numerous countries, would almost certainly be launched. Groener was again pointed in his criticism about Germany's absence in the competition.

"I find our lack of effort intolerable, Mr. President," Groener said, looking von Hindenburg directly in the eye. "The Prize is, in itself, pointless. It is the perception that is so important. We cannot allow Germany to be seen as a weak follower in the development of aviation technology."

Von Hindenburg groaned inwardly. How often had he heard the same useless rhetoric from other, even more useless, toy soldiers? He restrained himself from embarrassing the officer by responding directly to his challenge. Von Hindenburg, resolved from years of experience, thought it better to allow the idiot to make a fool of himself.

"Unless I am wrong, General, there have been no further attempts at a transatlantic crossing in either direction since Fonck's failure last fall, am I correct?" the President asked.

"Yes, that is correct, Herr President, nor do we expect another attempt until late March at the earliest," Groener replied. "It will more than likely be April before another attempt is made. That is why ..."

Von Hindenburg finished his sentence for him. "We need not make decisions as urgently as you would have us, am I not correct?" von Hindenburg said to the Defence Minister, knowing the General had no other recourse than to agree. "I refuse to consider this subject with any panic."

There was silence around the rectangular marble table around which sat the most accomplished of the German military as they witnessed their superior effectively cut off at the knees. The President may seem feeble, but only a fool would judge him by his aging appearance.

"Despite our distaste for Fonck," the President continued, "does he, or for that matter any of the competitors for the Prize, have any hope of securing it in actuality? Can a transatlantic flight be accomplished?"

Groener was silent, knowing, as did the President's son, that Fonck would have already made a successful trip across the Atlantic had there not been a carefully arranged conspiracy to sabotage Fonck's first effort in September, 1926. The two had become aware of Fonck's intentions only at the last minute and circumvented the President and his advisors using U.S. supporters of Germany to deliberately sabotage the landing gear of the Sikorsky-designed, Frenchman's aircraft. Had they been found out, the outcry for justice in the U.S. would have been immense with disproportionate response, such was the post-war hatred for Germany.

"General Groener, although it is always a pleasure to be in your company, I must admit you are trying my patience on this subject," von Hindenburg continued. "For the truth is, even if we wanted to launch a German effort to win this Orteig Prize, mindful of its importance only as a propaganda tool, we lack the physical resources. Dare I suggest that after nearly a decade of inactivity in the aeronautical sciences, I am relatively certain Germany lacks the intellectual ability to launch a feasible, if not laughable, effort? Does any one of you disagree?"

The President, watching the faces on the cadre of advisors to his left and right, including Oskar, who sat in silence, slowly began to understand that there were things he was not aware of. In fact, as they knew, the Balkenross, the black Greek cross on white that was the official insignia of the Luftstreitkräfte, had not been reduced to ashes as von Hindenburg, the German Parliament and the Western Allies had believed per accord of the Treaty of Versailles.

Without a word of response, von Hindenburg smelled the uneasiness in the room and seemed to turn slowly grayer as he studied each face. His left hand, perpetually grasping a large snifter of cognac, trembled.

"What exactly are you telling me, General?" he asked of Groener while staring directly at his son.

"Perhaps it would be best if I turned to General Ernst Udet, Herr President," Groener responded arrogantly. "As you know, General Udet heads the *Deutscher Luftsportverban,* the Air Sports Union, and as such is highly informed of the day-to-day flight operations and programs ongoing throughout our meager aviation resources."

The DLV was a paramilitary air force known and authorized under the Treaty as an entity responsible for the training of civilian pilots, primarily for the German national airline *Lufthansa.*

General Udet was indeed known to the German President as one of his country's true heroes of the Great War. General Udet's sixty-two kills during the horrific dogfight battles with French and U.S. pilots were second only to the "Red Baron," Manfred Albrecht von Richthofen's eighty confirmed kills. Both Udet and von Richthofen were awarded the Pour le Mérite, known informally during the war as the Blue Max, the Kingdom of Prussia's highest military order.

What the President did not know was that Udet was also in command of top secret development programs at Lipetsk where at least blueprints were being drawn for a new generation of aircraft that the German high command dreamt about, awaiting only new right wing leadership to allow the rebirth of the country's military aviation might.

Von Hindenburg's gaze turned to Udet, whom he had known and respected for more than twenty years, one of only several living recipients of his generation of the Blue Max, a German honor more coveted than sainthood. The President lit a large cigar, by action informing his staff that they were allowed to smoke.

"General Udet, my old friend. I correctly assumed that your presence at this briefing was not of a social nature. I am certain that the time of a man of such heroic proportions can hardly be difficult to fill with matters of far more urgency than the Orteig Prize."

Udet basked only momentarily in the President's honor. He had learned long, long ago that such prose, although well intended, hardly made up for the horrible scar tissue that covered ninety percent of his body and left him in perpetual agony, nor for his missing left eye.

"My President and Field Marshall, I would like nothing better to share hours before the fireplace with you, trading stories of our expeditions, many of which were linked," Udet smiled at von Hindenburg. "Unfortunately, our business today is more serious and pressing." He paused for a long drink from his cognac and a longer pull at his cigar before beginning again. "My time here with you today is hardly unimportant."

Von Hindenburg sat in silence, waiting for Udet to continue. Every eye in the room was on the disfigured war hero. "Herr President, I come before you today for two reasons. The first is at the beckoning of my superior General Groener and my colleagues around this table. The second is a plan for which only I can assume responsibility.

"I am embarrassed to utter the words *national pride* before one of our country's greatest statesmen, whose loyalty and sacrifice to the Fatherland cannot be questioned. Before I continue, let me share with you that I myself, after some years of service to Germany, of late have been mulling over the words *national pride*, and I have arrived at two conclusions.

"The first is that I am a broken-down old war horse who would have trouble climbing into a Fokker today, let alone flying one. The second is the recognition that it is time for the future of our great country to begin to be passed to the next generation of warriors so that they may have an opportunity to raise the might of Germany to the level of respect and admiration that I am afraid two soldiers such as we have failed at."

Von Hindenburg stared into his cognac for long moments without a word of response, his cigar ash growing cold. Unexpectedly, the President's only response was, "Go on, General."

Udet did not hesitate. "The country can ill afford another embarrassment, my President and friend. Germany must be first to conquer the Atlantic, especially in peacetime. I can assure you, a vast majority of the members of Parliament, many of whom I have spoken with regarding the Orteig Prize at one such social event or another, are in agreement. It must be the Fatherland that proves to the world that such achievements are within our grasp and reach and that we have not lost the courage or will to make it thus."

Von Hindenburg motioned to the officer with the cantor of cognac. He waited while his glass was being refilled, never taking his eyes off Udet. Suddenly, he turned to gaze at Groener. On his face for all to see was the disdain, bordering on contempt, he felt for the senior officer.

"General Groener, you never waste an opportunity to remind me of our distinct lack of preparation to attempt to win the Orteig Prize, and in so doing, in my leadership." He turned to address the whole group. "To be frank, I do believe my reluctance to discuss this subject with seriousness is more a symptom of the deficiency of your presentation and credibility than my lack of interest in the subject."

He paused only to relight his cigar. "Now, Groener, you enlist another," he paused again, "who frankly makes up for your weaknesses by his sheer presence to make the case for the Orteig Prize. While I am delighted to hear the thoughts of Herr Udet, I am embarrassed for you."

Groener appeared to have been shot in the heart, hanging his head in utter shame at the dressing down he had just received from the President of the Republic of Germany in front of the entire senior military staff. A bullet would have been merciful.

A vacuum filled the room. Even Udet, who had graciously accepted Groener's invitation to address the President, was silent, instinctively knowing there was no saving his superior. Groener would be retired by evening's end, and he himself was his obvious replacement.

"General Udet," von Hindenburg finally continued, "I, too, am aware of the desire of our elected officials to procure the Orteig Prize for Germany. Now that we have cut through all the rhetoric, how is it that you propose that we accomplish it at this late hour?"

Von Hindenburg paused for effect, allowing a smirk to emerge on his face. "Or am I correct in supposing the hour is not as late for us as I have assumed?"

"On that note, Herr President, allow me to introduce you to Hermann Goering of my staff, who will explain the two prongs of our plan to secure the Orteig Prize for Germany. Although you may not have met Herr Goering personally, I am sure you are well versed in his personal bravery as a pilot in the "Flying Circus", the wing man of the The Red Baron, Manfred von Richthofen, and his exploits as the Commander of the Jagdgeschwader 1 air squadron."

Goering, a tall, slightly rotund senior officer of the German paramilitary, stood up and snapped to attention, saluting the President. Von Hindenburg ignored the salute, preferring instead to stand and shake the General's hand vigorously.

It was only then that he saw the blue-enameled medal, the Blue Max, which was a Maltese Cross with eagles between the arms, hanging from the officer's neck. Goering seized the moment.

Von Hindenburg thought he saw the jugular vein in Goering's neck pulse as if his head was about to explode from intensity. "Herr President, it is my pleasure to brief you on project *Amerike*."

Seven

The Ryan Company, working closely with Lindbergh and almost exclusively on the *Spirit of St. Louis,* completed construction of the airplane in sixty days, exactly on schedule. The pilot was exuberant over the company's dedication to his project, particularly Mahoney and Hall, who had lived up to their every promise.

As called for, the *Spirit* was powered by a Wright Whirlwind J-5C 223-hp radial engine and carried four hundred fifty gallons of gas. A forty-six-foot wingspan topped the fuselage, and the aluminum engine cowling had been engine turned, meaning that a circular pattern had been burnished into the metal, giving it a jewel-like appearance.

Ultimately, the completed airplane was somewhat stubby, even with the elongated fuselage, because of the enormous wingspan. The landing gear tires were enormous at thirty inches tall, and the propeller, purchased from the Standard Steel Propeller Company and made of duralumin, had two blades with a diameter of eight feet, nine inches. The fuselage, with the exception of the turned metal engine casing, was completely covered with grade A cotton fabric finished with cellulose acetate dope in a silver color.

Understandably, as he would be the lone occupant of the *Spirit* for the duration of the previously uncharted crossing, Lindbergh oversaw every detail of the construction of the aircraft and each step of its assembly. He alone took it on every test flight. Man and machine were virtually inseparable.

Testing of the plane revealed some surprises. In flight, the *Spirit* was slightly unstable. Lindbergh soon realized that he would never be able to relax his clutch of the joystick fully, as the aircraft would quickly drift off course and dangerously descend simultaneously. The nose of the airplane would drift right and left without constant attention, and it also had a tendency to "porpoise," or move up and down in an unsettling motion. These were all problems common to newly designed airplanes and typically could be tended to. But Lindbergh told the alarmed engineers at Ryan to leave the problems alone. He was experienced enough to know that having to work the controls of an airplane aggressively was a great way to keep a pilot alert and awake. He would never be able to relax completely.

In fact, the young pilot's plan was to fly low during the day where the air was smoother. The close proximity to the usually active sea surface and speed of the approaching horizon was helpful in keeping the mind alert. At night, he would ascend to as much as five to ten thousand feet, depending on the weather, which would put him high enough, if he was overcome by exhaustion and fell asleep, to pull out of a fatal dive as building gravity forces would surely awaken him.

During the entire period he was airborne, Lindbergh could not allow himself to sleep. Aside from the stability and navigational issues, by design, it would be necessary each hour for him to replenish the nose tank with gas from the larger tanks in carefully distributed amounts to keep the airplane in balance. If the fuel supply in the nose tank ran out, the engine would starve and simply quit in midair, or the aircraft's center of gravity would change, causing a potentially fatal distribution of balance.

Finally, the *Spirit of St. Louis* was complete and ready for extended testing, which in this case would involve hours of local flight followed by a long, cross-country flight in multiple stages. Time was now of the essence, as several teams were in the final stages of readying their aircraft for attempts at the prize. Lindbergh scanned the morning papers daily looking for word of a takeoff.

The Contest Committee of the National Aeronautic Association, the overseeing body for the Orteig Prize, accepted the application for the *Spirit of St. Louis* and assigned it license number N-X211. The N was the international designation for the United States, and X signified that the airplane was of an experimental class. A sign painter in St. Louis was hired for the princely sum of ten dollars to display in black paint the number on the top of the right wing and the bottom of the left. The license number and RYAN NYP were also painted on the rudder and *Spirit of St. Louis* on either side of the engine cowling.

Lindbergh's instincts were correct; even as the sign painter's art was drying, a swarm of activity buzzed around the Orteig Prize in the spring of 1927.

On April 16th, a test flight of Commander Richard Byrd's Fokker C-2 monoplane, *America*, ended in disaster. Sponsored by A. T. Stewart department store owner Rodman Wanamaker, an early visionary of transatlantic commercial flight, Byrd's Fokker tri-motor airplane was nose heavy and failed to gain altitude on takeoff, resulting in a crash and serious injury to the crew. The ever-resilient adventurer Byrd suffered only a broken wrist, but co-pilot Floyd Bennett broke his collarbone and leg, and flight engineer George O. Noville required emergency surgery for a life-threatening blood clot.

Tragedy struck again on April 26, as U.S Naval pilots Lieutenant Commander Noel Davis and Lieutenant Stanton Hall Wooster were killed at Langley Field in Virginia during a test flight about a week before they were scheduled to attempt the New York-to-Paris run. Again, a huge fuel and overload problem was identified as the probable cause of the accident as their Keystone

PathFinder, *American Legion*, failed to gain altitude.

Neither investigation was complete. The investigators simply found no obvious reason for the wrecks but were not compelled to look for signs of sabotage. If the cause was indeed man made, the assailants had hidden their work well; for there were no apparent signs that anyone had meddled with either aircraft.

By now, the world had become captivated with the competition for who would be the first to make the transatlantic flight. Lindbergh began to emerge in the media as a dark horse, Minnesota farm boy versus the well-financed teams led by well-recognized aviation heroes. As competitors seemingly fell from the sky while testing their entries, Lindbergh took final delivery of his new monoplane. After several weeks of testing to work the kinks out of the sleek aircraft, his confidence in the new airplane was soaring.

Rigorous testing during the last days of April indicated that with maximum fuel load, the *Spirit* could reach Paris and fly at least six hundred miles beyond, but first he had to get his airplane back to New York from San Diego.

While making plans to do so, on Sunday morning May 8th, news came that the French team, comprising war aces Captain Charles Nungesser and Francois Coli of the French Air Service in their Levasseur PL-8 biplane, the *White Bird*, had abruptly left Paris' Le Bourget aerodrome. They were expected to land in New York sometime on Monday and in doing so to capture the Orteig Prize. The papers were full of news of the two dashing French pilots, both of whom had exemplary records in the French Air Force during the Great War.

Lindbergh was despondent that the delay in finding a manufacturer of the airplane he required would ultimately cost him the prize, but by Monday, May 9th, excitement surrounding the Nungesser and Coli flight began to turn to alarm. Various eyewitness accounts indicated the *White Bird* had last been seen over the coast of France and Ireland. By Sunday night, it was obvious that the Frenchmen must have crashed after running out of fuel, either over the Atlantic or the wilderness of Newfoundland or Maine.

Suddenly, the eyes of the world turned to Charles Augustus Lindbergh. It would seem he was the only flyer now ready to make such an attempt. But even as Americans began to look to Lindbergh, an alarming piece of news began circulating through the aeronautical community. It was the final findings of the probe into the disastrous René Fonck flight in September of 1926.

Fonck's Sikorsky-designed sesquiplane, although extraordinarily overloaded, had crashed on takeoff. Reportedly, it fell victim to the failed landing gear of the enormously overloaded behemoth of an airplane; but the plane's Russian-born designer, Igor Sikorsky, had never accepted the initial findings and continued to analyze the wreckage on his own, even as he was building a new aircraft for the transatlantic flight for Fonck. Sikorsky could not forget the screams of the two men who had been burned to death in a cauldron of twenty-eight hundred gallons of fuel. He replayed the moments before, during and after the crash over and over again in his mind. Something was missing and he was determined to find it.

With his excruciating attention to detail and inherent genius for design and load limitations, after months of agonizing effort to find the exact cause of the S-35 crash that had taken the lives of two of Fonck's crew members, Sikorsky found what he was looking for. The failure of the tri-motor's landing gear had not been mechanical or the result of metal fatigue.

The landing gear of the airplane had been deliberately sabotaged.

Eight

Like a pair of supremely agile hawks, the heavily armed, single-engine fighter aircraft pounced through cloudless skies on their larger but helpless prey two thousand feet below before its French crew members were even aware of the attack. The roar of the larger airplane's own giant motor drowned out the snarl of the lethal raptors that came at it with their backs to the sun. As the crew became suddenly aware of the assault from above and behind them, the blinding orb screened the identity of those intent upon sending the Frenchmen in their cumbersome, unarmed Levasseur PL-8 biplane to their fate in the cold-water grave of the North Atlantic.

Just moments before, *L'Oiseau Blanc* had been cruising some five hundred feet and one hundred miles off the swelling sea surface along the Irish coast, the wind-whipped whitecaps visible from the cockpit of the military transport that had been specially modified to compete for the Orteig Prize. Theirs was the second attempt, following Fonck's the previous fall, to be the first to make a transatlantic flight from New York to Paris from either direction in a machine that was heavier than air.

The French war heroes, pilot Charles Nungesser and navigator François Coli, seated next to him, had been completely unaware of the sudden presence of the two intruders above and behind them.

Hours earlier, after departing Orly Airport outside of Paris on May 8, 1927, they had reached the northern coast of France at Honfleur, where they waved off with

customary esprit-de-corps an honorary air guard of five
vintage war Nieuport-Delage NiD 42 Air Force fighters
that had accompanied them as the first French team to
attempt the transatlantic crossing.

Now some six hundred miles west of Paris, the two
French airmen quietly celebrated the freedom of heading
out over open ocean, leaving the Irish coast behind, with
thimblefuls of champagne drawn from a canteen carried
solely for that purpose. They were now bound for their
next navigational point of St. John's Newfoundland, just
under seventeen hundred miles away.

It was the longest and loneliest stretch of water over
the Atlantic and the most dangerous for pilots competing
for the Prize.

Nungesser and Coli had spent months preparing their
Levasseur PL-8 two-seat aircraft for the flight. By their
calculations, the airplane would need a minimum four
hundred fifty horsepower engine in order to lift its eleven
thousand pounds into the air. It had a forty-hour fuel
supply and incorporated a design that, once in the air,
would mechanically drop the landing gear to save weight.
The fuselage itself was accordingly waterproofed for a
landing in the ocean during an emergency or in New
York Harbor, should skill and luck be with them.

As professionals, they were an expert team.
Personally, they were as different as night and day.

Nungesser was an extraordinary pilot. Coli had
already proven himself to be a master of navigation,
having helped to set several other distance records since
the Great War.

Nungesser was a constant discipline problem for the
French military. He despised military discipline and
disregarded it openly at every opportunity. A decorated
pilot and ace, his handsome good looks and inexhaustible
taste for strong drink and loose women landed him in
trouble almost constantly. The French papers were nearly

as full of his escapades and flamboyance as they were of his combat exploits.

In the early days of military aviation, when young men willingly strapped themselves into canvas coffins as fragile as they were full of fuel, Nungesser was the quintessential example of the fighter pilots of his generation who enjoyed danger and a reckless lifestyle—and rarely lived beyond their twenty-fifth birthdays. On each side of the fuselages of the airplanes he flew, he had boldly painted a black, mocking death's head. Ironically, it appeared on *L'Oiseau Blanc*, as well.

Coli, on the other hand, was a man of discipline who possessed a rigid mind that was particularly well suited for the navigational requirements of record-setting flights that began in earnest following the War. In 1919 he established several long-distance records in the Mediterranean area, including a flight from Paris to Port Lyautey, Morocco, a distance of twenty-two hundred kilometers. By 1925, the Orteig Prize was beckoning him, and he made several aborted arrangements for an attempt. Finally, he hooked up with Nungesser in late 1926.

Even as Lindbergh was completing his initial testing on the *Spirit of St. Louis* in San Diego at the end of May, 1927, Nungesser and Coli were completing their final arrangements for the next attempt at the Orteig Prize. By spring, 1927, they were ready.

Even as the *White Bird* was rolled out if its hangar before dawn at Orly, photographers were catching their last snaps of the two veteran French pilots. France had grown particularly interested in their effort, and the two men were now national heroes. Orly Field administrators were expecting huge crowds to gather at the airport when, as opposed to if, they received word that the two men had successfully reached New York.

To onlookers, the weather for the takeoff seemed somewhat questionable. It was damp and rainy, two elements that would not help an already overloaded aircraft make air.

The dampness tended to retard the engine's power by slightly reducing its maximum revolutions per minute, while the rain simply caused the elegant, all white aircraft with the French national blue, white, and red tail colors to become heavier. The conditions clearly were not as favorable as possible, and long-range forecasts called for rainsqualls over Newfoundland and snow over Nova Scotia.

Nonetheless, at 5:17 a.m. on Sunday, May 8th, *L'Oiseau Blanc* began its long taxi down the Orly Field runway. At best, the takeoff was shaky as Nungesser nursed the heavily overloaded airplane into the air. It rose a few feet about halfway down the runway, then settled back down, its engine roaring at maximum revolutions, its tires noticeably flattened by the weight. Finally, after nearly half the runway was exhausted, the plane rose, faltered, then rose again, this time for good. When *L'Oiseau Blanc* disappeared from sight of Orly Field, it was no more than seven hundred feet off the ground and laboring for more sky.

Now, more than six hours after leaving Paris and roughly four hours after being last seen, *L'Oiseau Blanc* found itself with unwelcome company. Even as Nungesser screwed the cap back onto his canteen of champagne, he heard, then felt, the all-too-familiar shudder of machine gun fire strafing across the canvas of his upper wing. Then he saw the neatly lined tears through the fabric.

Nearly simultaneously, the fighter pilot's wingman let loose a burst of fire that struck Coli in the back, the wound exiting his chest and almost certainly killing him instantly. The weight of Coli's body fell forward against the flight controls, pushing *L'Oiseau Blanc* into a steep dive. The same burst of fire struck Nungesser across his lap, rendering his legs useless. A second later, fire broke out as raw gas from a pierced fuel line poured over the scorching engine, and the airplane instantaneously became a flying torch enveloping the two fliers in gas-fed flames.

Seconds before the aircraft exploded on impact with the ocean surface, Nungesser fired a single shot into his brain from a hand gun he had carried in his flight jacket.

Flaming fuel from the burning wreckage floating on the surface was quickly extinguished, and gaping holes in the fuselage allowed the carcass of *L'Oiseau Blanc* to sink rapidly. In a matter of moments, little evidence existed of the airplane or the two men who had flown her. Most cruelly, Nungesser and Coli never knew what had happened.

The two attackers, their mission accomplished, waved their wings over the site of the wreckage, saluted, and flew on.

By nightfall of the following day, those awaiting the arrival of the two Frenchmen in New York, as well as those awaiting the good news in France, knew that there would be no celebration.

Nine

Hurrying back to St. Louis from San Diego, in itself a record-setting, fifteen-hundred-mile flight, Lindbergh rested that night in a rented boarding house. He left Lambert Field for New York the next morning before eight o'clock.

Seven hours later he landed in New York at Curtiss Field on Long Island. Without realizing it, he had set a new record of flying cross- country in less than twenty-two hours of flying time. The *Spirit of St. Louis* was mobbed by a sea of reporters, photographers and airplane fans in general who met him as he taxied in.

The shy, reticent Lindbergh was becoming more and more uncomfortable with the media attention suddenly foisted on him. Without so much as acknowledging his achievement, his first words were a question regarding any news of Nungesser and Coli. They were still missing.

To escape the throng of reporters and writers now harassing his every move, the Curtiss Company provided the young pilot with a hangar in which to hide the *Spirit*. Still, he unwittingly found himself the subject of a press conference hastily arranged by representatives of the Wright Aeronautical Corporation, manufacturer of the airplane's engine. All Lindbergh wanted was a good night's sleep and clear weather for a morning takeoff for Paris. He escaped the mêlée as quickly as possible and retired to a small room in the Garden City Hotel for a much needed rest.

Unfortunately, there would be no Paris attempt for several days as the weather over the Atlantic and across the entire Great Arctic Circle route that Lindbergh intended to follow remained bleak. Knowing he would not be able to sleep once he began the long flight, perhaps thirty-six hours or more, Lindbergh tried to take advantage of the extra rest but found it impossible. The press continued to hound him, even in the privacy of his hotel. To make matters worse, his mother arrived unannounced, having traveled all the way from Minnesota to try and talk him out of the flight. He spent hours trying to alleviate her fears, but her presence frayed his own nerves even more.

When Lindbergh did manage to slip away from the chaos for a few hours of sleep, there was no escape from the precious few instruments in the small cabin of his silver bird whenever he closed his eyes.

Ten

I have to clear the trees at the end of the runway. Can I do it? It's so short. What else can I do to shed weight? My clothes, that will do it, I'll leave my clothes behind. But then I'll freeze, and it's already so cold at just a thousand feet.

If only I had more fuel. Four hundred twenty-five gallons seems like so little to go so far. But more gas would mean more weight, and then I'd never clear the trees. I'd crash like Fonck, and with all that fuel in front of me, the Spirit would be so nose heavy that she would spin head first into the trees, if not the gully at the end of the runway before the trees.

The cockpit is so small. It's too tight. I'll never get out if I crash. I'll burn to death like Fonck's crew. What were Clavier and Islaroff thinking as they saw the flames? Were they conscious after the impact? Did they know they were going to burn to death, that the fire would be so intense only their ashes would remain? Did they struggle to escape, knowing it was hopeless?

I need to cut down those trees and have the power lines removed. I should call my mother to see to it. No, I just need more power. The Wright Whirlwind radial engine is too small to carry me safely into the air. I have to remember to throw away the sandwiches I was going to bring. They're too heavy, more weight. No, I'll just take half the sandwiches. I'll need energy.

If I manage to clear the trees and head out over Long Island Sound, then I must follow a northeast course. That will bring me over Maine, Nova Scotia and Newfoundland before the Spirit can get to the open ocean.

Open ocean? What am I, insane? This is lunacy. My airplane is made of wood and cotton cloth and metal. The ocean will never let me across. It will reject such a contraption, throw me back where I came from or drop ice on me from the clouds that will make the Spirit too heavy to fly.

If I make it to darkness, then what? I'll have nothing but simple instruments to tell me how high I am or if I'm about to clip the whitecaps with the fixed landing gear. If the wheels hit the water, it will drag me nose first into a somersault. I'll cartwheel out of control.

I have my raft. I should throw it out. If I crash into the water, I'll drown long before I can get it out and inflate it. I wonder if Nungesser and Coli had a raft. They flew east to west, didn't they? Perhaps I will fly over them on their raft. Would they make room for me?

I should have spoken longer to Mother to tell her that I love her, but the Lindbergh's don't talk much about love. We are ... how did she explain it when I was a child and asked her why it was that father never said "I love you" to me? She said, "We come from an undemonstrative Nordic race, Charles. Your father is very proud of you and loves you very much. He just doesn't say such things." That's what she said. I wish I had told him, "I love you, Father." There must be some sort of Nordic way to say such things. Then he would have known.

I've got less than five thousand feet of runway. I must clear the trees. I must. Then I'll deal with the ocean. When the time comes for me to leave the land behind, to say goodbye to Newfoundland, will I be able to take the great leap of faith I'll need to go on? Will I be afraid and turn back, or will I take strength in the knowledge that no man before me or after me has ever been so truly all alone?

But first, I must clear the trees. Please don't let me burn to death ...

Eleven

He awoke with a start from the dream as imaginary flames were licking at his boots. Lathered in sweat, his hands shaking, it took him several minutes to shake off the nightmare and realize he had been asleep. It was 1:40 a.m., Friday, May 20, 1927.

Lindbergh rose and went to the window, drawing aside the curtains to peer out the window. It was raining heavily, the black pavement below glistening, an abstract red pattern reflecting the neon sign of his hotel. Low clouds covered the city, and he couldn't see the tops of its skyscrapers, which were completely enveloped in fog. He went back to bed for another twenty minutes, tossing and turning before admitting to himself that there would be no more sleep for him that night.

Just a few hours before, he had enjoyed a carefree evening with friends, all but certain that the forecast of heavy rain across New England would preclude him from making an attempt to lift off from Curtiss Field the next morning, or perhaps even the next. He took in the smash Broadway musical "Rio Rita," enjoying the exciting ambience of the theater on 42nd Street, then decided to check with the weather bureau one last time. One of the Ryan boys placed the call, returning a few minutes later to report that the latest updates would be in momentarily, but first indications were that the weather might be breaking along the eastern seaboard and into New England.

The group stopped for dinner, during which Lindbergh made some preliminary plans with his crew for a potential takeoff the next morning or later in the day, if the weather did change. Then he went out to the airfield to give some last minute instructions to the mechanics working on the *Spirit* before heading back to his hotel at midnight.

The revelry of the evening was gone now, and once again his thoughts turned to the flight, the darkened hotel room adding to his apprehension. Long-buried demons invaded his mind, bringing back memories of his childhood and his fear of the dark. He flipped on every light in the room and opened his window wide despite the rain. Moist air blew against his face as he studied the rain, which now seemed to be letting up a bit.

He needed to get out of the room, to get back to his airplane. Quickly, the young man bathed and shaved, dressed in his flying clothes, including Army breeches and lace boots, a light jacket and his favorite blue-and-red-striped tie, and then went downstairs to find some coffee. As the elevator doors opened, a sea of reporters who were camping out in the lobby jumped up and began shouting questions at him. Lindbergh's stomach churned as he realized that even as the world continued to await word of any rescue or sighting of Nungesser or Coli, the eyes of the media had turned to bore in on him.

He desperately scanned the crowd for a familiar face and spied his friend, Frank Tichenor, the publisher of *Aero Digest*, who quickly sized up the pilot's discomfort over the unwanted attention and hustled him off to his car. The two drove out to Curtiss Field in silence, broken only by Lindbergh's cynicism of the press.

"They're only writing about me because they expect me to fail, Frank, that I'll be the next victim," he complained. "Why can't they focus on the *Spirit* and what a wonderful airplane it is, or how the city of St. Louis is supporting me?"

"'Cause that don't sell papers, Slim," Tichenor responded grimly.

There was a steady rain again over Curtiss Field as they arrived just before three a.m. The runway was muddied and puddled. Lindbergh was shocked to find a crowd of nearly five hundred spectators wandering around the hangar where the *Spirit* sat awaiting its destiny. He could not believe the attention his flight was suddenly getting. "Don't these people ever sleep?" he asked Tichenor incredulously.

"They might ask you the same thing, Slim," Tichenor chuckled.

Ken Boedecker, one of the small Ryan crew that had followed him east from San Diego to lend a hand, rang up Dr. James H. Kimball, a New York meteorologist working late into the night at the Whitehall Building in Manhattan for the sole purpose of tracking the weather as best he could across the Great Arctic Circle route. To Kimball's surprise, and despite the fog covering the tops of the city skyscrapers, the weather over the Atlantic was slowly clearing, he told Boedecker. A sudden high pressure area was opening up spots of clearing over Lindbergh's intended path, the crewman repeated for Lindbergh's benefit. As the young pilot digested the news, he came to the conclusion that he had faced far worse conditions flying the U.S. Mail to Chicago.

It's time to swallow hard and go, he thought.

At four-fifteen, with no further consultation with anyone else, his mind made up, he ordered the *Spirit* pulled from its small hangar at Curtiss Field. Commander Richard Byrd, himself mired in legal problems with his financial backers that had prevented him from giving the transatlantic flight a shot already, was among the bystanders.

"Slim," he called out to the young Lindbergh, "let's talk about this."

Lindbergh was startled by the sudden approach of Byrd, who was famously antisocial. At first, he expected the famed explorer, who had been awarded the Medal of Honor for his claimed flight over the North Pole just a year earlier, to try to talk him out of the attempt.

The two men stood awkwardly outside the hangar in the rain, next to the *Spirit of St. Louis*, a tiny bird in comparison to the condor-like, four-man, three-engine air transport that Byrd was preparing for his own attempt. Byrd, for all his fame, had never gotten used to the spotlight and detested the press. He looked around, the rain dripping off the felt fedora on his head, assuring himself that his remarks could not be overheard by the news jackals that continuously hounded him, before he spoke.

Commander Byrd's own plane, the Fokker *America*, was safely ensconced in a large hangar at the adjoining, but much longer, Roosevelt Field, which he had rented out to prevent any other Orteig Prize hopeful from taking advantage of its longer runway.

Satisfied that the two men were alone and could not be overheard, Byrd continued. He did not know Lindbergh at all but had tremendous respect for the young man, who he knew was about to look death square in the face, just as he had done himself a few times.

"It seems kind of lonely over there at Roosevelt," Byrd began. "If the *America* could finally get some air under her and drop out a few dozen lawyers, we might make use of it ourselves tonight." He shook his head with disdain. "But that isn't about to happen. So how about you getting someone to throw a rope on that tail hook of yours and tow the *Spirit* across the way. It'll give you another three thousand feet or so to get all that gas in the air. Sure would break my heart to see such a beautiful airplane run out of room to make some history."

Lindbergh's draw dropped. He was speechless. Finally, he stuck out his wet right hand and shook the explorer's hand with the thanks that wouldn't come to his lips. The odds of getting the *Spirit* airborne, with an as yet untested full load of fuel, had just increased beyond calculation.

Without another word, Byrd turned to walk away. Then he stopped, turned, and said to his still-stunned competitor, "Make sure you send me a postcard from Paris. I'll want to show it to the lawyers." He smiled, tipped the brim of his hat, then walked on and disappeared once again into the crowd.

Hurriedly, Lindbergh barked orders that the *Spirit* was to be moved to the adjacent field. Hooked up to a dilapidated Studebaker pickup truck, the airplane, with its gem-like, machine-turned engine cowling wrapped in a tarp, was dragged to the end of Curtiss Field to a gravel road that connected it to the western end of Roosevelt Field. There, fittingly, the silver bird was aimed toward Paris.

By now, the rain had nearly stopped, and the continuing reports from Dr. Kimball indicated clearing skies over Maine, Nova Scotia and Newfoundland. A large truck carrying barrels of the *Spirit*'s fuel supply arrived, and the arduous task of hand pumping fuel into five gallon buckets, which were then poured into the airplane's five fuel tanks by hand, was begun.

When fully loaded, the *Spirit* — including its fuel and twenty gallons of oil, Lindbergh wearing his sheep-wool lined flight suit, five sandwiches, his passport and a bank draft worth about five hundred dollars — weighed in at approximately five thousand pounds. That was less than one quarter of the weight of René Fonck's ill-fated S-35 which had crashed the previous fall.

But even the light load, tolerable takeoff conditions and the extra three thousand feet of runway left

Lindbergh unsure of his ability to coax his untested airplane into the air. The *Spirit*'s total flight time since he first took her up over the crystal clear skies of San Diego was short of twenty-eight hours, less than the amount of time it would take him to make the crossing to Paris.

Amid the hundred last-minute preparations going through his mind was a gnawing in the pit of his stomach, a fear of burning to death, helplessly strapped into what amounted to a flying gas tank.

The thought grew heavier on his mind as the moment approached when he would attempt to lift the wheels of the *Spirit of St. Louis* from the muddy runway of Long Island's Roosevelt Field.

Twelve

Seamus McGill sat drifting in *The Lovely Mary* nearly one hundred thirty miles from the Irish coast, casting his nets for the herring that filled the waters this far southwest in the Atlantic. His thirty-five-foot trawler was named after his late wife, Mary Elizabeth, who had been taken from him by illness just the year before. When he had built the boat with his own hands some forty years ago, he had named her after his wife so that he would think about his bride every day they were parted as he plied the ocean for its bounty and their supper. Now, alone, he spent as much time on the aging boat as he could, if only to be close to her name.

McGill had been at sea for several weeks, fishing but also performing the daily task he had been hired to do by the stranger who had bought him a pint at Kerry's Ring the night before he weighed anchor out of Dingle Bay. For the princely sum of two hundred Irish pounds, the man required the fisherman to watch the sky, day and night, for airplanes. He was to report any sightings by using a complicated radio set he had been provided, which actually looked more difficult to operate than it was.

He had only used the radio once, perhaps a week before after spying a lone airplane several miles from where he anchored, flying low over the surface of the Atlantic in the early afternoon. *Was it the eighth of May?* He tried to recall.

McGill dutifully radioed the sighting of the airplane and its position to the frequency provided. Several minutes later, the radio had crackled a simple, "Thank you, that is all," in response.

The equipment had sat unused and eerily silent ever since.

Thirteen

Paul von Hindenburg — the greatest Field Marshall in German history, the man to which the leadership of Germany fell at its most dire hour, the warrior who banished a monarchy and established a republic — was tired. He was weary of the young men he commanded who insisted that the priority of the government must be to rebuild the military might of a country that desperately needed a climate of peace and aspiration. They wanted tanks, battleships and bombers. The aging President knew that what the nation needed was economic, industrial and agricultural growth, academic, social and moral revision and a renaissance of art and science. Unfortunately, he was simply too worn out to fight anymore.

He sighed, finally having come to terms with the truth. "General Udet," von Hindenburg said, more interested in a final cognac before bed than further discussion with the man who would now be charged with secretly rebuilding the German Luftstreitkräfte, "I leave this matter of the Orteig Prize in your hands.

"I am grateful for your exquisitely detailed briefing and compliment you on the thoroughness of your plan; but frankly, the whole matter, as I have made clear several times, does not interest me. Effectively, you are free to handle this matter as my official delegate with complete authority."

Udet beamed and turned to his subordinate, Gruppenführer Hermann Goering, who had just completed a briefing to his superior and the President on the progress of his plan to capture the Orteig Prize for Germany, as well as the intervening steps that were required to give the Luftstreitkräfte the time it needed to build its new airplane capable of a transatlantic flight from Berlin to New York.

"Nungesser and Coli were worthy opponents, Herr President, I assure you. I faced them myself in our rickety Fokkers many years ago over the trenches in France. They died quickly but with honor," Goring informed the President.

Von Hindenburg waved off the Luftstreitkräfte General's testament to the heroism of the fallen enemy with a wave of his glass and obvious disdain.

"I hardly think that ambushing two unarmed men in a dilapidated transport airplane overloaded with gasoline was an act we should be proud of, Herr Goering. Let us just say that it was a necessary step toward achieving our goal." He paused for a moment. "What I mean to say is the goal of the Reich."

Although he would not dare argue with the President, Goering was nonetheless proud of masterminding what amounted to the murder of the two Frenchmen; but his real achievement was how masterfully he had hidden the act from a world focused on the whereabouts of the two pilots.

"Yes, Herr President, as you see it," Goering responded. Udet was silent, knowing there was no need to intercede. Hermann Goering was simply the most intelligent, yet despicable, man he had ever known, capable of any act of cruelty or brutality and certainly not one to be intimidated by an aging general and politician in his last days.

Although literally disgusted by Goering as a human being, the thirty-four-year-old Gruppenführer was exactly the man Udet needed for the job at hand. A violent morphine addict, he was prone to fits of sadism and brutality that led him to a prolonged stay in the Långbro Asylum for the criminally insane in Sweden. So dangerous as to be sometimes straitjacketed, Goering's psychiatric reports claimed him to be a brilliant, yet hysterical and unstable personality, simultaneously capable of great acts of physical courage and moral depravity.

The man was incredibly insane, but he was useful for Udet, who could count on his subordinate to accomplish any task required that would boost his own personal career, for which he had much higher aspirations. The butchering of Nungesser and Coli was the perfect test for his protégé, and Udet had not been disappointed. The man who had won the Blue Max for his bravery, an honor associated with the valor and moral equivalent of knighthood, was also capable of cold-blooded murder.

Udet and Goering left the Imperial Chancellery together after being dismissed by von Hindenburg.

"How goes the design, Gruppenführer Goering? I trust we have adequate resources attacking the problem in Lipetsk?" Udet asked.

Goering laughed. "General Udet, you know me better. The requirements of the Orteig Prize do represent some challenges; but they are minor and I am convinced that we will overcome them shortly. We will have an airframe for testing within the next several weeks."

"In the meantime, should there be any further attempts at a transatlantic crossing by any other team or individual, we have our resources in place to handle the situation as we did Nungesser and Coli, Fonck and the others," Goering explained. "We have two heavily-armed Henkel floatplanes hidden along the Irish shore just outside of Dingle Bay. The plan worked quite well with the French. A radio signal from an Irish fishing boat alerted us to their arrival. The rest was uneventful."

"Well done, Gruppernfuhrer. As to the new plane at Lipetsk ..."

Goering did not allow him to finish. "I have my best minds working on various competitive designs, Herr Udet."

" Competitive designs?" Udet asked, confused.

Goering laughed. "I will tell you only that the team that submits the final design for production believes it will be allowed to go free," Goering responded, his face giving away not one ounce of emotion. Udet's stomach churned.

"The real challenges," Goering continued, "are in developing the horsepower for the relatively heavy vehicle we envision, with range enough and payload capacity to deliver on our real objective."

"The aerial surprise we will visit upon New York City?" Udet asked without sentiment.

"Exactly," Goering responded. "When I am done, there will be a new Treaty to be signed in Versailles, and the terms will be decidedly different." A vision of the burning skyline of Manhattan was never far from his mind's eye.

"I trust you have not discussed the full details of our plan with the President?" Goering asked.

"Nature is slowly taking its course with von Hindenburg," Udet responded. "By the time we are ready to launch our plan and prove not only the intellectual superiority of the German people, but indeed, their will to fight again, Herr President will be dead and buried, the victim of old age and too much cognac." He paused and held his colleague's sleeve. "If not, I will simplify matters the old-fashioned way."

Goering looked his commander in the eye, a grave seriousness crossing his face. Gradually, his look softened, and he broke into a grin, the likes of which startled Udet.

He suddenly felt as if he were looking into the face of Satan himself.

Fourteen

The first thing visitors would notice upon arrival to the Russian city of Lipetsk would be the nearly overpowering odor of minerals. It so happened that the city was built over one of the largest balneological deposits of minerals in the world. Lipetsk had been a gathering point for the sick and infirm of wealthy means since the early 1800s for treatments at its sulphate and chloride sodium therapeutic baths, in other health-restoring ferruginous springs, and through wraps of peat mud and other rejuvenators. It was located more than four hundred kilometers southeast of Moscow on the banks of the Voronezh River.

Despite its unique fragrance, the city of Lipetsk was also a carefully guarded metropolitan jewel of Russia, a fact carefully hidden by the extended royal family of Russian Tsar Nicholas II and those rulers who came before him dating back to the 16th century. It was a stunning center of culture and art, the treasures of which were hidden from the mostly poor population of twenty-one thousand. It was not until after the October 1917 Revolution and the subsequent years of upheaval that public libraries, museums, theater and the arts began to flourish in the city, substantially broadening the culture of its people.

Simultaneously, the Lenin government made massive investments in Lipetsk in a wide range of manufacturing operations and facilities and built colleges and universities to fill them with educated workers. Consequently, the great bulk of Russia's research, engineering, development and production efforts in the aviation industry also found its way to Lipetsk. Russia too had suffered enormously from war and revolution, but Lipetsk appeared to be one of the outstanding examples of communism at work.

Gruppenführer Hermann Goering cared little for the remarkable success of Lipetsk. The city was important to him only because it afforded him the opportunity and the resources to begin the process of rebuilding his beloved Luftstreitkräfte, which he knew was the first step toward exacting the vengeance he would reap on the Allied Powers that had so humbled the Fatherland.

The unexpected cooperation of the Russians, who were willing to trade the trust of the Allies for German technology in Lipetsk, gave him not only the educated engineers, development and manufacturing facilities he needed, but also a method to train German pilots in secrecy. These men were blended into the ranks of the official Russian 4th squadron of the 40th wing of the Red Army and could not be distinguished as members of the German Luftstreitkräfte.

Within hours of the meeting of the Kamarilla following Rene Fonck's disastrous takeoff attempt on September 21, Goering had wired orders to three distinct design teams at the secret Luftstreitkräfte Training School in Lipetsk to begin preparations of their own for a transatlantic crossing.

The orders were clear. Design teams from three German manufacturers -- Junkers, Focke-Wulf and Messerschmitt — were to begin competitive designs immediately to precise parameters. The plane was to be a super-long-range bomber that would have a range of ninety-five hundred miles. The four or six-engine aircraft was to carry a maximum payload of eight thousand pounds at a cruising speed of roughly two hundred twenty miles per hour and have a maximum speed of three hundred fifty miles per hour. In addition to its bomb load, it would carry heavy defensive armaments and a crew of between six and ten.

The airplane's single most important mission was to fly from a secret base in Berlin and follow the Great Arctic Circle flight path over Newfoundland and Nova Scotia and on to the east coast of the United States. The aircraft would then achieve its strategic objective before immediately returning to Berlin, nonstop -- a total flight time of more than sixty hours. The strategic mission for which the airplane was being designed was not specified. For the engineers considering the orders, the objective did not need to being spelled out in any greater detail.

German engineers from the three chosen manufacturers were aghast. The design parameters for the proposed airplane were preposterous. Further, it was a psychological challenge for which they were unprepared, for the target was plainly obvious: New York City. The objective was just as clear: to bomb Manhattan and begin war anew. More terrifying still, even if unspoken, was the price of failure for the teams whose designs failed to be selected. Although promised their freedom, they knew that no one who knew of the bomber's existence would live. The mission was a death sentence, win or lose.

Through that long first night, engineers chain-smoked their way through reams of roughly penciled designs. Hundreds, if not thousands, of questions remained to be answered, but within twenty-four hours of Goering's nightmarish orders, on paper existed the Junkers Ju 390, the Focke-Wulfe Ta 400, and the Messerschmitt Me 260. Each of the extraordinarily long-winged, multi-engine beasts represented untested theory, aeronautical concepts and designs that were far beyond the dreams of the most aggressive and confident engineers in the world. At best, the engineers were guessing at excessively high wing loads, unknown flight stability, engine performance and maneuverability issues, and the need for high takeoff speeds that might require augmentation such as a rocket sled.

Theoretically, each design was capable of fulfilling the mission assigned by Goering. If it could be done, it would. Unfortunately, what motivated the minds of the engineers working day and night to achieve the impossible was not reward, fame or even satisfaction. It was their very lives. The mission was a trap for all of them. They knew that no man with any knowledge of the bomber would be allowed to survive. The only hope of survival was more a game of slowing down the design process and dragging out the end result. With Goering leading the charge, there was little hope of protracting his iron-fisted schedule. There was little hope of surviving the trap, but hope was all they had.

Although they did know it, a quiet man among them offered a chance for survival, however slight. He would give his own life, if necessary, to ensure that they all failed.

It was possibly the only way to save their lives.

Fifteen

The slight, bespectacled man stood up to force the kink from his aching back and tapped his mechanical pencil hard on the drawing of the tail section of the Messerschmitt Me 260 section drawing. He had been bending over the drawing board of the detailed plans of the super bomber for hours. "We are off," he pronounced. "Our calculations are incorrect." He wiped the perspiration from his face with a handkerchief. "I must take a break -- a cigarette, perhaps."

"Go, Heinz. I will cover for you. Just make it fast," his colleague standing behind him offered. "Goering will be here soon," he said, reminding his friend of the morning's announcement of the Gruppenfuhrer's surprise visit later that day.

The man called Heinz, a German who "volunteered" to serve in Lipetsk to ensure the safety of his family, quietly left the room and the strong funk which had built up inside, the result of dozens of engineers working nonstop for hours in a windowless room. He stepped outside the door and waved past an armed security guard, holding up his cigarette package for the sentry to see. The guard nodded.

It was cold but not so bad for early winter on the river. He could remember worse. The fresh air felt good on his clammy skin. He walked a few yards away from the building along the bank of the river, removing the last cigarette from his pack. Luxuriating in the moment of peace and the bitterly refreshing taste of the tobacco, the engineer quickly finished his smoke, flicked the ash off the butt, and placed the now cool remnant into the empty cigarette package. Then he absentmindedly tossed it onto the river bank and left to rejoin the chaos and his place at the drawing board.

The Russian guard laughed to himself. *The German slob,* he thought to himself, *as if the river needs further polluting.*

Just at the changing of the guard some three hours later, the sun having long set, Goering's car entered the lot of the heavily insulated metal building that served as the Messerschmitt team's operations headquarters.

The outside perimeter of the building on the river bank was momentarily unguarded when a darkly clothed, unshaven Russian peasant, a street sweeper or other menial social worker from the looks of his clothes, appeared at the river bank. He reached into his inside coat pocket and pulled out a pint of cheap, yellow Russian vodka, unscrewed the cap and drank deeply.

Looking surprised as he gazed along the shoreline, he spied the cigarette package, leaned down and retrieved it. He laughed expressively, as if delighted with his new treasure, then opened the pack and found it empty. He shrugged his shoulders and then stuck the wet package into his coat pocket. After another pull at the bottle, he shuffled off down the river bank that would eventually lead him several miles up the road, to the small but warm shack in which he lived alone.

It was a quiet life, but as he closed the blinds to the few windows in his abode and checked the lock on the door, he reminded himself just how quickly his peace and quiet could become torture and imprisonment if he were found out.

Confident he was alone, he grabbed the metal frame of his bed and yanked it a few feet to the left, exposing a dirty rug that served as insulation under it and covered the bare concrete floor. He pulled the rug aside, revealing a wooden trap door which he pulled open with slight effort. He reached inside and pulled out a beat-up cardboard suitcase. Carefully opening it, he pushed back the top to reveal a short-wave radio, which he quickly turned on and allowed to warm up.

While waiting, he reached into his coat pocket and retrieved the empty pack of cigarettes. The cold, used butt was still there. It was the code from the engineer Heinz that he had desperate, urgent information to share, valuable enough to be worth blowing the cover it had taken him years to establish. He had to come out.

The man held the cigarette butt in his hand and stared at it for a long moment, mentally retracing his steps to be sure he had correctly interpreted the signal, then brought a small microphone to his lips, cranked the radio and made contact.

"Swimming pool here," he said, using the location code for Lipetsk and its sulfate baths.

Nothing. A moment later, a response.

"The water must be cold." It was the correct response.

"Quiet Man must come home to talk," the spy spit back into the radio, referring to the engineer known only to him as "Quiet Man". He knew little else about the man.

Nothing. Then the air crackled with a response. "Pack."

The radio went dead with the final word. The message had been received by London. British Naval Intelligence Lieutenant Commander Noel Breech would be extracted from Lipetsk by undercover British agents in slightly more than forty-eight hours while the sentries were busy with a changing of the guard. That first step would put other steps in motion.

Most importantly, in short order, Goering's complete plan would be in the hands of the British — and the Americans.

Sixteen

The American President sat by the fire in his enormous chintz arm chair, deep in thought as he sipped his after-dinner coffee and shared a large Cuban cigar with British Conservative Prime Minister Stanley Baldwin.

The air was full of spring in Washington D.C, and both men appeared to be in rare, relaxed moods. Such moments were few and far between for men who carried the weight of their nation on their backs as a matter of daily duty.

At age fifty-six, President Calvin Coolidge was comfortably ensconced in the middle of his second term and taking satisfaction in his unprecedented popularity following election in his own right. He was also enjoying the peace that had finally settled over the United States following the end of the Great War and the signing of the Treaty of Versailles in 1919.

Economically, the country was slowly recovering from one of its bleakest periods and enjoying the loose, carefree early years of the Jazz Age. Prohibition was a nagging issue, not one that he necessarily supported; but he intended to let his successor handle that can of worms, already having made up his mind not to seek another term as President.

The nation's Chief Executive was a man of painfully few words. Coolidge's conversations were marked by short, clipped sentences and, whenever possible, one-word answers. He was a popular president despite his shyness, owing perhaps to his contradictory style of sharing much information with the American people. In his Presidency, since March of 1923, he had held more than five hundred press conferences, allowing the media, and therefore his countrymen, extraordinary access to the man and the Office of the President.

Tonight, following dinner with Baldwin, a favorite ally and friend, their conversation was loose and random. The sixty-year-old Baldwin, in his second year as Prime Minister under the government of King George V, was not quite so relaxed as Coolidge, especially knowing he was about to inform the President of some disturbing news. He so hated to ruin an otherwise delightful evening.

Like Coolidge, Baldwin was a quiet man who did not enjoy stage lights but was a political genius. His hands were slightly fuller at the moment with issues at home. The economic recovery of the United Kingdom following the war was running out of steam; and unemployment was climbing at a steady, if not yet alarming, pace.

Of even greater concern to Baldwin were the recent indications picked up by British Naval Intelligence that Germany was toying with rearmament in strict violation of the terms of the Treaty, through various secret arrangements and agreements with other eastern European countries. To his surprise, Russia was among them. The Treaty of Versailles was not yet ten years old, and already it was in serious jeopardy.

In a brief respite of silence from their chat, the two men took pleasure in their cigars and the fire that roared in the great hand-carved Georgian mantle. Ironically, it had replaced one destroyed by the British in 1812 when the invaders burned the original White House and the city of Washington. Baldwin's eyes swept the large office of the man who, admittedly or not, was the most powerful representative of the most powerful nation on earth. America's last minute and successful intervention into the Great War that had enveloped the world had ended any questions about the strength of U.S. resolve.

He was envious of the spacious, oval-shaped office designed by Coolidge's predecessor, William Howard Taft, which was a lively space that encouraged discussion compared to the gloomy quarters of his offices at 10 Downing Street in London. However, he found the room's ornate Georgian Revival theme, with walls covered in a vibrant green faux sea grass paper, simply distasteful. Baldwin, like most of the world leaders who visited with the American President in the Oval Office, wrote off the dreadful decorative combination as that of a man who had inherited it and had much more important matters to tend. They were correct on both counts.

Just as the Prime Minister cleared his mind of the triviality and was about to speak, a black steward in full formal dress entered from a door to the left of the fireplace. He quickly refilled their coffee cups without asking and noiselessly retired through the same door, the hidden latch closing as silently as the door had swung open over the thick, green rug. Baldwin took note of how astonishingly still the room could be -- much like its chief occupant.

Baldwin quickly collected his thoughts before proceeding. It was only ten days before that he had received a lengthy briefing from his British Naval Intelligence Attaché and a rather odd Lieutenant Commander of the Intelligence Service. The latter was an experienced agent who had, over a period of several years, penetrated the Lipetsk industrial complex in Russia under the guise of a German aeronautical engineer. Upon the success of his requested extraction by British Commandos, knowing that he must get his considerably important information in detail to his highest superiors, he shared with them a remarkably alarming tale. The Lieutenant Commander reiterated his own observations along with the information he had collected with his collaborator, the German "Heinz".

That story, and additional information hurriedly collected from sources all over Europe indicating German activity relating to rearmament, had caused the Prime Minister to request an immediate meeting with the President. The Prime Minister had come to Washington aboard the dreadnought *HMS Rodney*, the Royal Navy battleship's first transatlantic journey to the United States, having been commissioned just months before.

"Mr. President," Baldwin began. His sudden change to official formality signaled Coolidge that what was coming was serious. "I have a rather serious matter involving German attempts at rearmament that I must speak with you about."

Coolidge winced. Since assuming the Presidency, with the signing of the Treaty of Versailles long over from an American perspective, he had done his utmost to keep the U.S. out of European affairs. He had been nearly overwhelmed by the full domestic economic fallout of U.S. involvement in the war and was just now seeing signs of a revitalization of American spirit. The very last thing he wanted to discuss was German rearmament.

But Coolidge had long ago forged the respect for Baldwin to know that what the British P.M. considered serious was indeed serious. Nonetheless, in keeping with his inordinately quiet and introverted personality, he responded simply, "Ah, finally we hear from the Germans."

The Prime Minister breathed deeply. "Yes, the Germans, old friend. I'm afraid we both knew this day would come, given the remarkable failure of sensitivity employed in drafting that worthless document in Versailles."

"So what are they up to now?" Coolidge inquired in a tone of voice he might have used to ask about the well-being of the P.M.'s grandchildren.

"It's not what they're up to. What I am about to tell you will probably sound more preposterous than when I first heard it," Baldwin responded.

Coolidge quickly tired of mysteries. "Then what is it?" he asked, his voice rising an octave.

Baldwin flicked an ash toward the fireplace. "It is war that the Germans seek again, Mr. President; and they are planning for it now through various means, which until recently, and I must add embarrassingly, have escaped our notice."

Coolidge stared at his friend, too stunned to speak. Finally, he said the inevitable.

"Mr. Prime Minister, we have both long known that the Treaty of Versailles is not worth the paper it was drafted upon," he said. "It is only a matter of time before Germany raises its viper's head once again to start the whole bloody mess over, only this time on a grander and far more murderous scale. It has been my daily prayer that more sensible heads would intervene long after you and I are gone, and true and lasting peace would be possible. From what you indicate, it appears that will not be possible.

"On a more practical scale," the President continued, "it will take the Germans years to rebuild their forces. Their navy has been scuttled, and every Luftstreitkrafte aircraft wearing the iron cross has been destroyed. How is it that the Germans believe they are in a position to threaten war now?"

Baldwin exhaled deeply, wishing his coffee was a strong brandy.

"Mr. President," the P.M. responded, his voice low and apologetic, "there is perhaps nothing more humbling for a leader than to recognize that he has been duped. I, Sir, sit beside you, a fool."

"Based on our most recent intelligence reports, the Germans are hard at work rebuilding their naval fleet through shipping companies of convenience in countries throughout Europe. Submarines are being built for the Huns in pens in Holland. Tanks, trucks, gun barrels, small weapons, and even poison gas, are being produced in German factories disguised as casting facilities, trucking plants and chemical firms under the guise of agricultural products."

"Some of the largest companies in Europe are involved in the funding ... Krupp in Russia, Pintsch in Holland, and Solothurn in Switzerland, just to name a few. The Germans are using their own operations that existed in neutral countries before the war for some of this production, which, by the way, is a gaping hole in the *Treaty of Versailles* that none of us saw. To pay for it all, it appears that German banks are routing government funds to the industries in these off-national locations. The governments of Spain, Turkey, Austria and Finland are also known to be involved, although to what extent has yet to be determined."

The President was silent.

"The bottom line, old chap," the Prime Minister continued, his face ashen, "is that everyone is working with the Germans, everyone is making money, and the Hun is rearming at a rate of production that in some areas will exceed their highest production levels achieved during the great war of less than a decade ago."

Without hesitating, Coolidge, usually not a drinking man, rang a small hand bell next to his chair. Immediately, the steward appeared carrying a bottle of scotch and two crystal goblets.

For the next several moments the two world leaders sat in silence, allowing the anesthetic qualities of the fine twenty-year-old liquor to help them through the difficult conversation still to come. President Coolidge stared intently at the three-by-five foot oil painting hanging above the fireplace, the 1870 *Rocky Mountain Landscape* by American artist Albert Bierstadt. It was on loan from the Metropolitan Museum of Art in New York and had been hand picked by the President himself.

It was a montage created by Bierstadt, who traveled the American West painting for some thirty years, and Coolidge liked to believe that it was a scene an American frontiersman might have come upon. For the President, time stopped with this image, a moment frozen for an instant. He often contemplated the painting, wondering how to freeze himself in those rare, fleeting moments of world peace he had experienced in his lifetime.

"There is more," Baldwin added. He took a long swallow from his scotch before continuing. Coolidge sighed.

"Apparently, the Germans have most recently revived their attempts to stir up their hornets, the Luftstreitkräfte," Baldwin continued.

"You will recall that at the end of the war, the Luftstreitkräfte had proven itself an amazingly dangerous new element to warfare and the Germans particularly adept at advancing aeronautical technology at a pace far superior to the Allies combined. I shudder to think what would have happened had they not run out of time and resources and had been able to transfer some of their designs from the drawing table to the airfield. Some of the engineering drawings we discovered were truly remarkable … and frightening."

Baldwin had Coolidge's complete attention. "We, or I should say British Naval intelligence, believed that these efforts had been eradicated and the key engineering resources scattered throughout civil aviation operations, especially Lufthansa, the German national mail and passenger domestic service, and other commercial aeronautical companies."

He paused, angry with himself for allowing the situation to get so far out of hand. "We were wrong. The best and brightest of Germany's engineers have been drawn together again under the guise of several commercial airplane and component manufacturers — Junkers, Focke-Wulfe and Messerschmitt, to name just a few — and subsidized by hundreds of hand-picked, technically accomplished prisoners of war who were hidden from the Allies. Together, they are working feverishly, Mr. President, as we speak."

Coolidge was alarmed, but as always, his practical side calmed his emotions.

"So they are back at work," the President scoffed. "It will be a decade or more before they could reconstitute the operations, development, testing and manufacturing backbone they would need to build even the simplest of aircraft, let alone assemble an industry and a fleet of the super planes found on their drawing boards."

"Not to mention the various rocketry sketches we unearthed," Baldwin added. Coolidge shook his head in silence.

The Prime Minister downed the last of his scotch and stared into the fireplace, saying nothing. The President patiently waited for Baldwin to begin again.

Baldwin continued. "Unfortunately, and quite inexplicably, the Russians have proven most gracious hosts for our friends, the Germans, willingly supplying them with everything they need to launch the aviation industrial complex needed to support a major and near-term war effort. It is in a small Russian city known as Lipetsk, roughly five hundred miles southeast of Moscow. You may have heard of it. The Russian communists are most proud of its achievements since the October Revolution."

Coolidge drained his own scotch and poured another for each of them.

"Yes, I have heard of Lipetsk," Coolidge replied. "It seems to be the one place in the whole of Russia where communism has indeed worked; although, obviously and as usual with the Russians, there has been an alternative motive."

They were silent together for many minutes, each deep in thought. The steward appeared again, tended to the fire and left. It was like having an alter-ego, Baldwin thought to himself, watching the man. The President no sooner thought of something than it was taken care of. If only peace in Europe could be so easily managed.

"Why now, Prime Minister?" Coolidge asked. "You still haven't given me a reason for the German's abrupt interest in rebuilding the Luftstreitkräfte, let alone the rest of their military might. There must have been a trigger. I thought we might at least trust von Hindenburg during his last few years."

"Von Hindenburg is not the problem," Baldwin said without hesitation. "It is the youngsters beneath him who are gradually assuming his powers as he ages and who are still chafing at the goddamned Treaty," Baldwin responded without hesitation. "Damn my bloody blindness in allowing that fool business to be ratified," he tortured himself.

The Americans had been just as blind, Coolidge thought, although he had not yet been in the political picture when it had been drafted. Nonetheless, when it came to spreading blame for the tool of vengeance that the Treaty of Versailles was in actuality, he was never prone to claim American innocence.

"You ask me what the trigger was, Mr. President?" Baldwin responded. "You could not guess it in a million years." He paused for a moment, collecting his thoughts, before continuing.

"Since the signing, no adversary has slighted the Germans or advanced upon their territory," Baldwin said. "No new and more egregious demands for postwar reparations have been made. Not even von Hindenburg's mistress has been left off *Vanity Fair*'s most well-dressed list. The slight is far more dangerous, I am afraid."

"Then when is it, man?" the President nearly shouted, his patience for the long windedness of the Britain almost at the breaking point.

Baldwin leaned forward in his chair, shook his head slightly and said, "It is the German ego, Mr. President, and it has to do with the famous Raymond Orteig prize."

"Raymond Orteig," Coolidge repeated trying to place the name. "You mean the New York hotelier? Now it's coming back to me. You can't be referring to that silly grandstanding, or should I call it barnstorming, prize for the first crossing of the Atlantic he has proposed?" Coolidge asked, incredulously. "It has to do with the first crossing between New York and Paris, am I not correct?"

"You are absolutely correct, Mr. President ..."

"Has the world indeed gone mad?" Coolidge interrupted, furious at even the thought of such nonsense.

"As to the sanity of the world, Mr. President, I can only guess," Baldwin moved to calm the President, who was red faced, "but you underestimate the value the Germans place on this achievement.

"You see, it is intolerable to those of the German Luftstreitkräfte who failed in 1918 to see upstarts like the U.S. and the French, especially the most hated French, to become, from at least a public perspective, the leading aviation power on earth. They plan again to have the most powerful air force on earth.

"That is another of those entitlements the Germans seemed to have inherited, and by God, they will do anything to prevent any man, woman or nation from being the first to accomplish what you see as a grandstanding attempt. Yes, it is a matter of national pride, especially as to the seat of power. Had the Orteig Prize been established for transatlantic flight from New York to Berlin instead of Paris, the overreaction might not have been so great. As it is, to suggest that Paris is the seat of greatness in Europe is far more than the German military can swallow."

"Good God, man, how ridiculous." The President dropped his head to his hands as if he had a sudden headache. "It is almost adolescent."

Baldwin drank from yet a third scotch and gazed up at Bierstadt's *Rocky Mountain Landscape* over the still-raging fireplace, wishing he were anywhere else. "My sentiments exactly, Mr. President, except that the German plan to retaliate to ensure that no one successfully crosses the Atlantic before a German airplane can do it from Berlin."

Coolidge turned to face Baldwin squarely and looked him in the eye, slightly confused. "Your British Naval Intelligence," Coolidge responded with a touch of ridicule in his voice, "believes that will be enough to launch a second world war?"

Baldwin didn't hesitate a second. "It will be," he answered, "if the Germans are successful with what we believe is their well-advanced plan to bomb New York City on a round-trip transatlantic flight from Berlin with the first of their super bombers, code named *Amerike*."

He turned and stared into the fireplace, ignoring the sound of the President's glass shattering on the floor.

Seventeen

The tide had taken the bow of the *The Lovely Mary* on a due southwest course over the days since McGill had seen the solitary airplane pass over his boat and he had used the radio his new friend at Kerry's Ring had provided him some weeks before.

He had provisions on board to stay at sea at least another few weeks and was indeed in no hurry to return to Dingle Bay and the loneliness he felt there. At any rate, his holding tank was less than a quarter full. He'd better do some serious fishing over the next several weeks if he was going to turn any profit on the trip other than the money the stranger had paid him in the bar.

As was his custom, after a lunch of cod or mackerel or some such game fish he had caught by line for the sheer pleasure of it during the morning hours, he would take to the bridge, tie off his ship's wheel, sit on his well-worn leather captain's chair, and take a nap for a half-hour or so. He found that the few minutes of sleep revitalized him for the afternoon and early evening, when the winds and the whitecaps were more likely to pick up, and even helped to get him through those sleepless nights when the north Atlantic, sometimes out of nowhere, kicked up her mighty and terrifying heels, sending twenty-foot waves smashing across the bow of his old ship throughout the long night.

He never felt fear during those lonely storms, when it seemed God himself was intent on cleansing the surface of his ocean. Seamus had faced the worst storm of his life in losing his beloved Mary, and he knew the meaning of real fear. Nothing would ever make him afraid again.

He was sleeping at the ship's wheel as he did now since spotting the solitary airplane days before, when he was awakened as if by instinct. There was something in the water, something floating ahead of the *The Lovely Mary*'s bow. He jumped up from his seat and grabbed a long fishhook before it went under the bow. He pushed it off to the side; and as the boat slowly passed by the flotsam, McGill reached out and dragged in a long section of what appeared to be a remnant of some kind of cloth. When he pulled it aboard, it was clear that the material was varnished canvas, a white color. There were no markings to distinguish it, just a long tear as if it had sheared off a sharp edge, and there appeared to be soot stains along one side. He didn't know what to make of it.

He motored ahead a bit and came upon another but larger section which was also a length of white canvas or cotton, obviously painted or varnished in some way so as to be stiff. But this piece was stretched over the remnants of shattered wooden spars of different lengths that were jagged, as if they had been snapped off. The cloth along the sculpted surface of the remnant was smooth and rounded to cover the sculpted edge, as if it was shaped to fit the wooden spars beneath it. The entire piece measured some eight feet in length.

It was a strange find in the middle of the ocean, hardly the kind of thing that would be thrown overboard as trash from one of the big commercial or passenger boats. What finally caught Seamus' eye was a series of small holes, each a shilling around in size, every ten inches or so across a six-foot length of the entire scrap. They were clean holes through the cloth but jagged below. Where the holes had hit the scraps of spar, the wood was completely shattered.

It suddenly hit him that they were bullet holes from a machine gun. McGill was no stranger to the work of a bullet, having volunteered for the Irish Infantry Regiment of the British Army in 1916, the only year since he was a boy that he had not spent at sea and the only time in forty-seven years he had been separated from his Mary.

At first, he thought that he had come upon a piece of long-lost wreckage from the Great War, but that hardly made sense. First, he was too far from land, and second, the sea would have disintegrated the cloth, if not the wood spars as well, years before.

No. What he was holding in the grasp of his long fishhook was the remnant of a section of wing, the wing of an airplane that had recently been crisply and cleanly shot off.

Then it came to him.

The airplane that had passed over his boat two days before was white like the pieces of scrap. In his hands he was holding wreckage of that airplane, he thought, which apparently had been shot down somewhere over the horizon and out of his sight after he had made the radio call identifying it.

Panicking, he pulled the larger piece of scrap onto the boat and secured it. He tied a rope line to his waist and dove into the cold water in search of more wreckage. The water was cold, but an icier chill ran through his veins when he realized he might come upon the bodies of the pilots. He dove as deep as his lungs would allow, but found nothing but bottomless blackness. He kicked to the surface, breathing heavily, and dove twice more before convincing himself there was no more to be found at that spot.

Through the remainder of that afternoon and into the early evening when the sun finally set, he crisscrossed *The Lovely Mary* over the location where he had found the section of wing. He was looking for more wreckage, but the sea had swallowed it all.

Chilled to the bone by the North Atlantic waters, he broke open a quart of cheap Irish whiskey he kept on board for medicinal purposes and wrapped himself in a blanket. His mind traced back over the last several days, especially the moments when he had spied the airplane and sent the radio message. Who was it he had sent the message to? He was racked with guilt. Had he played a role in the crash? Were there pilots on board? Of course there were, he told himself. Who was it he had radioed?

He thought back to the conversation at Kerry's Ring, well into his cups with the stranger who had asked him to take aboard the radio "as a scientific experiment," as he had called it. Why hadn't he asked for more details? The money had simply looked too good and too easy.

He had to do something, he told himself. He had no idea what he was involved in but had to find out. The question was, how?

He couldn't use the radio. The frequency was preset; and if nothing else, he would give away what little he knew and probably where his ship was located. He wasn't sure he wanted to do that. He simply didn't know whom he was dealing with, but whoever it was seemed to consider violence a reasonable option.

His mind wandered through his own options as he brought the bottle to his lips several times to get the blood moving in his veins again. His first thought was to turn for the Irish Naval Base at Fenit, the Port of Tralee near Dingle Bay. Touchy subject, that. The Anglo-Irish treaty of 1922 gave Ireland responsibility to police its fishing boats, but the damned British hung onto control of policing Irish waters.

"Oh, bloody hell," he thought, giving momentary thought to cutting his line and letting the wreckage join the rest of the airplane several thousand feet down. "Who would know?" he said, half aloud.

He would.

An idea suddenly came to him. He remembered a war relic he had been ferrying around on *The Lovely Mary* since recommissioning his boat upon returning from Dingle Bay after the war. It was a small crystal set radio, a heavy little bugger, which he had been assigned responsibility for carrying with the 1st Lancashire Fusiliers in the trenches near Beaumont Hamel, Somme, France in 1916.

He had stored the wooden box containing a General Radio BC 14A crystal set in his forward cabin, wrapped in waterproofed canvas under his bunk, for some imaginary emergency, knowing that he would never be able to afford one of the new Marconi marine sets that were standard equipment on the newer fishing boats. The emergency had come. He only hoped he remembered how to fire up the thing.

He dragged out the box and cranked up the power supply, letting the communications relic warm up. As luck would have it, he still had the code book of frequencies, its pages smeared with mud from the Beaumont Hamel trenches, and quickly located Tralee. He dialed in the frequency and held his breath.

"Tralee Naval Base, come in, please," he called into the small microphone, then added quickly, "Over," to signify the end of his statement. There was no response except the crackle of empty airwaves. He tried again.

"Tralee Naval Base, come in, please. This is the Irish fishing boat *The Lovely Mary* in need of assistance. Over." He waited again, recalling the days when he had shouted into the mouthpiece, seeking a response as artillery shells whistled over his head and small arms fire buried their rounds in the Sommes trenches, thick with red mud and blood. He could be a little more patient now. The call of an Irish fishing boat was hardly enough to set off alarms at Tralee.

Suddenly, the vintage radio lit up. "Come in, *The Lovely Mary*. This is the Tralee Naval Base, Ireland. Over."

McGill responded quickly. "And it's a fine evening to hear your voice Tralee. Over," he traded with the Naval communications officer.

McGill thought he heard a laugh as the receiver clicked. "What is the approximate location of *The Lovely Mary*? Over," the sailor asked.

"I would believe to be about one hundred thirty miles southwest of Tralee, wishing I was enjoying a pint and a warm, red-headed lass. Over," McGill responded.

"What is your name, sir? Over," the voice came back without hesitation.

"I am Seamus McGill, captain of the thirty-five-foot fishing vessel, *The Lovely Mary*, hailing from Dingle Bay. Over," McGill said proudly. "As fortune, good or otherwise, would have it," McGill continued, "I have recovered a large section of wreckage. It would appear to be a section of a wing from a small airplane. Over," McGill said.

"How large is the section, Mr. McGill and can you provide details as to its construction? Over," the sailor responded. McGill thought he detected a hint of interest in the voice of the obviously young man.

"It is approximately eight feet by four feet in dimension, and the surface is a canvas or cloth of some sort, either painted or varnished white to make it brittle. The underside has a wooden frame, comprising spaced, evenly spread wooden spars. They have substantially heavy damage, machine gun bullets, from the looks of it. Over," he finished.

There was a prolonged silence from Tralee. Then, "*The Lovely Lady*, please stand by for further instructions. Over," McGill heard. The Irish fishing captain sat patiently waiting, wrapping himself tighter in the blanket and taking another nip of the whiskey to stay warm.

It would be a cold night, McGill thought; and the wind was beginning to whip the surface into small whitecaps, although the seas stayed relatively calm. The last of the sun was setting, darkness quickly descending on his bobbing boat; and once again, McGill found himself alone in the vast sea with nothing but his treasured boat and the memories of his beloved.

"Come in, *The Lovely Mary*, this is Tralee. Over," the radio suddenly sparked after about fifteen minutes of silence. McGill had begun to worry that he had lost the signal.

"*The Lovely Mary* awaits your instructions, Tralee. Over," said McGill at once, happy for the continued contact.

"The British Government requests that you lay up for the night, taking precautions against potential loss of the wreckage you have come upon. Over," the young voice said. "Her Majesty's Ship, the heavy cruiser *HMS Lion* is steaming in your direction and should arrive by 0600 hours. Over," the transmission continued.

McGill whistled aloud. The *HMS Lion* was one of the most well-known, battle-hardened British cruisers to sail the Irish coast, and the sight of her would take a sailor's breath away. She was more than twenty-six thousand tons and could do thirty knots, which meant she was well north of *The Lovely Mary,* if it would take her until six o'clock the next morning to arrive.

McGill was so surprised by the response he did not immediately reply. Whatever the hell it was he had found, it must be important to attract such incredible attention.

"*The Lovely Mary*, this is Tralee, please confirm. Over," the radio suddenly barked again. McGill, startled back to reality, immediately responded. "Yes, Tralee, *The Lovely*

Mary will maintain position and await *HMS Lion*. We are proud to receive her. Over," he jested with the sailor.

"Thank you, *The Lovely Mary,* for your cooperation. Over," Tralee responded. Then, surprisingly, "Captain McGill? Over," the young sailor added.

"Yes Tralee, this is McGill. Over," McGill responded.

"Should you have any uninvited guests prior to *HMS Lion's* arrival, please take extreme personal caution. Over and out." The transmission went dead, leaving McGill grateful for the warning but wondering what in the bloody hell he had gotten himself into.

He took another swig from his bottle, threw on a heavy sweater, and doused the boat's running lights from bow to stern, including the cabin overhead, as a precaution. The morning light would make *The Lovely Mary* clearly visible for the British cruiser. She'd not need to be seen before that, and she was well east of the shipping lanes that would put her in danger of a moonless night's collision.

Until then, taking the young Tralee sailor's advice to heart, he intended to spend the evening alone curled up on his bunk, rifle by his side. But sleep didn't come easily. He had too many unanswered questions to rest easy — as well as a strange sense of guilt.

Eighteen

Rising even before the sun crested over the horizon, McGill manned his eyeglasses and scanned the far-off edge where the world dropped off, hoping to spot the famous warship as she bore down upon him. It wasn't every day *The Lovely Mary* hosted such a visitor as the *HMS Lion,* and he literally could not wait to share this story with his mates at Kerry's Ring.

The *HMS Lion* filled the mind of every schoolboy who was just old enough to follow her exploits during the war. The daily Emerald Island newspapers tracked her as closely as possible because of the number of Irish seamen who voluntarily manned her wooden and steel-plated decks.

She was a battle cruiser of the Royal Navy, launched in 1910, and served as the flagship of the Royal Navy during the early years of the war. *HMS Lion* distinguished herself in action in the battle of Heligoland Bight, the first major naval battle of the war off the coast of Germany, as well as the pivotal battle of Dogger Bank. During the cataclysmic battle of Jutland off the mainland of Denmark in May 1916 -- in which nearly eighty-seven hundred British and German sailors perished in a single day in the largest naval battle in recorded history – the *Lion* was hit by heavy shells no less than nine times. Somehow she survived and led Britain's decisive and last major naval battle of the Great War.

Seamus McGill knew all this by heart. For, although he was a foot soldier who had survived not only the bullets but the disease and pestilence of the filthy trenches of France, in the heart and mind of this seaman was etched the history of the great naval battles, especially those involving the United Kingdom. There wasn't a sailor in Dingle Bay who could not recite the history of the Battle of Jutland from memory with the aid of a pint or two.

Shortly after 0600 hours, just as predicted, the twenty-six-thousand-ton, seven-hundred-foot-long seagoing monster, *HMS Lion*, bristling with her heavy guns, appeared on the horizon, her forty-two boilers at full steam, trailing great bellows of black smoke.

She's in a hurry, Seamus thought, although still unsure why, even if it had been an airplane that had been shot down. *With the steam she's making, you'd be swearin' the bloody Prime Minister himself was in the pilot's seat,* he thought, immediately thinking poorly of himself for making light of the fate of the man or men who might still be strapped in the contraption below his boat.

As the great ship drew closer, he could not help but notice the still visible battle scars of the *Lion*, ten years on, despite her fresh coat of paint. A more impressive sight he had never seen; and he could not help himself as a tear came to his eyes.

Twenty minutes later, *HMS Lion* was calmly anchored some seventy-five yards from *The Lovely Mary*, and a small launch was on its way to intercept McGill's boat. The chop was light with an easterly breeze, so not even a mist greeted the visitors.

"Welcome aboard, Sir," McGill greeted the first man with gold stars on his collar. "*The Lovely Mary* has rarely had such important visitors."

"Thank you for your hospitality and your cooperation," an older gentleman, wearing the braided cap of Royal Admiralty, said as he stepped forward, his hand extended in greeting. "Your message and its details were a great surprise to Her Majesty's Government, as well as the Palace at Versailles."

McGill took the man's rock solid hand but could not hide his confusion. *Versailles?*

"I am Commander David Culloch of Her Majesty's British Naval Intelligence, the officer said, "and this," turning to a bearded gentleman some years younger, "is my colleague, Lieutenant Commander Geoffrey Hughes, also of Naval Intelligence. The Captain sends his regards, but I am afraid his attentions must be elsewhere aboard ship at the moment." A half dozen sailors accompanied the two men.

"Pleased to make your acquaintance, Sirs, and to offer my cooperation," McGill said, "but I must admit to being completely befuddled by your visit, as well as the flotsam I discovered on the ocean's surface."

"I'm sure you are, Captain McGill, and I will do my best to explain as best as possible," Culloch said, a calming gaze on his face. He wasn't about to give anything away until necessary. "Would it be possible for us to examine the wreckage now? We are most anxious to see it."

Without saying a word, McGill moved to *The Lovely Mary's* stern and yanked a heavy canvas off the long wooden wreckage. As he did so, he thought again about the conversation he had had between himself, the bottle and the unused radio openly on display below decks several times the evening before.

"Get rid of it. Drop the bloody radio over the side, and no one will know the better for it," his inner self had told him after a drink or two. "No one need know that you had a hand in these troubles."

But he could not bring himself to do it, for reasons he could not explain. He had never considered himself a man of moral convictions; but by God, if he had sold out the lives of some poor wretches for the price of a couple of hundred pounds, he could not live with it, or especially the act of hiding his actions. He had no excuse. He'd obviously made a deal with the devil. Better to stand before God and man and live with the consequences than be haunted by the truth for the rest of his life.

"Here 'tis, Commander," McGill uncovered the wing, "just as I found her not a hundred yards from here, floating on the surface. I dove the spot several times looking for more," he said, then hesitated. "I could find nothing but the devil in this, I thought. It was just too big and too strange an object to have been thrown from a passing ship. Besides, it hardly looks like it came from a ship yard, so I had my doubts that it was any part of a vessel, large or small."

The two Naval Intelligence Officers bent over the wing without another word. Hughes picked up one end of the span and lifted it to test the weight. Together, they flipped it over to examine the spars. The inspection took but a few moments before they had reached a conclusion.

"I'd bet on my mother's grave that's the section of the upper starboard wing closest to the cockpit," Culloch said to Hughes. "The holes, no doubt from a large caliber machine gun, would have torn up anything over the next several feet, meaning into the pilot's cockpit. I'd say the bullets came from a German 13.2 mm TuF round, wouldn't you, Geoffrey?"

The Lieutenant Commander responded without hesitation. "No doubt it's the lousy kraut round," he said, fingering one of the holes. "The Springfield .30-06 round would have made a larger, more ragged hole in the doped cloth, and the Browning would have shot clean and neat through the spars. The German bullet's self-rimming cartridge has left strakes on the wood. It's German, all right, the sons of bitches."

"These were let go from close range. The poor bastards never had a chance," he concluded with a look that would have put fear in the heart of a rock.

McGill shook on his heels at that last statement -- *bastards*, as in plural?

"Commander Culloch," McGill protested quietly as the deck hands who had accompanied the Naval Intelligence Officers began transferring the wing section into their launch. "I'm not usually afraid of a fight, but it's obvious you're not going to tell me if one was involved here. But as just a lowly fisherman to an officer of her Majesty's Royal Navy, I beg of you to explain. I know I just came upon this mess by accident, but please do me the courtesy of explaining what in bloody hell you're talking about!"

He was on a roll and couldn't stop, his guilt feeding his desperation for answers. "You mean to tell me the Germans shot down an airplane? What is the reason? Why? What could possibly cause them to do such a thing?" Culloch was surprised by the fisherman's building rage.

" With all due respect, Sir, what the bloody fuck are you selling?" McGill finished, his emotions and the secret he was holding inside getting the better of him. "I've been at sea for several weeks. Are we at war again?" he asked, knowing how ridiculous he sounded.

Culloch said nothing, kicking at the white canvas hanging in shreds off the remnant off the wing. The silence was deafening. "I have my orders, Captain McGill. It is hard for me to be clearer."

He finally looked up at the hapless seaman and suddenly had a sense that the grizzled fisherman might know more than he had had the chance to say.

"You got a bottle on this old tub?" Culloch asked.

"Several," McGill responded. "And careful, she's named after my late wife, old tub or not."

Culloch smiled without laughing. He had a sense about this man that he didn't get from many of the intelligence crud he had learned to work with. "You might grab a couple of them bottles, Captain. This could take a while," he said, motioning Hughes into the cabin with him and dispatching his crew to offload the wreckage and return for them upon his signal.

"So, let's talk," Culloch said, finding a spot near a porthole lest he need to signal his men quickly.

Nineteen

They no sooner had entered McGill's small cabin than the two intelligence officers spied the sophisticated radio that the fisherman had taken no effort to hide.

"That's some radio for a small fishing boat. Bet it set you back a few quid," Hughes said first.

"I didn't buy it," McGill said. "It was given to me."

"Given to you?" Culloch asked, not hiding his surprise.

"Yah, by a bloke I met in a bar, Kerry's Ring in Dingle Bay, a few weeks ago. With a pint and two hundred Irish pounds he gave me to take it on board."

Culloch said nothing but simply raised his eyebrows. He waited for McGill to continue. If there was anything he had learned from two decades of life in the British Naval Intelligence, it was to let a man do the talking when he had something to say.

"It was late April, I think. I've been out several weeks now, the dates are a blur. But I met this bloke. He seemed to come out of nowhere one night at the Ring while I was sitting at the bar minding my pint. Dingle's small. You know most folks. I didn't know this chap. He says, 'Let me buy you a beer, you look a bit lonely today.' I remember him saying that because he thought I looked lonely. Lonely? Hell. Without my Mary, every day is lonely. I didn't answer him but figured since he guessed right and didn't come across as a fag, I said what the hell, so long as he was paying."

Culloch asked if the man was Irish. McGill laughed. "I don't know if he was Irish. He might have been Irish or a

Mick, a Scot or a Welshman. You hardly don't ask when someone else is buying the beer. He wasn't a swine Hun or a wop, if that's what you mean. He just seemed like a regular sort. We talked about a lot of things, laying net for herring, if I remember. It's kind of blurry. I was in my cups.

"But I remember he told me he was a scientist, a bloody scientist, can you believe it, in Dingle Bay?" McGill continued as he cracked open a bottle of whiskey and poured three fingers into each glass. He was suddenly in a three-fingers mood. Hughes downed his quickly and saluted McGill so he'd follow suit. They poured another while Culloch sipped his.

"I remember he told me he was doing some sort of experiment, counting whales or some such malarkey," McGill continued, "and he had a friend who was using an airplane to help him with the counting. Said he needed help, someone to keep tabs on the airplane and whether or not the bloke was doing what he promised. He asked me if I was interested in the job of looking out for the airplane.

"I told him to fuck himself, I did, that I had better things to do than babysit an airplane flying around a port the size of Dingle. Christ, a schoolboy could do the job. Besides, I was leaving with the next tide to do some herring fishing around Baileybunnion, I told him."

Hughes had seen to it that McGill was already half drunk. It wasn't hard to get someone drunk if he thought he had a drinking partner, and drunks talked more. If McGill had something to hide, it was about to come out. Culloch played along. They'd been at this game a few years together. He'd barely touched what looked like his third heavy drink.

"Anyway, the bloke is serious. He buys us another pint and offers me two hundred Irish pounds to load a radio on my boat and ring him up if I see the damned airplane. Two hundred pounds! That's a lot of herring and a lot of diesel. I told him okay and met him on the dock with the radio within the hour. There she is."

"Have you used it?" Culloch asked gently.

"Once," Seamus grimaced. "Goddamned white biplane made a pass about a hundred yards portside less than five hundred feet off the caps." He paused. "I called it in, God help me. The voice on the other end just said, 'Thanks.' I haven't heard a peep from it since." The elderly fisherman hung his head in shame.

"When was that, Seamus, what day? It's important," Hughes dug. "And what time of day was it?"

"Hell, who keeps track of days anymore?" McGill answered. He reached for the bottle to fill his empty glass. Culloch pushed it away. He needed an answer to the question.

McGill stared at the officer, angry but afraid to answer the question.

"Hell, what's today?" he paused, thinking. "It was Sunday. God himself knows the date. It was the late afternoon, when the sun is at its golden best and crystal clear."

Culloch and Hughes exchanged glances without saying a word. That would have put L'Oiseau Blanc just off the coast of Ireland, heading for open water. "Were there any colors on the plane, Captain?" Hughes asked, pushing the bottle back to McGill.

"Yes, she was a pretty thing, with the pilot and copilot sitting side by side. I'd never seen that before. But on her tail was the French Tricolore, no mistaking it. That's how I knew it was the plane the bloke at Kerry's Ring was looking for. He said she had French markings."

There was silence in the cabin for a few moments as all was digested. Seamus had spilled his guts but felt worse than ever. The Naval Intelligence Officers were beginning to pull the pieces together.

"Would you recognize this chap if you saw him again, Captain?" Hughes asked.

"He's been a face in my dreams the last several nights, Commander. I'd have no trouble picking him out of a battalion," he said, deeply troubled that he had allowed easy money to land him in this pickle.

Quiet again. "What happened?" McGill asked. "You owe me that."

Culloch swallowed hard, knowing he was about to break every rule in the book for feeling terrible for the lonely fisherman who had simply reported seeing an airplane.

"The airplane you saw was manned by two French pilots, both decorated war aces, who had left Orly Airport earlier that day to attempt to become the first men to make a transatlantic flight from Paris to New York City in the United States," Culloch said. "A prize has been offered for the first airmen to accomplish the flight. Perhaps you have seen an account of it in the newspapers?"

"There's not much reading to do at Kerry's Ring, Commander. I was unaware, not that it would have made any difference," McGill offered.

Culloch continued. "The contest would seem harmless enough on the surface," he said, "but British Naval Intelligence has learned that the Germans have taken particular exception to the escapade. It seems they feel it would place undue honor on Paris as the capital of Europe. They have sworn to prevent any person or persons from making the attempt successfully and fully intend to do it themselves."

McGill did all he could to hide the anger that swept his face. "You mean that radio message I sent informed the Germans that the French had cleared Ireland and were, I would guess, headed for Newfoundland?"

Culloch reached for the second bottle and uncorked it open without answering.

"Precisely," Hughes answered for him.

McGill's face was ashen. For a few pounds of greed, he had sent two men to what must have been a horrifying death. "There was no way you could have known, Captain McGill. It appears the Germans shot down the French pilots Nungesser and Coli in their airplane, *L'Oiseau Blanc,* in cold blood shortly after your radio message. They would have been unarmed."

That would explain the orange, fire-like glow over the horizon less than an hour after McGill's radio message to the stranger. "The British, U.S., French and Irish navies have been searching for them since Monday morning, when they should have made landfall over Newfoundland," Hughes added.

"I assume it doesn't end here, does it?" McGill asked. "This will make world headlines. Will the Germans be made to pay?" It dawned on him that he had a price of his own to pay. Like it or not, he had blood on his hands. This was different from fish blood. The stains would never leave his hands.

Culloch thought for a moment, mulling over the strong Irish whiskey in his glass, saying nothing. McGill hung his head in his hands. He would have put a bullet through his own head given the chance.

"Perhaps, dear chap, but unfortunately, the time is not right for the rest of the world to know," Culloch finally said. "Unless we stop the bloody bastards, we can expect the Germans to continue their murderous game while they make their own preparations for a crossing, and any attempt at a transatlantic crossing from either direction will end the same ... so long, that is, as the Germans believe *The Lovely Mary* is their eyes and ears."

"What? McGill said. "Am I hearing you right, or is it the whiskey?"

Hughes grabbed the fisherman's huge bicep. "He's right, McGill. So long as you stay on this track, the Great Arctic Circle, the Germans believe you will spot any airplane attempting to make the crossing. This close to shore, the planes will be flying low, looking for land. The fucking Hun bastards have you right where they want you and need you."

The seaman drained his glass, not even the whiskey warding off the wave of shocks that were pounding his head. *Jesus Mother of Christ,* he thought, *where are you, Mary Elizabeth when I need you, my darlin'? I'm just a small fisherman, not a goddamned hero.*

An hour later, after naval seamen had loaded his small cabin with additional radio equipment, McGill bade farewell to Culloch and Hughes. Together, they had hashed out a plan, subject to approval of the British Naval Intelligence hierarchy and the French Government. Neither of the two senior intelligence officers anticipated objections from either government. What they were more worried about was the mental well being of the Captain of *The Lovely Mary.*

As the half-drunk, heartbroken captain watched the pride of the Royal Navy steam over the setting horizon, he reached into his pocket and removed the wad of bills the stranger had given him that night at Kerry's Ring. He looked at the money, ten ugly, twenty-pound Irish notes that had placed his finger on the trigger of the machine gun that murdered the Frenchmen as surely as the sad day he was born.

Without hesitating, he tore the bills to bits with his bare hands, one by one, and sprinkled the colored shreds of paper across the sea. His pay would be the vengeance he would help extract from the murderous German pigs who had robbed two brave young men of their lives, and the sleepless nights he would suffer for the rest of his life for helping them to do it.

Twenty

Gruppenführer Hermann Goering carefully climbed down the steps of his personal military transport and saluted the waiting commanding officer of the Lipetsk Aircraft Development Consortium, a cover for the German military activities in the Russian city. The two shook hands then stood at attention as the German national anthem was played by the base military band. The incongruity of the German anthem being played on Russian soil did not escape Goering.

"How was your flight, Hermann?" Colonel Rainer Janzig politely asked his friend of more than a decade. They had served together in the air war over France in its final eighteen months, and Goering had been his commanding officer in the famed "Flying Circus", the Jagdgeschwader 1 squadron of which Manfred Albrecht Freiherr von Richthofen, the Red Baron, was the most celebrated member with eighty recorded kills.

Janzig had often served as Goering's wing man, and he had shot down nineteen Allied fighters in close aerial dogfights. Besides the Iron Cross, he was awarded the Zaehring Lion with swords, the Karl Friedrich Order, and finally, in May 1918, the coveted *Pour le Mérite,* or Blue Max.

Goering had personally appointed Janzig to the Lipetsk post, a clear indication that the Luftstreitkräfte leader was grooming him as his successor. He trusted Janzig like no other, and in return, Janzig had never failed his superior. Janzig was the only man in the

Luftstreitkräfte who would dare address the powerful
Gruppenführer by his first name.

"Yes, Rainer, the Junkers G23 is convenient but hardly
tolerable for flights of this duration," Goering replied. "I
feel my years after sitting in her cramped belly for more
than two hours. Nonetheless, the old war horse serves its
purpose, although it is a pity that we cannot showcase
some of the excellent designs coming out of Lipetsk under
your command. I trust you could outfit your
commanding officer with a transport far more
comfortable."

"No doubt, Hermann, but it would be too risky to
parade our newest aircraft in front of the watchful eyes of
the Allies. When we are ready, however ..." The base
commander let his words trail off.

"That will be soon, my friend. The world is in for quite
a surprise, hey?" Goering smiled at his friend, sharing his
frustration with their covert world.

"Yes, Hermann, and you, my Gruppenführer, will
lead the parade. Now, come. I am eager to show you the
progress we have made on *Amerike*. You will be
impressed, I assure you."

"That is good news, Rainer, but I am hardly surprised
that my most trusted Luftstreitkräfte officer has anything
but progress to report to me. You are a remarkable
manager, my friend."

"Thank you, Sir, but you have provided me with the
resources to get the job done," Janzig replied, always
careful to massage his superior's fragile ego. "It is
unfortunate that so many of my best men are slaves, but
their engineering skills more than make up for their
pronounced lack of enthusiasm in serving the
Fatherland."

"They are long-forgotten prisoners of war, Rainer. I
trust you have educated them well that they are
disposable," Goering responded sarcastically. He felt no

compassion for the POWs, men with considerable technical education and proficiency who had been hidden from the Allies after the signing of the Versailles Treaty. "How many of the aliens do you now employ here?"

"There are twenty-three POWs remaining, Gruppenführer, in addition to the Brigade of four hundred engineers and a security detail of one hundred fifty men who are under my command." Janzig could not help but feel a tingling sensation of pride. He had come a long way since the poverty of his youth, working eighteen-hour days with his father on their farm when he was only a boy. As a young cub, he had watched helplessly as his beloved father worked himself to death at the young age of thirty-four while struggling to feed his family off the rocky soil of their farm. When his father finally succumbed to a massive heart attack while driving the farm tractor in the field, the boy had been sitting on his lap, playfully steering the machine. To the child's horror, his father's lifeless body crushed him against the steering wheel. It was several hours before he was rescued by his hysterical mother. He winced at the memory.

"Yes, Hermann, we keep the slaves on their toes; and so far, they are performing well. You will see," Janzing replied and motioned the Luftstreitkräfte commander to follow him into a gigantic hangar on the southwest side of the fifteen-hundred-meter concrete airstrip.

Escorted by armed guards front and rear, Janzig led Goering through a side door to the forty-thousand-square-meter, metal-clad hangar. In the front, facing the airstrip, massive hydraulic doors, thirteen meters high by sixty meters wide, were closed and locked, hiding the top secret work being conducted inside. Goering had not yet visited this hangar, and its immensity made him catch his breath.

"*Mein Gott!*" he cursed as he entered the brilliantly lit hangar. "I have never seen such a facility, Rainer. Perhaps we are giving you too much in the way of resources?" he chided the base commander.

"Do not judge the barn before you see the horses inside, my good friend," Janzig laughed. "You will see that a building of this scope is a requirement of a project of this magnitude and complexity." He was nearly yelling at Goering. The noise inside from innumerable cutting and fabrication machines, welding torches, hammers and the din of hundreds of workers communicating made normal conversation difficult, at best.

As Goering scanned the interior, he noticed a large aircraft parked to one side of the hangar. It was a 1916 Gotha G.I. bomber, which had seen duty during one of the few bombing runs the Germans had attempted over England during the Great War. The fabric-covered biplane was huge with a wingspan of more than twenty meters and a length of twelve meters. It had held a crew of three; and with its twin 110 kW Benz Bz.III engines, it could make a maximum speed of 130 kilometers per hour. It had a maximum payload of fourteen hundred fifty kilograms of ordnance and was armed with two Parabellum MG14 machine guns. To the former fighter and ace, the airplane not only looked like a turkey, he recalled that it flew like one, as well.

Janzig caught Goering's gaze at the ancient bomber.

"Ah, Hermann, I see you have spied our antique," he said. "It is a Gotha G.I. that flew in the raid on Dover in 1916. She caused considerable damage, my Gruppenführer, even if her crew was terrified that she would fall apart in midair over the English Channel."

"What is its purpose here?"

"I have ordered that each of our engineers study this airplane, nearly the first of its kind. I believe that one can only create for the future if he understands the creations of the past," Janzig replied without hesitation. Gruppenführer, perhaps you will recall the bombs we first dropped on the Allies in 1915?" he asked.

"A test, Rainer?" Goering cocked his brow in surprise but smiled. He was more than up to the challenge. "If I recall, they were not bombs at all but thin steel darts known as fléchettes. Am I correct, Commander?"

"Precisely, Gruppenführer," Janzig replied, impressed at his superior's recollection of a time so long ago. "Soldiers in the trenches were more afraid of the fléchettes than of explosive bombs. Come, I want you to see what our new technology looks like."

Goering followed the base commander into the hangar. In the center of a whirlwind of activity, large, off-white muslin drapes hung from the ceiling to the floor, surrounding the aircraft that had brought Goering nearly eighteen hundred kilometers from Berlin to inspect. The drapes were intentionally opaque to hide the activity behind them further.

Goering followed Janzig as he led him past row upon row of machine tools and workers hunched over fabrication benches. They entered the draped area only after the base commander showed his credentials to the sentry assigned to the single entry point.

"Security is high, Rainer. I am pleased," Goering complimented Janzig.

"Yes, Hermann, we take no chances. There is too much at stake."

As they entered the work area, Goering stopped dead in his tracks. He was momentarily stunned by what he saw. He had been anticipating an advanced biplane design, somewhat based on the Gotha G.I. bomber in the hangar. Never in his wildest dreams was he prepared for the vision in front of him.

The aircraft was an all-metal, high-wing, four-engine heavy bomber. It was unlike anything Goering had ever seen or dreamt of. All of its exterior surfaces were coated in gleaming black paint, and engraved across the forward fuselage on each side beneath its cockpit was the word *Amerike*. The Luftstreitkräfte senior officer thought he had never in his life seen a machine so purely evil. It was the devil with metal wings.

Goering was speechless. Janzig allowed him a few moments to absorb his creation, then interrupted his superior's gaze.

"We finally decided to go with the Messerschmitt design, model designation Me 260," Janzig told him. "I believe this aircraft will meet your every expectation and more. It is the ultimate creation of all we have learned about aircraft technology over the last decade, and it is truly a weapon of mass destruction. Even her ordnance is advanced. I will explain later."

Goering was astonished. The Me 260 before him had not only leapfrogged the technology advances of his lifetime, it had soared over many more generations of development. By comparison, the Gotha G.I. bombers and the advanced, bright red Fokker Dr.I Dreidecker triplanes that he and his squadron had used to escort the fragile behemoths were toys, their design and technology almost childlike in comparison to the Me 260.

Janzig motioned for Goering to follow him to the front of the bomber. He explained that the plane's fuselage was circular across its cross section, resembling a long pipe with a tapered nose. The nose of the aircraft was completely glazed below the cockpit, adding to the airplane's striking overall resemblance to a bullet. Here, Janzig pointed out, was where the crew would rest on missions of super-long duration. The all-glass cabin contained bunk beds and a small galley.

"What is its range?" Goering probed, his mind racing.

Janzig did not hesitate. There was nothing he did not know about this airplane. "She has four twelve-cylinder, twelve-hundred-fifty-kW BMW 801G engines, Hermann, with a maximum range of fifteen thousand kilometers."

Goering stared at him, unbelieving.

"Enough for a round-trip, Berlin-to-New-York-City mission with eight crew, a ten-thousand-kilogram payload and a fuel margin of fifteen percent," Janzig bragged, his eyes gleaming with pride. "We shall see, but I believe the *Amerike* bomber may have the range to reach even the west coast of the United States.

"You will discover as you study the aircraft that we have applied advanced aerodynamic devices to the wing and tail surfaces," Janzig continued. "The wing incorporates a swept leading edge and a straight rear edge, and the tail has double fins. With a wingspan of nearly forty-three meters, she has by far the largest lift surface ever constructed by man. These innovations all contribute to her remarkably long range."

Goering pointed to a bulge beneath the fuselage. "What is that, Rainer?"

"Come, I shall show you," Janzig replied excitedly, leading his superior up a set of wooden stairs that led to the rear cargo hatch of the airplane. Inside, workers were welding and using cutting torches on the massive frame, as well as reinforcing the wing mounts with steel collars. Janzing pointed forward, and Goering followed him to a small hatch in the floor of the aircraft, in an area just forward of the overhead wing. He opened the hatch and invited Goering to step down inside.

The rotund Gruppenführer eased himself through the relatively narrow hatch into the belly of the airplane and slid into a padded leather chair, complete with shoulder, lap, and anti-submarine safety belts. He suddenly realized that in front of him were the firing controls for twin 4 × 13 mm MG 131 machine guns, and he was surrounded by thick armor plating.

"No need to put on the belts," Janzig called down. "Engage the pedals at your feet, Herr Goering," Janzing instructed. "Press the left pedal, and the turret will move to the left. Press down on the right, and you will swing to the right. In this way a gunner can control the left and right movement of the machine gun turret, and the weapons will move up and down, as well, independently of the turret. There is no angle of attack by the enemy to which the gunner cannot respond."

Goering quickly mastered the controls and found that he could actually move the turret through a full three-hundred-sixty-degree sweep. "*Unglaublich!* Commander Janzig, this is an incredible advance. How many of these turrets are designed into the aircraft?"

"There are a total of eleven guns in five turrets, Gruppenführer," Janzig replied. "There is one in the nose, one in the tail, waist turrets on either side of the fuselage aft of the wing, and the belly turret that you occupy. *Amerike* is bristling with weapons, and her gunners will be well protected behind heavy steel armor plating. No other aircraft has ever been so well armed."

Goering reluctantly climbed out of the ball turret, thoroughly enjoying the exercise. "What is her speed, Rainer?"

Janzig rattled off specifications with an ease that impressed even Goering. "She will do five hundred sixty kilometers per hour if necessary but cruises at two hundred seventeen with a maximum takeoff weight of fifty-six thousand kilograms," he said. "Her service ceiling is eight thousand meters, and *Amerike* will climb at a rate of one hundred twenty meters per minute.

"Frankly, Herr Gruppenführer, there has never been anything like her, and I doubt that the French, British or Americans have even dreamed of such an aircraft. The world will be shocked at our capability and the unmatched intellect of our engineers."

Goering was deep in thought, contemplating the proper moment to unveil the startling new airplane to his superiors.

"When will she be ready for testing?"

"It is my hope that we can commence testing within sixty days, Hermann. I personally will take *Amerike* up for her first flight," Janzig bragged. "I hope you will agree that there is no better test pilot, my Gruppenführer."

Goering smiled at the unintended slight of his subordinate. "Perhaps there is one, Commander Janzig."

"Ah, yes, Sir," Janzig replied, smiling sheepishly, color coming to his face. He brushed the *faux pas* aside. "Now, Gruppenführer, I would like to brief you on the new ordnance we have developed for project *Amerike*. Let us retire to my conference room. I have a special cognac waiting for you."

Janzig's office complex was Spartan by comparison to Goering's sumptuous headquarters in Berlin, but it spoke well of the man. The base commander was obsessed with the success of the *Amerike* project, and his imprint on the final design and the extraordinary management of the construction of the *Amerike* bomber was visible to Goering's eye. The Luftstreitkräfte leader was very pleased with all he had seen. He wondered what new development Janzig had up his sleeve.

As they sat around a long, metal conference table in a sparse room adjacent to Janzig's office, a white jacketed steward, a Spaniard, Goering thought, poured a tall cognac into crystal snifters.

"Herr Goering, the glasses are practically the only luxury I have allowed myself here in Lipetsk. I hope you do not object," Janzig apologized for the extravagance. "But one can hardly drink a cognac of this quality in canning jars, hey?"

"Hardly, my friend. I salute your taste," Goering responded, holding the snifter up against the light and inspecting the contents. "So, this is a special bottle?"

"Hermann, this one bottle cost me a week's wages. It is a Martell Cordon Bleu from the French Chapeu family in the Borderies which I acquired from a merchant in the city. Do you remember it?" Janzig explained.

"Rainer, another test?" Goering raised the glass to his nose and took in the bouquet. "It is the cognac you and I shared after every mission, is it not?"

"Your memory is remarkable, my Gruppenführer. Yes, you and I shared many bottles of this fine spirit, celebrating our many kills together. *Prost!*" Janzig toasted his superior, and they both drank deep and long.

"Ah, Ranier, impeccable," Goering said, savoring the traditional nutty taste of the Borderies region cognac. "Too bad we must fill the rest of the afternoon with business, hey?"

"Yes, Herr Goering, but after I show you my next development, you may wish to drink again."

"Proceed, please, as I am intrigued, Commander," Goering said, raising the glass to his lips again.

Janzig stood and walked to the head of the table. An aide took a position next to a large standing easel.

"Gruppenführer Goering, as you know, a separate division of engineers here in Lipetsk has been exploring the science of packaged explosives. I speak, of course, about aerial ordnance that can be delivered to a long-range target by the *Amerike* bomber."

Goering nodded.

"While we have been able to advance the conventional aerial bomb that was used in the Great War to a point where it is more reliable and has a greater explosive yield, these weapons are bulky and weigh, on average, nearly five hundred kilograms. This weight vastly limits the number of weapons that may be carried on any bomber, but particularly the *Amerike* bomber, because of the extraordinary long-distance missions for which it has been designed.

"I am pleased to inform you, Herr Gruppenführer, that we have achieved a major breakthrough, one which will allow the *Amerike* to carry twice as much explosive payload, because the bombs in its bay will weigh half as much as the conventional weapons with which you are familiar."

Goering was ecstatic. "This is extraordinary, Commander Janzig," he said, reverting to formal salutation for the benefit of the military aide and another man, a stranger to him, seated near the front of the table. "Has it been tested?"

"Yes, Gruppenführer. As you will see in a demonstration shortly, it not only works, but we have achieved a yield per bomb that is roughly one hundred times greater than a conventional aerial bomb of twice its size."

"*Mein, Gott!*" Goering cursed. "This is impossible. Surely you exaggerate, Commander." His face was suddenly flushed, irritated by Janzig's wild claim.

Taken aback by his superior's reaction, Janzig was immediately on the offensive. "I assure you," he replied calmly, "there is no mistake, Gruppenführer." He turned to the stranger. "Rather than waste time, allow me to introduce Herr Dr. Mario Zippermayr, who has led the development of this new weapon.

"Dr. Zippermayr joined us here a year ago at my invitation to oversee the new weapons development program. Among his many academic credentials, he earned his doctorate from the University of Florence, where he studied with the great Italian physicist, Enrico Fermi, and also was tutored by Albert Einstein at the University of California in the United States. Despite being a Jew, one must agree that Einstein is a brilliant physicist and has had a profound effect on the thinking of Dr. Zippermayr."

He motioned to the man, who immediately stood. Tall and slight of build, the bearded scientist appeared almost gaunt. In fact, Goering thought he was ill. He was slightly stooped, although he did not appear to be much older than his early thirties.

"Thank you, Herr Janzig," he said quietly following his introduction. He turned and faced Goering, who immediately noticed the scientist's eyes. They were perhaps the deepest shade of blue that he had ever seen on a man. In fact, Goering was somewhat repulsed, as they appeared almost feminine in their brilliance. While his long, unkempt beard and slightly wild, lighter blond hair gave him a look of eccentricity, his eyes seemed to imply a softness of character and suggested a deep unhappiness. Goering was immediately put off by his appearance, despite his academic credentials.

"Gruppenführer Goering," the scientist began, "I thank you for this opportunity to share our progress in the development of advanced aerial munitions." He stared directly at Goering, looking him in the eye, a trait that always made Goering uncomfortable and raised his guard.

"Yes, Zippermayr, please get to the point. Herr Janzig has made some bold pronouncements. You will back them up?" Goering responded, obviously irritated and impatient.

"I will try, Gruppenführer,' the young scientist responded. He turned to the easel and motioned for Janzig's aide to flip over a chart. On it was a formula of some sort.

"As Commander Janzig has explained, the problem of weight and low explosive yield has been a limiting factor in the value of aerial warfare since the introduction of the bomber aircraft in 1914 by Germany. It has been our mission to find a new bomb, one that will weigh considerably less while possessing extraordinarily lethal powers. Herr Gruppenführer, we have found it," the scientist said without fanfare.

Goering was not impressed. "Yes, go on please. I do not have all day."

Unperturbed by Goering's boorish reaction, Zippermayr continued.

"What we have developed is the world's first fuel air explosive. In its simplest form, it is a combination of liquid air and an explosive chemical compound such as coal dust, black powder, gasoline or even propane."

Goering sat up in his chair, listening intently.

"Our first experiment was with a mixture of sixty percent brown coal dust and forty percent liquid air. We used a total of eight grams of powder and mixed the two ingredients in a small, thin container. Using an incendiary fuse, the mixture was ignited. The resulting explosion was, to be honest, astounding to us, and far more lethal than we had anticipated. For a range of between five hundred and six hundred meters in all directions, the earth was completely scorched, and all trees, vegetation and wildlife were incinerated. Extreme damage was noted as far as two kilometers away."

Goering stood up from his seat, unable to contain his building excitement. "Go on," he demanded.

"Upon analysis, we determined that if the explosive compound was first spread out over a wide area, the resulting explosion would be that much greater. Consequently, we designed a metal container containing fifty grams of compressed powder that was hoisted thirty feet into the air and released. Upon impact with the ground, the container acted somewhat like an aerosol dispenser, causing a rapid dispersion of explosive dust over a wide area. It resembled a cloud." He hesitated for effect.

"Roughly one-quarter second later, a small charge in the metal cylinder was exploded, which in turn ignited the dust. The ensuing event was quite possibly the largest manmade explosion in history."

Goering's head jerked back. "What are you saying, Herr Zippermayr, that you have created a super bomb?"

"Precisely, Herr Gruppenführer. We have created the mother of all bombs," the scientist responded. Janzig nodded his agreement to Goering.

"The resulting explosion virtually incinerated everything in its path in an area of four to five kilometers. Incredibly, brick structures at six kilometers were reduced to stone dust, and wooden structures as far away as twelve kilometers burst into flames. Unfortunately, we tested this bomb on an airfield about forty kilometers from here and unwittingly destroyed it. We have told the villagers that the explosion was caused by a meteorite strike."

The frail scientist was spent and sat down on his chair, not bothering to ask Goering if he had any questions. The Gruppenführer was nearly too stunned to speak. He stared at Janzig for long moments, making the base commander uncomfortable. Although he had never personally experienced Goering's wrath, he was well aware of his explosive and sadistic bent.

"Are you sure, Herr Janzig? It works?" Goering finally asked.

Janzig did not hesitate. "I would stake my mother's life on the veracity of this claim, Herr Gruppenführer, but words are hollow. If you will follow me, we will take a ride out into the countryside, far away from prying eyes, where we have arranged a demonstration for you. Dr. Zippermayer will drive out ahead of us."

Janzig waited until the scientist had left the room before continuing. "Before we go, Gruppenführer Goering, let us share another cognac together, yes? I believe we have given you much to consider for your next chat with Obergruppenführer Udet and our beloved President."

"Indeed you have, old friend, indeed you have," Goering responded as the steward reappeared with the crystal decanter of prized cognac. He took his glass and raised it in appreciation to Janzig.

"I can always rely on you, Commander. We shall celebrate again when you complete the flight testing. Perhaps, Colonel, there is room on your uniform shoulder boards for some gold braid," Goering teased, suggesting the possibility of a promotion for his loyal ally to the rank of a junior grade General or *Brigadeführer*.

"Thank you, Hermann," Janzig replied, somewhat surprised by Goering's candor. "All in due time as there is much work still to be done; but I assure you, we will bring home the *Amerike* project, so let there be no doubt. It occurs to me that our work here in Lipetsk is not the biggest challenge that lies ahead for you, Gruppenführer."

Goering raised the glass to his lips again, savoring the silken smoothness of the superb cognac and the warmth in his chest. "What do you mean, Colonel?"

Janzig had not meant to be so direct, but there was no turning back now.

"What I mean is that I wonder how long you and Udet will be able to keep the real mission of the *Amerike* project from von Hindenburg?"

Twenty-One

Pipon Decker, head of the French Intelligence Agency, sat with his counterpart, British Naval Intelligence Commander David Culloch, and French President Pierre-Paul-Henri-Gaston Doumergue at the Presidential Palace at Elysée'.

The exquisite 16th century structure, located on the Rue du Faubourg Saint-Honoré in Paris, not far from the charming and idyllic Champs-Elysées, was the official residence of the President of the French Republic. The president's office was located there, as well as meeting facilities for the Council of Ministers.

Gaston Doumergue never felt particularly comfortable in this room, its pretentiousness an embarrassment to him when entertaining heads of state or important visitors such as Culloch.

His strict Protestant upbringing and extensive service in the French colonies overseas, where he served in political positions in impoverished Indochina and Africa, always reminded him that not all men were blessed to have been born into wealth. Consequently, he was unprepared for the life of opulence and overbearing attention that was foisted upon him when in Paris. Even little things bothered him about his perquisites. He despised his desk, a priceless antique handmade by the private artisans of Napoleon III, as an example of excess that he found particularly distasteful.

Gaston Doumergue longed to work out of his simple flat on the Left Bank, where he had a suite of simpler offices that he shared as work space and as his personal quarters for more intimate life with his new bride. He had married Eloise while serving as the thirteenth President of the Republic. This single fact made him one of the most popular leaders ever to assume the presidency of France. He was sixty-three, handsome, newly married and wildly popular. Life was good. So why were these two spies in his office about to ruin his day?

"You mean to tell me that Nungesser and Coli, two of the most admired heroes of the war who somehow survived the fighting in those ridiculously dangerous wooden and canvas contraptions were slaughtered by those German sons of syphilitic whores? " the President lashed out after receiving the news from his visitors. "For simply attempting to set a flight record? You are telling me this with indisputable certainty?" Gaston Doumergue exploded with a passion that Decker had never envisioned possible for the man.

His face crimson and the jugular vein in his neck bulging, the French President struggled to control his rage. He swept his arm violently across a 17th century French, hand-blown decanter, commissioned by King Louis XV, sending it flying across his desk and shattering it, shards of the rare crystal flying everywhere. Culloch winced, caring not for the priceless antiquity but despairing that the hundred-year-old brandy it had contained had been wasted.

"This is madness!" the French President screamed, completely overcome with fury. He searched fruitlessly for some barbaric countermeasure to protest the German action and satisfy the blazing hot stream of vengeance coursing through his veins.

His wrath brought him to the brink of insanity. "I order you to identify immediately two visitors of German descent and arrest them … tourists, priests, I don't care," he ordered in mock justice. "Pick them off the street, and arrest them on some trumped-up charge. We will hang them publicly as retribution for the murder of Nungesser and Coli," he shouted, his voice still quivering with fury.

Neither intelligence officer said a word. Out of respect for the President who was first and foremost a loyal Frenchman, they would not rob him of this moment of insane logic. Such reactions had already passed through their own minds. Silence descended upon the room as Gaston Doumergue paced, gradually regaining his composure.

"My God, what have we come to?" he asked. He wrung his hands in anguish, as if there were something he might do. "May the Lord have mercy on them. Do their families know?" he asked.

Decker responded. "The families, as well as the French people, believe the two pilots have been lost at sea in the Orteig attempt, that they have paid the tragic price of fame and adventure," the intelligence officer responded. "There has been no speculation of sabotage. Only the luck of the Irish fisherman who witnessed it and had an unknowing role in the plan has led us to this conclusion. We have no intention of releasing any information to the press," he said.

"You realize that this is an act of war?" Gaston Doumergue yelled, his wrath unleashed. "Does von Hindenburg have any idea what he has done and the retribution he will likely bring upon his nation? The Allied call for revenge will be immense. Can he possibly believe this is a solution to the inadequacies of the Treaty of Versailles?"

Culloch answered after a polite pause. "Mr. President, let us be clear. We have no idea if von Hindenburg even knows or if he is still in control of the German command. He is quite elderly. It is possible that he is uninvolved or even unaware."

"Have President Coolidge and Prime Minister Baldwin been informed?" Gaston Doumergue asked.

"Yes, Mr. President, they have been intimately informed. They have also been briefed with additional information that we must also share with you," Culloch continued.

"I do not understand," the French President responded. "Why is it that Coolidge and Baldwin are not present for this conversation to plan our response?" he said with some irritation and surprise in his voice. It was not his ego that had been bruised. This matter required both efficiency and immediacy.

"There is an explanation, Sir. Neither the American nor the United Kingdom leader wishes to alert the Germans who, you can be assured, are watching for signs of any sudden meeting of the three of you."

Gaston Doumergue mulled this over for a moment. "What is this vital additional information I must receive?" he asked.

Decker and Culloch exchanged glances. Out of respect, Culloch allowed Decker to respond.

"Mr. President, what I am about to tell you is the product of firsthand information. It has been acquired by many resources in Germany and throughout Europe who have risked their lives to ensure that the Allies are able to do their utmost to maintain peace. Understand, please, that they are often working with people or in environments that are dedicated to the contrary. I ask you to consider all this in the framework of what Commander Culloch and I are about to tell you. Your complete confidence is vital."

Gaston Doumergue said nothing but simply sat down to prepare himself for the kind of national crisis he hoped to avert during the final years of his political career. His sixty-three years suddenly felt like a century. Long minutes passed.

"Gentlemen, you have presented me with a most urgent matter of national security," the beleaguered

French President said. "I hope you are here to provide me a solution as well."

"Mr. President," Culloch responded, "there is one promise I swore to many years ago when dedicating my career to public service and especially to the man to whom I swore allegiance as the head of national intelligence. I am certain Monsieur Decker has taken the same oath."

Culloch paused, and Gaston Doumergue waited.

"And that would be?" the French President inquired.

Culloch took the liberty of lighting a cigarette and taking a deep drag before responding. A cunning smirk came across his face.

"Never, *never* hand the chief a problem without a solution."

Twenty-Two

Seamus McGill carefully packed away the antique crystal frequency set that had put him in touch with the British. Those long days of carrying the wooden box while slogging through the mud of the French trenches had certainly paid off, if not at the time, certainly a decade later. He patted the varnished plywood box with respect before rewrapping it in waterproof canvas and storing it away in his foot locker under the bed.

His small cabin was beginning to resemble a radio station with both the Germen equipment he had sailed with from Dingle Bay and now the British set he had acquired after the visit by British Naval Intelligence people earlier that day. The plan that he, Culloch and Hughes had worked out just had a chance of working, and the thought of returning the murderous favor to the Germans was one his mind was mulling over in double time.

To think he had been duped into participating in the murders of the two Frenchmen was beyond him. He was still unable to come to grips with his rage and constantly fantasized about meeting up with the bastard who had involved him in the mess. Oh, what he would do to the treacherous kraut bastard, he thought. It would not be a pretty sight, but he had learned over the years as a fisherman that not all things extraordinarily satisfying are necessarily pretty.

It seemed, if the British were correct in their assumptions, that he would have at least another week at sea before the action began. There were no attempts at a transatlantic crossing planned during the next seven days, largely because of uncooperative weather.

He had gotten over the loneliness of being so far off the mainland long ago. He was quite comfortable with his own company now and enjoyed the constant motion of the weather, no matter how horrifyingly at odds it could be. In his lifetime he had witnessed some of the most glorious mornings on the planet, the golden orb of the sun rising over the horizon and warming the day with amazing speed. He had also seen daybreaks as black and cold as night, as if Satan himself had taken full charge of the world and all that happened within it.

He no longer feared those black mornings but had learned to prepare for them, because at some point, he knew his courage and skills would be tested, usually almost simultaneously.

For the moment, he would prepare as best he could for the coming manmade storm, and he would be ready when the time came, God willing. Until then, he would tend to his nets, go about his day as he normally would, and dwell on those moments he had shared with the only person who had ever really cared for him and he for her.

When the time came and the action began, no matter the role life would have for him, large or small, he would be ready. Secretly, he had made up his mind that it didn't matter, so long as the mission was accomplished.

Inwardly, he prayed to God to give him the opportunity to stare one of the murderous bastards in the eyes as he cut his throat from ear to ear.

Twenty-Three

The time had finally come.

Released from the tow hook of the truck and positioned correctly on the runway, the *Spirit* was being positioned at the base of Roosevelt Field. Lindbergh kicked at the muddy ruts caused by the airplane's wheels, wondering how much drag the soft field would have as he gunned the monoplane for all it was worth toward the sky with its enormously full fuel tanks, seeking freedom from the earth's grasp.

It had stopped raining, or at least the torrential rains had stopped, but there was still a fine mist in the air. It was no more than heavy dampness, but it accumulated on the shining doped skin of the *Spirit of St. Louis* and trickled down the silver paint. Lindbergh had donned his flight suit now, a full leather jumpsuit lined with sheep's wool. It would be cold up there, even at low altitudes, but his experience with mail delivery told him he'd be warm enough. He would pee in paper cups. He kept a bag for the used cups so as not to pollute the countryside when he made land. He would not want to offend any foreigner.

Tucking the white wool scarf his mother had given him tightly around his neck, he fixed the uppermost button of his flight suit tightly. Since the *Spirit* had no fixed side windows, but celluloid curtains that had to be fixed into place, he planned to fly without the windows to allow a strong flow of air through the cockpit that would help keep him awake through the long and lonely flight. The night hours would be the worst, he knew. He would need to stay awake more than thirty hours, possibly a lot closer to forty if he encountered difficulties with his plan to navigate using the stars and a series of instrument measurements to guide him. He'd flown for long stints before, but he was unsure if he could make a day and a half or more without sleep. If he couldn't, he thought to himself, he'd never know.

Lindbergh walked slowly around the outside of the plane, stopping here and there to run his hands over the wet surface, almost caressing the machine. He spent minutes inspecting the struts on either side of the fuselage, making sure no damage had been done with all the trucking of the aircraft. Finally, he checked one last time to make sure he had his passport; then shook hands with his loyal crew from Ryan. He turned to the crowd and waved unceremoniously and almost apologetically for all the fuss. A lot had happened in a short time for such a young man, and he made a mental note to write a letter of thanks to every living soul who had helped him reach this moment after he landed in Paris.

Without a word, he made the climb in his awkward flying suit through the single, left-hand door, having already donned his chin-strapped leather helmet. One of the Ryan crewmen adjusted the booster magneto to give the engine a hotter spark in the dampness, then gripped the duralumin propeller and spun it. The engine sputtered to life immediately, turning over with an ear-splitting growl as it quickly warmed up to operating temperature. Lindbergh opened the throttle until the engine was roaring. The small plane, held in place only by the wooden chocks blocking its thirty-inch wheels, began fighting against the obstacles as if waiting to be set free. Lindbergh's crew held the wing tips to take some of the stress off the fixed landing gear and the struts.

The pilot closed the throttle and let the engine drop down to idle speed. Lindbergh was all business now. His last act was reaching through the window and taking from one of the Ryan boys the five sandwiches and the thermos of hot coffee he had packed for the trip.

He checked his instruments to see that all were working, especially the large tachometer centered on the simple instrument panel. It was turning at fourteen hundred seventy-five rpms, some thirty revolutions lower than usual because of the dampness. He hoped that it would increase another fifty rpms or so as the engine warmed. The engine was designed for as much as eighteen hundred rpms.

Much more worrisome was the fact that the plane had never been tested at takeoff with a full fuel load. The accidents that had happened thus far in the attempted transatlantic flights could mostly be attributed to untested weight, with the exception of the Sikorsky-designed Fonck accident where the landing gear had been deliberately sabotaged.

He did a quick mental checklist. The conditions for taking off weren't as favorable as he'd prefer. The plane was wet and heavy. He wasn't pulling maximum rpms from the engine when he needed power the most, there was a slightly dangerous tail wind blowing from west to east, and yet he knew the time was now or never. Another few hours and one of the other teams might be ready to go, or the weather could change … or a hundred excuses might present themselves to make him change his mind.

As was his custom before taking off with one of the open airmail planes, he stuffed wads of cotton in his ears, cinched up his safety belt, pulled his goggles off his helmet and down over his eyes. He shrugged his shoulders and waved to the crowd.

"What do you say? Let's give it a try," he called out to the hundreds of adoring and fascinated fans in his farm boy best, mostly to people who wanted to say some day, "I was there the night Lindbergh did it." He nodded to the Ryan crew who waved and simultaneously pulled on the ropes attached to the wheel chocks, pulling them away. Like an unbroken wild stallion, the *Spirit of St. Louis* was released from the lasso holding it.

The silver plane jumped with the sudden freedom, and Lindbergh slowly opened the throttle on his air cooled, nine-cylinder, two hundred-twenty-three-horsepower Wright Whirlwind J-5C engine. At this moment, the performance of the five hundred pound motor meant life or death for the twenty-five year old pilot. Now, as the crowd parted way for the silver bird, Lindbergh realized that finally, it was just the two of them -- man and machine.

There could not have been a more oddly arranged marriage. His airplane was miniscule in size, power and fuel capacity compared to any of its competitors. He was a pilot from the American Midwest who up until the last several days had been all but unknown compared to the heroic European aviators he was challenging. He had made nary a mark on the world of aviation other than being recognized as one of the most capable airmail pilots ever to brave the clouds.

But here they were, together: a shy, gadabout pilot and a remarkable silver debutante who had barely been introduced but were about to confront history together.

Twenty-Four

The light on the miserable daybreak of May 20, 1927, was hardly encouraging in itself. It was simply wretched.

Some believe that great things occur on the brightest of days, when the air is full of hope, when the combination of warmth, sun rays and the slightest of breezes invigorates the mind and fills the heart with determination and ecstasy at being alive. It's on this kind of glorious day, when a person can actually feel his soul and even give in to the urge to run or jump or scream with joy, that the utmost accomplishments are made and the most amazing achievements recorded.

If, in fact, that were true, Lindbergh thought from the cockpit of his now soaking wet airplane, dressed from head to toe in a dirty, damp, itchy, sheepskin-lined, raw leather jumpsuit, feeling already hungry, exhausted and completely miserable, today would have been a good day to roll over and stay in bed.

But that was not Charles Lindbergh. It was true that the greater the challenge, the more alive and invigorated he felt. He may have looked like a boy, a characteristic that seemed to exaggerate his bravery; but there was nothing about him that wouldn't surely have made his father nearly burst with pride. He was a man in whatever ways make men good and strong.

He was also a realist; and for every moment of satisfaction in his life, there was also a problem solved or a mechanical riddle untangled. Hope for Charles Lindbergh had nothing to do with sun and warmth and breezes. It had to with clear skies and wings free of ice.

Those times, high above the world in the flimsiest of contraptions, were the moments that invigorated his mind and filled him with determination. There was nothing concerning ecstasy and romance about Charles Lindbergh. Hardly. There was simply a life well lived and close enough to the edge that most people would fall off.

Now, as he brought all his concentration to bear on the mud-drenched and grass-soaked airfield before him, with nothing but four hundred twenty-five gallons of intensely flammable aviation fuel, an engine that was running a bit rough, and a two-bladed duralumin propeller between him and the freedom of flight, the realist in him asked a question. Did he know what he was doing, or had he completely lost his sanity?

It took him only a second of reflection to answer his own question. What he was doing was what he was born to do -- to embark upon and achieve the virtually impossible, and leave the jumping for joy to someone else.

Hundreds of onlookers cheered him on. Some were there for the unspoken thrill of knowing they were about to witness a man triumph or die a horrible death in the next few seconds. The time for hesitation was over. Lindbergh mashed his right rudder pedal to the floor, yanked the control stick to the right in order to dead center the airplane on the runway, then gunned the Wright Whirlwind engine for all it was worth, willing every last ounce of power out of every component of the hand-machined and assembled motor.

The tail hook of the airplane skidded in the mud from the terrific sudden torque that shook the airframe as it turned and sent some onlookers scurrying back from the spraying mud. The *Spirit of St. Louis* began its agonizing journey down the straight runway, aided by the efforts of several of the Ryan men lifting up the wingtips and under the struts. The extra muscle helped to free the airplane's oversized wheels from sticking in the mud.

Watching the Ryan crewmen straining to push the aircraft free of the muck, physically giving him all they had left, Lindbergh never forgot the look of supreme satisfaction he saw on their faces as the silver bird picked up speed. He turned and watched as he left them behind, falling on the wet runway, covered from head to toe with mud, cheering and screaming for their lives, pounding the grass with their fists with elation, looking up for one last glimpse of the airplane they knew part by part – and the pilot they knew in their hearts.

The final push was all the *Spirit* needed to begin to move under its own power, picking up the speed it so desperately needed less than a mile away. If this silver-skinned monoplane was to have a chance to beat the challenges of the heavens and make it thirty-six hundred miles to Paris, it first had to clear one small hurdle, a long, muddy runway at Roosevelt Field, Garden City, Long Island.

It was a nightmare of a run down the soggy strip. With no forward vision because of the bulkhead fuel tank, it was a take off only a fool or a very brave would man attempt. The thought made Lindbergh chuckle as he realized it was a little bit late for it. As the young man reached down and pulled tighter on his seat belt, pushing him down even further into the small, intentionally uncomfortable wicker pilot's seat he had installed to save weight and help keep him awake, it suddenly dawned on him that the cockpit wasn't long enough for him to stretch his legs.

And Paris was only forty hours away.

Twenty-Five

With the exhausted ground crew now far behind, the *Spirit* began picking up real speed on its own but continued to fishtail down the mud-soaked runway as the plane's wheels struggled for traction. After a thousand feet, he still felt no control of the airplane in the cockpit. The stick would not respond. He barely had lift under his wings. Occasionally, he felt the familiar surge telling him he was getting closer to liftoff speed, but he was running out of time.

At two thousand feet, he was still too slow but could begin to feel the wind building consistent lift under his wings. At the very same time that he was gaining some control over his airplane, he was also at the point of no return and had to make the split-second decision as to whether to stay the course or abort.

There were two end results of making the wrong decision. If he didn't have enough lift to clear the telephone lines, the *Spirit* would explode in a rather spectacular manner twenty feet off the earth and fall to the ground, a mound of smoldering wreckage. If he was unable to lift off, he would end up in the same gully as René Fonck and probably suffer the same fate as his crew members who burned to death in their fuel-laden aircraft.

The third option was to stop, but that had to happen now to have any chance of saving the plane. It never entered his mind. He made the only decision his determination would allow him to accept once he felt the sensation of wind beneath his wings.

He pulled back even harder on the yoke, virtually willing the *Spirit of St. Louis* into the air.

The yards went by in seconds. Another thousand feet passed, the telephone polls and their wires looming. Still, he would not stop. In the cockpit of the *Spirit*, he was bouncing around, painfully banging from side to side in the cramped fuselage, which measured only thirty-six inches across. The lap safety belt he had cinched around his waist was so tight that it had already cut grooves into his leather flying suit. Observers watched as Lindbergh, with limited side-to-side visibility through his open side windows and the periscope all but useless with the jarring movements, constantly course corrected the airplane by fluttering the rudder pedals and preventing yaw that would rob the airplane of speed by wobbling its course.

At this same time, the young pilot could feel the plane begin to gather enough wind under its wings to launch it momentarily into the air, then lose the lift and settle back down on the runway, its engine still roaring. The *Spirit of St. Louis* bounced once into the air, settling back down on its muddy path, bounced into the air a second and finally a third time until it seemed to grasp hold of the invisible air and stay aloft — but just barely.

Those few who had the discipline to glance at their watches read that it was 7:52 a.m. as the lone monoplane finally cleared by a scant ten feet the gully that had devastated Fonck and the guillotine-like telephone wires by twenty feet.   He was airborne by the slimmest of margins, and he was tempting history with either the greatest barnstorming scam or the bravest, loneliest act the world had ever known.

The aircraft carried the name of a single city; but it carried the hopes and pride of the entire country as well. Everyone from small children barely able to grasp the fact that there was another side of the world, to the aged who never dreamed that flying from one continent to another could be possible in their lifetimes, cheered together all over America. It was a moment more people would remember than the victorious news of the U.S. Expeditionary Forces declaring victory in Europe.

In France, too, despite the nation's continued mourning for the loss of their heroes, Nungesser and Coli, men, women and children cheered on the lone, lonely American pilot.

Word reached Paris by wire within minutes of Lindbergh's successful takeoff. The French government ordered the huge light beacon at the village of Cherbourg, one of the ports of embarkation for the great passenger ocean liners plying the North Atlantic between Queensland, Ireland; Liverpool, England; France and past the Statue of Liberty and Ellis Island into New York harbor, to be lit to guide Lindbergh to the French coast and on to Paris.

If all went well, and the prayers of millions were heard, the silhouette of the *Spirit of St. Louis* would be seen near the Eiffel Tower before midnight of the following day, preparing to land at Le Bourget Aerodrome in Paris, France.

Although the news was that Lindbergh had actually taken off, only the first major step had been achieved on the long trip. Men cheered him on, women wept for his safety as if for a son, and children held Lindbergh as their hero. But the odds were against him. Not even Lloyd's of London, the great, eccentric insurance house, was quoting odds on Lindbergh, begging off the whole thing as just too risky.

Lifting the enormous fuel load into the sky was a huge accomplishment, the very thing that had doomed the planning or actual attempt at just about every other transatlantic crossing effort. Six men had already lost their lives in the attempt.

It appeared that Lindbergh's bet that attempting the flight with a single-engine airplane, versus the multi-engine approach which required far heavier fuel payloads others had depended on, had paid off. That was, of course, if he, as a single pilot, was able to remain alert and awake for the estimated forty-hour flight and his single engine and self-oiling device performed flawlessly over the length of the flight. Success also depended on his marginally tested navigational skills without even the aid of a sextant. Of course, there was always the chance that he might encounter some freak, unexpected weather pattern that could blow him off course. Or his wings and fuselage would load up with tons of ice and send him hurtling into the ocean without a chance... there were so many "ifs" to go.

When it had finally come to making the decisions about equipment he would need aboard the *Spirit* to have any chance should he have to ditch at sea, he had hardly thought seriously about it. He flew without a parachute, a radio or a sextant. He allowed himself a small rubber raft, which was very surprising, as he admitted privately that he would carry no life jacket and would likely drown before he could inflate the raft. He did, however, allow himself the pocket knife he had earned as a Boy Scout.

As he flew farther from Roosevelt Field, across Long Island Sound and over the wealthy Connecticut shoreline mansions, "Lucky Lindbergh", as the media had taken to calling him, was in a winner-take-all, loser-take-the-fall situation. There was no in-between. He would simply succeed and live in triumph or fail and meet a forgettable death. If anything, the grey mist over the Connecticut shoreline near Madison kept his celebration of being airborne in check. The ugliness of the day simply dampened excitement.

Even so, the Connecticut coastline, lined with summer cottages and year-round mansions, was breathtaking.

Lindbergh, the farm boy from Minnesota, had not been exposed to anything quite like it. It was a far cry from the places he had lived as a boy. Although he had been born in Detroit, his father, future republican congressman Charles Augustus Lindbergh, a Swedish emigrant, and his mother, Evangeline Lodge Land Lindbergh of Detroit, had moved their young family to Little Falls, Minnesota, along the banks of the Mississippi River when he was very young. There, Lindbergh often recalled living the life of a 20th century Tom Sawyer.

The Lindbergh's' was not a happy marriage, and rumor had it that C.A. ran for Congress just for the opportunity to live apart from his wife, who was pushing him for a divorce. He set himself up in Washington, D.C., leaving Charles and his sisters in his mother's care in Little Falls. The boy felt his father's absence acutely, and Charles A. Lindbergh, Jr., despite the boyish looks that would mark him until his middle years, became a man at a very early age.

Now, flying low over the Connecticut coast, he forced himself back to the present and berated himself for the lack of discipline so early in his flight. *I am far too busy to be reminiscing about my boyhood,* he thought to himself as he scanned the instrument panel of the *Spirit* for any signs of trouble.

For the moment, he was winning. The engine had spun up to a comfortable seventeen hundred fifty rpms, the altimeter showed him at two hundred feet, and his air speed indicator indicated he was traveling at just over one hundred miles per hour. He hoped to average somewhat faster than that by journey's end. By 9:00 a.m. he was flying at five hundred feet toward the Rhode Island coast. He hit a bit of turbulence over Connecticut, but the flight over Long Island Sound was relatively uneventful.

At 9:15 he passed over Plymouth Rock and a few minutes later, the small town of Marshfield,

Massachusetts, the last bit of land he would see for
several hours as he headed out over the Atlantic for the
first time. By noon, he was over the small fishing village
of Tusket, Nova Scotia, still averaging one hundred miles
per hour in the gray, but otherwise clear, sky.

Only thirty-five hundred miles to go. He began thinking
about what he should say when he landed at Le Bourget,
then quickly erased the overconfident thought from his
mind. He reminded himself that the trip was not quite
over.

Lindbergh knew he would be surprised by how fast
the Maine coastline would appear, when he would leave
land for an extended period for the first time on his way
to his next landmark, Nova Scotia. Once he got
comfortable that all was well in the plane, Lindbergh set
to work on his navigational tasks. He settled into the
wicker chair, which really was terribly uncomfortable. He
was having second thoughts about it already.

He pulled out his maps and the Mercator charts he
had purchased in the shop in San Diego so many months
before; then set the needle of his earth inductor compass,
a relatively new technology, to its first setting of sixty-five
degrees.

Developed just three years earlier, the earth inductor
compass Lindbergh had Ryan install in the *Spirit*
determined an aircraft's direction using the magnetic field
of the Earth. It replaced the magnetic and gyroscopic
compasses generally in use, which had proven
troublesome at high altitudes. Lindbergh knew that
mastering the instrument was crucial to his ability to
navigate the vast North Atlantic accurately. The unit he
was using had been hand built by his friend Ray Simpson,
a leading innovator in the burgeoning test instrument
panel field, of Lac du Flambeau, Wisconsin. Simpson was
hoping that the notoriety gained from Lindbergh's flight
would help him find the investors he needed to found

Simpson Electric. Lindbergh knew all too well the difficulty of finding people to invest in dreams.

Satisfied with his course, he began experimenting with the controls of the somewhat finicky airplane. He worked the horizontal and vertical stabilizers gently to smooth out the inherent pitching and yawing movements of the *Spirit* for the most efficient flight possible. Lindbergh had spent hours during his recent cross-country flight working on the same problem but was not yet satisfied with his performance. The airplane's flight control idiosyncrasies weren't going to change, he knew. It was the pilot who had to change the way he flew the airplane—and he had a very long way to go indeed.

Twenty-Six

At almost the same moment word arrived in Paris that Lindbergh was airborne, the news was also picked up in the British and Irish embassies, setting into motion a series of dramatic actions that, once initiated, would be almost impossible to reverse. The first began at a small, cleverly hidden airfield to the south of Dingle Bay, just along the sandy coast of the peninsula. It was a short grass airstrip that had been constructed at the height of the Great War as a training field for English pilots. Later it was used as a launch base for U-boat search operations operating in the North Atlantic off the Emerald coast.

The airfield, really several dozen acres of farm land that a French farmer had voluntarily abandoned in support of the war effort a decade ago, had sat nearly unused since the end of hostilities. There was virtually no military aviation activity by the English that far south; the Irish had no air force, and the French, like the English, had little use for it. The grassy, briar-filled airfield, which was now so overgrown as to be almost unusable, saw only occasional use by private pilots and there weren't very many of those.

As well, there were few military pilots left from the war who had any stomach for flying, and as a sport, the hobby was enormously expensive, difficult and dangerous. The sole hangar at one end of the field was actually more like an overgrown metal barn that leaked so badly that any plane stored inside had to be covered with canvas tarps. Starting an airplane stored in such conditions was an hours-long affair because of the moisture and the difficulty of getting a good spark from a damp magneto. There wasn't a qualified airplane mechanic within one hundred fifty miles. Any support the Army needed had to come from within. The field was nearly seventeen miles outside of town, so only a few of the locals were even aware there was renewed activity at the Dingle Airfield.

Today, the air around the old grass landing strip was almost electric with the activity of the French Air Force, which had suddenly appeared with a fleet of four vintage SPAD XIIIs, the most advanced Allied fighters which had enjoyed a great degree of success over the skies and trenches of France during the latter part of the Great War.

For the French Army personnel who had served then and were assigned to this mission, the abandoned airfield unleashed a torrent of long-buried, but never forgotten, emotions. One could almost smell the excitement, as well as the heavy scent of fuel, oil and grease, cordite and gunpowder. Even though only a handful of the most senior officers there knew the true intention of the mission, the rank and file speculated that the whole production was some sort of odd training exercise, likely to show up in the press to be used as a recruiting gimmick. Either that or something very strange was up.

The center of attention at the field was the SPAD XIIIs, just four of the eight thousand legendary fighters that had been produced by France during the War. It was so successful in aerial combat that most of the Allied nations fighting the War adopted it for their own use. Even the U.S. Government used it to substantial advantage. American war ace and hero, Lt. Frank Luke, shot down fifty-four German planes in a SPAD XIII and posthumously won the Medal of Honor with his heroics in the French aircraft. Besides being one of the most capable fighters of the war, it was one of the most successful. The SPAD XIII had a two hundred horsepower engine, Vickers machine guns and an operating range of more than five hundred miles. Nearly a decade after it had gone out of production at the war's end, the French military command was hoping it was still as lethal.

The problem was there weren't many left from the War. The four SPAD XIIIs waiting in the hangar were the best the French had left in their arsenal and had been chosen for perhaps one of the most vital peacetime missions in aviation history. They were the centerpiece of the first step in a larger strategic plan devised by the leadership of four Allied nations. If all went according to design, it would be one of the best-kept secret military actions of all time, designed to devastate the enemy's self-confidence with limited deployment of military assets and, above all, without risking another world war.

On this day the flag flying from the ramshackle, rusted old maintenance hangar at Dingle was not the Union Jack of the British but the Tricolore of France. Although the English had volunteered to do the job — and with some emotion had actually lobbied for the work of vengeance -- the nation of France would simply not allow another to avenge the barbarous murder of its two heroes.

The fact that the Germans were responsible for the murders of Nungesser and Coli had been carefully hidden from the French population for fear that it would incite a call for bloody retaliation that would become a roar for yet another all-out world war. No, the French President Doumergue had properly briefed only the most level-headed and trustworthy advisors and representatives of the government. His handling of the situation, despite his own personal struggle with an appetite for vengeance, was superb.

With cool heads at the helm, a plan of retribution had been quickly devised by French, British, Irish and American military leaders and approved by the heads of state. Most senior government officials of each country thought that a second world war was eventually inevitable, but to a man, they did not want it to start over the folly of insulted German military idiots who refused to consider lasting peace if it did not include their domination of Europe, at the least.

Veteran French military mechanics, those who had kept the airplanes flying daily during the Great War, had been handpicked for the assignment. These were the same men who not only repaired the bullet-ridden aircraft, but who had also removed the bodies of maimed pilots from the cockpits of their SPADS and washed the blood from the seats. Their memories were long and motivation still fresh. Each of them worked overnight on the old birds that had been carefully stored for just such unwanted but necessary use. They had not wasted a moment since the airplanes had flown in from a military air base south of Paris over the English and Bristol Channels to Dingle Bay. The SPADs had arrived not a moment too soon. At the abandoned Irish airfield, the aircraft were tuned to the highest level of performance the old planes could muster under the meticulous efforts of mechanics that lived, drilled, caroused and got drunk with the pilots who would fly them. Not a screw, bolt or wing nut escaped their inspection or repair, such was the effect of their brotherhood.

Now, the four hand-picked French pilots who would fly the mission to avenge Nungesser and Coli waited with their superbly ready weapons of destruction. It might be a week, a day, or an hour before they would get their chance to even up the score, but they were ready.

The French had been given the assignment despite the ambitions of the American military. Realizing that the American involvement in the Orteig Prize effort would likely and eventually put a U.S. pilot or pilots at similar risk if the Germans were unchecked, the American Army

Air Force Command was itching to get its planes and resources into play.

But the insufficient time and sheer lack of American resources on European soil frustratingly would not allow them to satisfy their eagerness for justice. The French, with vengeful spirit decades old, were only too happy to resolve what they saw as a French problem anyway.

Under the command of a French Lieutenant Commander, Laurent Marciél, the four pilots at Dingle, ready to take on the mission, were the best he had ever known. He was not completely comfortable with their technical proficiency, as only one had actual combat experience, nor the old equipment available to them to accomplish the operation. But he knew that each of the pilots had suffered a grievous loss during the former conflict, of one sort or another, and had not since lived a day without the thought of an opportunity to share the pain they felt with an enemy they would despise forever.

They were motivated. Two had lost fathers in the skies over the French trenches, one a beloved uncle, and a third, a brother. Not only were the Germans dissatisfied with the outcome of the Versailles Treaty, the French thirst for German blood had yet to be sated.

Unbeknownst to Marciél and the French pilots, some thirty hours remained before their mission would be launched. They still had plenty of time to prepare for their operation, which was clear, precise, and nearly foolproof in that it was dependent on the highly reliable resources of the British Naval Intelligence Service and their own intelligence operations.

By now, three hours or so after the warm spring sun had cast a golden glow over the airfield at dusk, word had whispered through the night to the local Dingle farmers that a contingent of French fliers had suddenly and mysteriously appeared at the old, nearly forgotten airfield. Early the next morning, from an ancient, rutted dirt road that led directly to the airport from the center of Dingle Bay, an army of small trucks full of dozens of villagers and children excitedly riding their bicycles filled the path. A great brown cloud of following dust gave away their arrival and brought uncertainty to the instincts of the sentries stationed at the airfield's rusted gates. Their orders were to allow no one through -- no one.

The lead truck was stopped by the French sentries, and a conversation was attempted between a soldier who spoke French and a farmer who spoke a combination of Irish Gaelic and English bastardized by long years of English occupation. An argument ensued between the two; but it suddenly stopped in its tracks when a small blond-haired, blue-eyed lass of perhaps ten years old crawled out from the middle of the front seat of the antique Riley, wooden-bed stake truck. It was at least thirty years older than its littlest passenger.

Brushing aside the soldier, she spoke to the commanding sergeant. After shaking his head in confusion, he shrugged his shoulders and sheepishly escorted the peasant girl to Lieutenant Commander Marciél's makeshift tent headquarters, incongruously holding a heavy rifle in his left hand and the young girl's arm in his right. The appearance of the weapon aimed at her head was almost obscene, and the sergeant looked hopelessly embarrassed.

"Sir, they just appeared out of nowhere. There was nothing we could do," the sergeant stammered before his commanding officer. "Perhaps we can round them up and hold them as prisoners in the hangar," he offered, completely befuddled by this child, who continued to attempt to speak to him in English with a heavy Irish brogue, which further confused the soldier.

Marciél looked sternly at his sergeant, unsure of how to respond to his subordinate for his failure. He leaned down to the little girl, who was clutching a large, reed, woven basket covered with a red-and-white-checked linen cloth.

His frown quickly melted as he kneeled at the little girl's eye level. Despite his determined efforts to look angry, he couldn't help smiling at the girl. "What is your name, little one?" he spoke in near perfect English with a strong twist of cockney, a gift of the English who had employed him in Liverpool for several years after the war in the back-building chore of breaking enemy ships. She giggled and carefully removed the cloth covering from the basket, revealing freshly baked breads, homemade cheese, fruits, and bottles of black Irish stout.

"My name is Elissa," the child responded, beaming, knowing that her intentions were finally understood. "Mister General, we have brought much more for your soldiers. We are so happy to have you visit," she said, revealing an innocent smile and wide blue eyes that reminded him of his own beloved daughter Lillé, awaiting his return to their home near the Orly Aerodrome and airfield on the outskirts of Paris. He felt his eyes moisten.

Commander Marciél, smiling and unconsciously puffing up his chest in mock honor of being referred to as a General in front of his amused subordinates, some of whom were doing a poor job of stifling laughter, grabbed her hand. He emerged from the tent holding Elissa's hand and gently leaned down to pick up the small child. He gave her a tiny peck on each cheek and hugged the girl as if she were his own. A cheer arose from the parade of farmers and villagers, and there was not a member of the French military on duty that day who did not gain respect for their superior officer for his kindness. He was a hard man who had never been known particularly for his gentleness; but on this day, he had recognized the beauty of peace between peoples.

Still enjoying the mock tone of a General, he barked orders and instructed his sentries to open the airfield gates wide and allow the Irish farmers to join them. The children on their brightly colored bicycles let out yelps of glee and raced through the open gates, immediately heading closer to the SPAD VIIIs for a closer look. In most cases, this was the nearest they had ever been to an airplane.

While the conversation was sparse, as few knew English or Gaelic and fewer still the French language, the laughter and camaraderie between the soldiers and farmers were as real as the bread, cheese and stout they devoured together. The adults, in particular, celebrated a decade's worth of overdue remembrance with the fine dark brew the farmers had produced from wheat, barley and hops grown in their own fields and aged in barrels they had made with their own hands.

There were moments when common men such as these celebrated the victory of war, but triumph was officially measured by those who counted which side lost the most amount of blood. Only the generals and politicians who counted the bodies took real satisfaction in such conquests. For those who actually waged the battle –pulled a trigger, thrust a bayonet, dropped a bomb or tossed a hand grenade – the elation of *victory* often evolved into the nightmares of *horror*. Marciél seethed at the thought of his own nightly struggles.

For those who had lived the reality of war, the cause or outcome was never of real consequence. What was important was that victory ultimately ended the mindless slaughter. That was why few soldiers who survived truly ever felt joy again. War taught them the meaninglessness of life. For the remainder of their lives, the elation of living came only in fleeting moments. For the sake of his veterans, the Commander hoped this was one such moment of jubilation.

At British Naval Intelligence, there was only one
potentially weak link in the orchestrated plan on this day.
It involved the simple Irish fisherman, known only to the
English, who was now waiting some one hundred
twenty-five miles or more off the Irish coast in his small
wooden fishing boat. It was the fisherman's personal
responsibility to send the radio signal that would engage
the intelligence, men, machines and desire of four nations
simultaneously to defend the lone, twenty-five-year-old
pilot.

The British, as the U.S., French and Irish probably
would have done if they were closer to the issue,
questioned the fisherman's personal suitability to the
mission. They doubted his understanding of Lindbergh's
unwitting political role. As well, they thought him naïve
in grasping the lengths to which war-minded men would
go to satisfy their own personal egos and ambitions,
under the pretense of national interests.

At the same time, this uncertain leadership of four
different nations did not know the Irishman whose
intelligence and courage they questioned. Seamus McGill
was neither an educated man nor an expert to any degree
in world, or even Irish politics; but blind and uneducated
as he might be, once he took a vow, he was unshakable.
At the wheel of *The Lovely Mary*, the Irishman remained
vigilant, awaiting a signal from the British he was certain
would come.

McGill knew he had but one role in the game once it
began and that was to help reverse the deception, set the
bait, and lay out the hook. What the doubters also did not
understand was that his integrity and sense of justice
more than made up for his lack of schooling. Nor did they
recognize that his soul, nearly dead since the loss of his
wife, was aflame again in anticipation of his small but
vital role in gutting the fish they hunted. For the first time

in many months, he felt full of anger and hatred — and fully alive.

There were few men living whose word could be trusted as much as that of Seamus McGill. Unfairly, but necessarily, the old Irish fisherman would have to prove that to men who considered themselves his better.

The character most unwittingly and unknowingly involved in the game was the young pilot who was now entering the sixth hour of his flight across the Atlantic. He was just now making landfall over Nova Scotia. Lindbergh's own fight dealt with the limitations of nature, the body and mechanical physics. Combined, these forces did not constitute a willful attempt to defeat him, yet they were real and not completely in his control. Nature could overcome him by simply changing the weather environment to a degree where his machine could not survive; he could physically fatigue at the controls, or a sudden mechanical breakdown could rob the *Spirit* of the wind beneath its wings.

Ultimately, however, it wasn't the challenges he could not control that were against him. His real enemies were those who believed that only bullets and bloodshed could shape Lindbergh's destiny and fulfill their own.

Twenty-Seven

At a little past three in the afternoon, Lindbergh's *Spirit of St. Louis* was flying low over the tiny hamlet of Mulgrave on the Strait of Canso just before Cape Breton Island. The pilot saw storm clouds beginning to gather ahead, so he increased his throttle, pulled back on the joystick, and took the airplane to eight thousand feet to climb above the storm.

Less than three-quarters of an hour later, he flew over Main-á-Dieu on the coast of Cape Breton Island, the most easterly point of Nova Scotia. It was a landmark for which Lindbergh had been searching to check his navigation. While researching the path of his intended flight, he had come upon the small town of lobster fishermen and saw that its French name translated to "Hand of God". He thought perhaps that flying over the port would remind him to pray for his safety before heading out over the immense and forbidding North Atlantic Ocean.

Despite being airborne for more than eight hours, the *Spirit of St. Louis* was still quite fuel laden; but the airplane and its young pilot had successfully crossed a number of hurdles. The plane had effectively hoisted more than twenty-five hundred pounds of fuel into the air. It had performed flawlessly across all of New England and Nova Scotia, and its heading was dead on. Given the universal failure of his competitors on takeoff or within the first few hours of flight, Lindbergh's success instilled confidence in British Naval Intelligence that the American pilot actually had a chance, and it launched the first element of the Allied plan into action.

"The Lovely Mary, come in, please," the navy military radio crackled in the small cabin of Seamus McGill's fishing boat. It was the call the fisherman had been awaiting patiently for more than a week while he put his boat through the motions of casting nets for herring. It was now 7:00 p.m. on the Irish Coast, and the sun was just beginning to settle over *The Lovely Mary's* bow.

McGill had been topside, scanning the horizon for signs of other ships, when the radio call came and breached the evening silence over the calm waters. The lapping of water against the hull and the occasional cry of a seagull were about the only company he had this far off shore. Strangely, he found comfort in this quiet, just as he had in holding his Mary's hand and looking into her eyes, not saying a word.

He climbed down from the upper deck two rungs at a time and reached quickly for the microphone of the British Navy's radio, which had already broadcast the call sign a second time.

"The Lovely Mary at your service, Sir," McGill keyed the microphone excitedly. "Over."

Silence followed for about thirty seconds. "It's good to hear from you, Captain," the familiar voice of Commander David Culloch responded. "Over."

McGill keyed the microphone. "As it is here, Commander. Over," replied the fisherman, who had yet to get over the fact that an officer of Her Majesty's Navy would pay him the respect of referring to him as "Captain." Mary would have been proud of him.

"I take it the fishing is good, Captain. Over," Culloch responded to McGill in a prearranged coded question that inquired if all was well with him and his ship.

McGill did not hesitate. "Aye, Commander, my holds are not full yet and may not be for another ten days or so. Over." It was another code for the status of *The Lovely Mary's* well-being and how much longer she could remain on site without attracting the attention of being reprovisioned by a naval vessel. Culloch wanted to avoid drawing any undue attention to the small fishing boat unless absolutely necessary -- the craft being a key element of their complex plan.

"This is good news, Captain, as we understand the fishing may become very active within the next twenty-four hours your time," Culloch said.

McGill immediately understood that Culloch was giving him the signal that Lindbergh had successfully lifted off and made it to the Atlantic. He had no idea if the *Spirit* had yet flown over Newfoundland to begin its two-thousand-mile trek to the Irish coast, but no matter. The American airplane was on its way, and at some point, the paths of *The Lovely Mary* and the *Spirit of St. Louis* would cross.

In the back of McGill's mind, that fact reminded him that the poor American bastard was now the target of the same murdering scum that had done in Nungesser and Coli.

"Not if I have anything to do about it," he mumbled aloud with the microphone closed.

"I thank you for that information, Commander. Over," McGill added. "A full hold would be a welcome way to greet the spring, my friend. Over," he said letting Culloch know that he was now fully alert to look out for the French or Brits and to provide any other assistance that may be asked of him. Sleep would not come for the fisherman tonight for fear that he would miss the airplane. Nothing could come between the commitment he had made to the British Naval Commander, and in another sense, to those millions like him who wanted to live their lives, hard as they sometimes were, in peace.

Culloch responded immediately. "It's the least I can do for a man who's offered to buy my beer at Kerry's

Ring, old friend. We must make a pact to meet there again on return port, aye? Over," he said.

McGill was actually pretty good at this game. "See here, Commander, you'll be the first to know if I fill my hold within the next day," he said, "but it's your turn to buy the beer, whether you outrank me or not. You should expect to hear from me soon. Over," he ended.

"Fine, *The Lovely Mary*. I'll be waiting to hear from you. Until then, may your seas be calm, the skies clear and your hold full of fish, Captain. Do not hesitate to raise me on this frequency. Over and out," Culloch signed off.

The first part of the trap had been sprung. Culloch was banking on Germany's desperate requirement for invisibility of their murderous intentions. He was equally confident that *The Lovely Mary* would not only be on Lindbergh's route, but also would be at the far edge of the range of the German fighters. Seamus McGill would be the eyes and ears that would tell the French when to launch their SPADS to intercept the Germans before they could get to Lindbergh. It was a long shot, but it was also a huge ocean to cover. The British Intelligence Officer was willing to bet his plan was the only shot Lindbergh had at survival.

Radio transmissions off the Irish coast were routinely monitored by the local villagers and commercial and navy vessels. Aside from the jesting, there was nothing overtly out of the ordinary about the transmission from *The Lovely Mary*, especially to the German pilots who had been eavesdropping on their own radio at a hiding place on the Irish coast, just north of Dingle Bay. The Germans listened carefully to the broadcast, near their Heinkel 59 floatplanes which rocked gently in the shallow waters of a salt marsh set back a hundred yards from the ocean. These were advanced fighters the world had not yet seen which had been designed, developed and produced in Lipetsk.

The two aircraft had remained hidden here for more than a month, but the planes had flown only twice. They had been carried by train from Lipetsk across Russia to Leningrad, then loaded onto a German commercial freighter for the long journey through the Gulf of Finland. They passed the Swedish islands of Gotland and Oland and the Dane's Bornholm Island before making port at the German coastal city of Kiel.

There the airplanes were loaded onto flatbed rail cars and transported by train through Germany to Bremerhaven, where they were once again loaded onto a freighter flying a neutral flag for a surreptitious passage across the North Sea. They skirted the Netherlands and Belgium before passing between France and Great Britain on the English Channel.

Finally entering the North Atlantic, the ship sailed around the southernmost tip of Ireland, laying anchor one hundred miles off the coast. Under cover of darkness, the Heinkel pontoon planes were unloaded and reassembled, then flown by German pilots to a spot just north of Dingle Bay. There they taxied the airplanes into a salt marsh guided by an undercover German agent with a torch.

The spy was one of hundreds placed strategically throughout Europe by the German military. By day he was the proprietor of a small book shop in the village. He guided the pilots toward the deepest edge of the marsh which bordered a heavily wooded sanctuary where they could make camp. The hiding place was far from any road or path out of Dingle Bay, and save for the persistent attacks of mosquitoes, the Germans were safe and in no danger of being discovered.

There, hiding in the shadows of the marsh, the Germans had waited patiently for the French try at the Orteig Prize. Eventually, their opportunity to ambush and murder Nungesser and Coli came. The pilots eagerly reported on the remarkable performance of their seaplanes and laughed at how easy it had been to shoot down an unarmed aircraft traveling at half their speed. They had been on station ever since, awaiting instructions to intercept and shoot down other non-German Orteig Prize participants. The pilots, who had not seen action for nearly a month now, were bored.

The Heinkel 59 was one of the most advanced aircraft the Germans were developing in secrecy in Lipetsk. It was a floatplane, meaning it could take off and land in the water and that each of its pontoons was used as a fuel tank. Each pontoon was large enough to hold an amount of fuel to give the plane a range of over four hundred sixty miles.

The airplane had two, four-bladed, fixed-pitch propellers and a wingspan of nearly twenty-four feet. Two BMW VI six-liter water-cooled V12 engines developed over six hundred sixty horsepower, giving it a gross speed of nearly two hundred thirty-five kilometers per hour at more than sixteen thousand feet and an ability to climb at a rate of six hundred fifty-six feet per minute. It was simply a spectacular airplane and a sign of German aeronautical technology to come if unchecked. Positioning the airplanes in Ireland was perfect. The Heinkels were just far enough off the coast to do their treacherous work without danger of being seen.

Nungesser and Coli had been sitting ducks. In fact, ducks might have had a better chance. As a lethal fighter, the Heinkel 59s could best be described as high-performance race cars, and their competitors were hot air balloons. If the four SPAD XIII pilots, waiting patiently at the air strip in Ireland, had been fully briefed on the performance ability of their enemy, they might have enjoyed a few more pints of Irish stout and spent time with their parish priests before considering their futures against these monsters of Bavarian brilliance.

The Germans, both young men in their early twenties, were as bored as their French counterparts just a few kilometers away. At least the French could pass the time with the Irish farmers, especially their red-headed daughters.

For the two young Aryan pilots, however, life was about to get a little more exciting.

Twenty-Eight

Into his ninth hour in the air, the lanky young man who normally enjoyed an insatiable appetite felt the first twinges of hunger in his stomach. The excitement had him too keyed up to eat, so he settled for a drink of water from his canteen. He drank sparingly. If he was forced down at sea his need for fresh water would be much greater.

Having successfully skirted the storm he had encountered over Nova Scotia, Lindbergh nosed the *Spirit* lower just as he passed over the outlying island of St. Pierre et Miquelon just off the coast of Newfoundland at the Grand Banks. He soared over the rocky coast of the Burin Peninsula and into the fishing village of Marystown, then crossed over Placentia Bay en route to St. John's.

The J5C engine propelling the *Spirit of St. Louis* droned on like a Gregorian chant, smooth and elegant with all the percussion tuned to accentuate its vitality. Satisfied that all was well with his single engine, Lindbergh notched up the throttle a bit to seventeen hundred rpms to compensate for the drift he was picking up through a small mountain range over the Avalon Peninsula. He slowly began to climb to eighteen hundred feet to smooth out.

He wondered if anyone in the villages he had passed over had radioed the news back to New York that the *Spirit of St. Louis* had been seen over Nova Scotia. Did it make a difference, he wondered, when he was not even a quarter of the way there? He was far more worried about everything else. He had to stay awake, alert, functioning; or he'd end up swimming for his life.

He was tired already but almost ashamed to admit it. Things had just been too hectic in the days before he left; there had been too much to do. He should have been more adamant about getting rest, letting Ryan's crew handle the small stuff.

For now, he was all right. The sun was shining, and visibility was almost unlimited. He dipped lower again to five hundred feet which gave him plenty of visibility of the rolling hills of Newfoundland and its small villages to keep his mind busy. He kept his hand firmly on the joystick. The dangerous times came when you had to fly above the clouds or at night, when a pilot literally lost contact with the earth and his only real bearing disappeared. That's when your grip really tightened on the joy stick. You just hoped it was tightened in the right direction.

Lindbergh snapped to full alert some thirty minutes later. The sky was slowly darkening, and a cumulus cloud could be seen here and there until a solid layer of cover drifted in from above. The sunlight turned grey, streaks of which could be seen across the horizon. He hoped the change didn't signal a storm over what remained of Newfoundland.

He took the *Spirit* down to one hundred feet. Below him, gale force winds of forty to fifty miles per hour were whipping whitecaps on lakes and ponds. This alarming shift in weather jerked him back from the complacency he had been feeling only moments before. Warm sunlight and the smooth flight across Long Island to Nova Scotia had driven the possibility of dangerous turbulence from his mind since leaving Roosevelt Field, but now things were getting very rough as the storm clouds appeared.

He looked out the side windows and watched as his wingtips flexed, and he bounced around inside the cockpit. His pangs of hunger quickly turned to uneasiness in the pit of his stomach as he worried about the effect of the turbulence on his overloaded airplane. True, the *Spirit* was already five hundred pounds lighter since takeoff, but it was still dangerously fragile because of the enormous weight it was carrying. A strong gust of air could snap a spar or fitting or even a wing, he thought. No airplane could tolerate this kind of violent abuse for very long.

Despite the danger of his situation and the worsening weather ahead, he was heavily fatigued now, and drifted off into a light sleep. He began to dream of a happy time when he was a boy walking along the banks of the Mississippi River with his mother, skimming stones across the Great Muddy.

The day suddenly went from warm yellow to a chilled gray mist. He and his mother took cover under a great Cyprus tree, thinking the storm would pass over quickl; but if anything, it seemed to worsen.

A whip of wind suddenly grabbed a huge branch on the tree, which frightened them both. Since the house wasn't more than a few hundred yards away up a grassy embankment, they decided to make a dash for it. It seemed like a good idea until they left the cover of the tree after about seventy-five feet. A cloudburst suddenly let loose followed by a screaming wind that the boy thought would wrest his hand from his mother's. It lasted perhaps only a minute, but he seriously thought he would drown in the ensuing torrent.

A great crash of thunder came down upon them, and the boy and his mother were truly frightened. Sensing this, she scooped him up in her arms and ran the last hundred yards holding him over her shoulder, her drenched head pressed against his chest. They made the landing steps and held each other on the verandah catching their breath, both shaking, she from the sudden chill and the boy from fear.

Not thirty seconds later, the rain came to an immediate stop, and the wind died down to nothing but a soft breeze. The whitecaps on the great river disappeared, and the sun suddenly appeared again, only it seemed ten degrees hotter. They sat down on the porch together, finally, and his mother said, "Now what was that all about?" with a gentle laughter that made his fear disappear instantly. They went inside, changed out of their wet clothes, and by the time they reappeared outside, you wouldn't have known it had rained.

Lindbergh snapped out of it, the memory fading as he was jostled awake by a strong gust of wind that threatened to turn the *Spirit* sideways in midair. He forced himself to concentrate and spent long minutes studying his situation. As squalls go, it wasn't a particularly large one; but with each heavy gust, clouds were growing darker and the brilliance of lightening flashes stronger. He quickly decided to turn eastward rather than to run through the center of the storm, and he began looking for a way around it. He flew all over the sky looking for a clearing, stumbling upon one, then just as quickly finding himself in a new downburst.

Rain was beating down heavily now, but at an altitude of nine hundred feet, visibility was not so much of a concern. Lindbergh scanned the ground below him, looking for things to occupy his mind and to help him stay awake. He saw that mud roads below were washing out.

Slowly the storm let up as he continued forward towards Newfoundland. He checked his instruments every few minutes from habit and noticed that the wind had subsided to only ten miles per hour, and the *Spirit* was still making better than one hundred miles per hour despite the weather. It was a little before noon.

His mind drifted again, and he wondered what it would be like to dip down at about seventy-five miles per hour and reach out and touch the ground.

That's the trouble with flying, he thought. *You can see the geographical features of the land all around you, but you really*

*can't connect with the earth, you can't feel it. I can see the birds
in flight, even fly close to a pine tree and touch the needles, but
the ground and tree are still two separate entities. One does not
want to come into contact with the other, at least at speed.*

*There's little in the way of telling what lies beyond a storm.
The gray curtain of rain is consistent and unrelenting.
Sometimes I fly lower to catch the rain reflecting off the muddy
roads and farmhouses to get a sense of how heavy the rain is,
but the only thing that gives it away is the ragged streaks of
foam and whitecaps on the lakes and ponds.*

Patches of blue sky ahead brought him back over the
wilderness of Newfoundland. Lindbergh was more than
one thousand miles closer to Paris and he became more
optimistic about the weather. The pilot was feeling
refreshed, too. The rain-cooled air and the fresh breeze in
the cockpit had renewed his confidence and quieted
down any second thoughts he had about the need for, or
usefulness of, a parachute.

Twenty-Nine

In his tenth hour, Lindbergh was flying at six hundred feet, and visibility was unlimited again over the eastern edge of Newfoundland near St. John's. The *Spirit* was doing ninety-six miles per hour, and the wind was blowing gently at fifteen miles per hour south-southwest. Looking for things to occupy his mind, he found it curious that he saw nothing moving below him.

There's not a sign of life anywhere, and I'm sure the sound of my engine has scared the wildlife into hiding. The rivers look fast. This is wild country; yet there's no way to feel it. This large blue sky separates us.

The edge of another storm is blowing gradually toward us; gray and white clouds billow upwards thousands of feet. This morning, I left Long Island in the spring on a muddy but grassy airfield. Now we're flying over the last vestiges of snow-covered, dirty river banks.

After the coast-to-coast flight and over nine hours after boarding the *Spirit of St. Louis* at Roosevelt Field, the tiny cockpit had become Lindbergh's home. His legs had lost most of their feeling from not being able to stretch out, and the wicker pilot's chair felt like a cactus; but he didn't regret his decision to use the lightweight seat. The weight saved in exchange for extra fuel more than made up for the discomfort.

It was actually quite warm in the cockpit, and several times Lindbergh contemplated lowering the upper half of his leather flying suit, eventually deciding it was more trouble than it was worth. He began to struggle with fatigue again and fought to stay awake. From time to time, he would climb higher or descend to an altitude just over the green hills to keep from falling asleep.

Only a few miles now separated the *Spirit of St. Louis* from the challenge of the enormous North Atlantic, a puddle jump compared to where he had come from and the vast distance yet to be traveled. He flew over St. John's about 6:00 p.m. New York time and looked down at the city, taking in the last sign of land he would see for more than twenty hours.

He lingered for a few minutes over St. John's, dipping low over the wharves and ships in its harbor. As he passed over a row of buildings in what looked like the center of the city, he thought he saw several people waving at him, but he could not be sure. The early evening light was fading fast.

He savored the moment, exhilarated by the recognition of how far he had flown already, but said a silent prayer as the *Spirit* passed over the rocky shoreline into the North Atlantic where he would be completely alone, completely out of sight. The sun was low now, and the waves were tipped gold by the last vestiges of its warm light. He looked down at his instruments for one last check. All gave him positive reinforcement to continue. If one had indicated any problem, he would turn back to the safety of dry land, he thought, but there was no turning back now. He leaned out the window and took a long look at the horizon. For as far as he could see, there was nothing but water; and he knew that was all he would see for at least the next twenty hours. A shiver ran through him as he thought of the alternative.

Behind him, St. John's Harbor steadily sank into the sea, and the tall mountain range of the island eventually disappeared from view altogether. At sunset, there was nothing ahead of him but dark air and gathering fog clouds. He brought the *Spirit* slowly up to five hundred feet to fly over them, but was startled to notice large white shapes looming up ahead of him on the ocean surface. They were icebergs, thousands of them in every direction. The fog clouds began to join together, and soon his visibility dropped to zero. He pulled back on his stick and pushed the airplane up over them, to his relief finding clear air at twenty-five hundred feet.

By 8:00 p.m. New York time, stars began to burst into view as the sun set and night fell. Seven hundred fifty feet below him, the ocean was now completely covered by a dense fog. The moist air felt good as it whipped through his open cockpit and helped him to remain alert. He tightened his grip on the joystick as the airplane porpoised through the air, the result of some chop in the cloud and the idiosyncrasies of the *Spirit*'s aerodynamics. She was lighter now, with nearly a third of her fuel burned off, but there was still enormous load on the airplane's wings.

Working his left and right rudder pedals with the ease that came with his now intimate feel for his airplane, Lindbergh countered the yaw and slowly increased the throttle to ascend. The *Spirit*'s nose lifted in a gentle climb as he pulled back on the joystick, careful not to increase the stress on his still fuel-laden wings. He leveled off at seventy-five hundred feet, high above the clouds billowing up from the sea surface. He felt slightly refreshed from the maneuver, which cleared his head. He momentarily considered fitting the windows into place as the temperature began to drop in the nighttime sky, but he thought better of it. The cold would help keep him awake.

Lindbergh suddenly remembered his maps, suffering several anxious moments of panic as he was inexplicably convinced that he was terribly off course. *We could be hours off now,* he worried, punishing himself for his lack of discipline. He quickly used the earth induction compass to check his course and then double-checked his findings with dead reckoning, an art he had mastered with his arduous experiences flying the mail across the United States, often at night in zero visibility.

He recorded his instrument readings and began calculating his heading, distance flown, the time, wind direction and his ground speed. Ten minutes later, to his great relief, he determined that he was only slightly off course, two degrees or six miles, having drifted somewhat northward. To compensate, he kicked in his right rudder and gently banked the *Spirit* into a slight turn southward, checking the faint nighttime glow over the horizon to ensure that he was level.

Feeling drowsy once more after almost thirteen hours of flying, he was shocked back to full awareness as the airplane was suddenly rocked by vicious turbulence. It was not something he hadn't already experienced many times before, but the suddenness and ferocity of the change startled him. He was pummeled by simultaneous increases in lift and weight, causing the *Spirit* to buck up and down in a huge yawing motion seventy-five hundred feet above the cloud still hanging over the North Atlantic. Lindbergh was violently tossed around inside the airplane, banging his head and shoulders on the fuselage walls. He glanced nervously at his wings, which were flexing abnormally, even though the airplane was much lighter now as the fuel load was burning off.

Collecting himself, he slowed the *Spirit*'s thrust by decreasing his ground speed and let drag build up on the tail of the airplane as he nosed it downward.

He felt the skies suddenly go smooth at five thousand feet and leveled off the *Spirit* at ninety miles per hour. *That was close,* he told himself. Another few minutes of excessive pressure on his wings might have doomed him. He silently vowed to remain alert and tightened his grip on the joystick.

He glanced at his watch. It was 11:00 p.m. Lindbergh looked down at the surface of the North Atlantic to find fog still covering the sea. He stuck his head out the left window, despite the whipping wind, to get a perspective on the skies ahead just as he flew into a thunderhead. Calmly, he increased his throttle and bored into the towering cloud, now respectful but unafraid of the difficult turbulence that he would almost certainly encounter.

After twenty uneventful minutes, he was alarmed to feel the controls go heavy in his hand. He looked nervously up at his wings and found ice covered the fabric surface on both sides. He berated himself for being stupid.

Quickly he increased the throttle and pulled back on the joystick, desperately attempting to bring the *Spirit* higher. He knew that descending was out of the question with the sea surface completely covered by fog, which would only increase the ice on his wings and probably reach up and suck him out of the air into a crash landing in the North Atlantic. At ten thousand feet, the air suddenly became calmer, and he leveled off, hoping and praying that the ice would melt in the drier altitude. It was his only chance.

Ever so slowly, he began to feel the controls begin to lighten, and he poked a small flashlight out the open window up at the wing. The ice was melting, he was sure of it. Regaining his composure, he checked his fuel gauge. It read nearly empty -- another silly mistake. He had forgotten to siphon more fuel from his left wing tank into the main tank in the fuselage in front of him, just behind the engine. Quickly, he reached up and turned the valve to let gas flow between the two tanks and watched cautiously as the fuel gauge began to climb. He closed the valve when the main tank was once again full, berating himself a second time for such a careless mistake.

Out of nowhere, the fatigue was on him again after his adrenalin had spiked. The sudden excitement had taken its toll. Fighting to keep his eyelids open, he twisted about in his seat trying to get his blood flowing and revive himself back into full awareness. He was aching, too. His legs had long ago fallen asleep, as he was cramped in the cockpit and could not stretch out fully. Desperately, he increased the throttle and pulled back on the *Spirit's* nose to force the airplane into a steep climb. The wind whipped through the cockpit, cool and moist, smashing into his face as the *Spirit* climbed higher and faster. At twelve thousand feet, he dipped the nose and dropped his ground speed back to one hundred miles per hour, resuming level flight.

Feeling slightly refreshed, he forced himself to check his dead reckoning navigation indicators again to ensure he was on course. Despite his grogginess, he was pleased to find he was only half a degree, or a mile and a half, off course and adjusted the *Spirit's* direction accordingly to south-southeast. It was midnight New York time.

By two o'clock in the morning, Lindbergh was now eighteen hours into the crossing. He had cause to celebrate as he realized that he was probably halfway to Paris; but instead of celebrating, he was filled with a sudden anxiety.

He was sure that he needed to stay awake for at least another eighteen hours.

Thirty

Seamus McGill awoke with a start. He had fallen asleep in his wheelhouse chair while watching the skies for Lindbergh. He, too, was dangerously tired and had no idea how long he had slept. He jumped down from his seat and made his way to the bow of *The Lovely Mary*.

The sea was calm and the air cool and clear as he stood on the forward deck, scanning the sky for the lone pilot. *Visibility is excellent*, he thought. *If he flies over me, there's no way I can miss the lad.*

The Lovely Mary was well positioned, now one hundred fifty miles off the coast of Ireland. He wondered how he might go about getting the pilot to see him. Pulling out a chest from under his unused bunk, McGill pulled a half dozen well-aged red flares from the trunk, carefully laying them on the bed. *These will get his attention,* he thought, *no matter how high he's flying.*

What McGill didn't consider was who else might be attracted by the flaming torches he lit to attract the attention of the American pilot.

Thirty-One

Daylight burst through the cockpit window, jerking Lindbergh out of a deep trance. He was confused. It was only 3:00 a.m. New York. He was momentarily refreshed by the sudden brightness and rejoiced that he had made it through the darkness. Of course! He had forgotten that he had flown through several time zones as he crossed Nova Scotia and Newfoundland and was chasing the sun.

His relief was short-lived, however, and gradually the fatigue returned. The pilot fell asleep for several minutes. A slight bump in the air jerked the *Spirit's* nose up two degrees, startling the pilot back to consciousness. He quickly leveled off the airplane, his mind racing in panic.

I have at least 17 hours to go, he thought. *To come all this way, do all the preparation, spend all the years dreaming of this moment; and it will be lost unless I can find a way to keep myself awake.*

He slapped himself in the face several times with his gloved hand and took a long swig from his canteen. He splashed some water on his face, too. The cold water felt good, and his eyes began to widen as he came back to full alert. His right hand was numb, he noticed, from holding the joystick so tightly. He released his grip for a moment, flexing his fingers. After several minutes, he felt life again in the hand and resumed his hold on the joystick, gradually tightening it again. The *Spirit* flew on with Lindbergh now fully awake in the cockpit.

At 5:00 a.m., after twenty-one hours of nonstop flying, the fatigue returned with a vengeance. Lindbergh continually fought to stay awake but fell asleep repeatedly with his eyes open, sometimes for as much as five to ten minutes. Then he would awaken, startled to find that he had been unconscious and had no memory of blacking out. He began to hallucinate as the minutes passed. His eyes shut again, and he dreamed of his father.

C.A. Lindbergh was at his side, lying on a gurney in a doctor's office. He was holding young Charles' hand, gripping it tightly. The eight-year-old boy watched, terrified, as a doctor took a scalpel and pierced his father's abdominal cavity. The elder Lindbergh gritted his teeth, refusing anesthesia. He had asked his son to come with him for what he described as minor surgery. Instead, what the boy witnessed was major surgery to correct an abdominal blockage. For the hour and a half that the surgery lasted, C.A. Lindbergh talked to his confused son about international banking and the Federal Reserve System, which he violently opposed. When the doctor completed the procedure, C.A. put on his hat and coat and drove forty miles home with his boy over sun-baked, rutted dirt roads. By the time they arrived, blood had soaked the large bandage wrapped around his waist, horrifying the child. His father comforted him and told him it was nothing to be afraid of. He would be all right.

He began to ask his father a question, but violent turbulence snapped him out of his trance. He came to in the cockpit, sweating despite the cold air which circulated around him. Lindbergh reached for his canteen and splashed more precious water on his face in a desperate effort to stay awake.

The young pilot quickly checked his instruments and calculated his position. He banked the airplane slightly southward to correct a drift that occurred when he blacked out. The *Spirit* was completely surrounded by fog, which Lindbergh could not seem to get above no matter how high he took the airplane. He leveled off at ten thousand feet, hoping to reach a clearing. Lulled back to complacency by the monotonous drone of his engine and zero visibility, he once again fell asleep. He awoke seconds or possibly minutes later. It was impossible for him to tell the difference. He continued this pattern for more than an hour, somehow each time awakening after only a short nap.

Finally, his desperate need for sleep caused him to black out completely. He was unconscious for as long as ten minutes, but in his deep sleep, far away, he began to hear a sudden coughing and sputtering, but could not make it out. Something within him forced him to crawl back to consciousness. As he struggled to clear his mind, he realized that the sounds were coming from his engine. The droning roar of his motor had become raspy and choking. He panicked, his eyes furiously scanning his instrument panel for a cause for the failure; but it took precious seconds for his vision to clear. The engine was about to quit as he came back to life and gripped the joystick with all his remaining strength. He was dizzy and incapacitated for several minutes as his mind raced to force his body to respond to the crisis. Finally, just as his engine stopped, Lindbergh regained his faculties.

"My engine, what ..." he said, hardly recognizing his own voice. It was the first time he had spoken out loud in some twenty-two hours alone in the cockpit. While he desperately looked for the cause of the failure, the now powerless *Spirit of St. Louis* began to fall. Then he found it. The gas gauge read empty. He had again neglected to fill the *Spirit*'s main fuel tank in the nose from the wing tanks. Quickly, he reached for the valve and opened the line from his right wing. Gas flooded into the main tank even as the airplane fell into a deep dive from the lack of power.

Lindbergh pulled out the choke and pressed the starter button, hoping against hope that his engine would fire again. The engine whined but did not turn over. He checked his altimeter gauge. The *Spirit* had already dropped two thousand feet. He pressed the starter again.

The engine roared back to full power, and the airplane leveled off as he pulled back on the stick.

Lindbergh dropped back into his hard wicker seat, drained from his failure to monitor fuel consumption. He chided himself; but at the same time, he felt fully awake. The scare had chased the sleep from him, and he was wide eyed again. The *Spirit* continued on, making slow progress toward Paris.

By 8:00 a.m., he had found clear skies again and was relieved to be feeling awake and alert. As he glanced at his watch, he realized that he had now been flying for twenty-four hours, an entire day in the sky. Two hours later, now flying at two thousand feet, Lindbergh spotted a black shadow on the water ahead. As he came closer, he realized it was a fishing boat and silently rejoiced. Where there was a boat, land could not be more than several hundred miles away, at most. He dipped the nose of the *Spirit* and aimed for the small fishing trawler.

Thirty-Two

His conscience still reeling from his unwitting role in the murders of Nungesser and Coli, Seamus McGill stood on the bow of the *The Lovely Mary* and scanned the sky with binoculars. He was determined to find Lindbergh. It was slightly after 10:00 a.m., and the morning sun found the skies clear and cool and the seas calm. He had perfect visibility to see the lone pilot anywhere within ten miles of his boat. "Come to me, son," he whispered aloud, knowing that the young man would probably end up like the two dead French pilots if he failed to find his airplane.

He had been scanning the sky for hours since daybreak. As he peered out over the horizon, straining his eyes looking for what he knew would just be a speck in the white cumulus clouds above, he spied something, at least eight miles away, maybe more. Was it a bird? He couldn't be sure.

Excited, he continued to track the speck of dust flying low beneath the clouds, and then at once, he knew it. It was an airplane for sure. He raced to his cabin and cranked up the radio the British Intelligence people had given him in the event he sighted the lad. The radio hummed as McGill seized the microphone and attempted to reach Commander Culloch.

"This is *The Lovely Mary* calling," he excitedly said into the open microphone. "Over."

There was agonizing silence as McGill heard nothing in response. He repeated his call. "Come in, please."

The radio crackled with a response. "Yes, *The Lovely Mary*. Please identify yourself. Over," a young voice responded.

Thank God, he thought. "I am Captain Seamus McGill of *The Lovely Mary*, approximately one hundred miles off the coast of Dingle Bay," he said. "Please put me through to Commander Culloch immediately. He is awaiting my report. Over."

"Very well, Captain. Indeed he has been waiting for you. Please hang on. Over," came the instant reply.

McGill waited for what seemed like an eternity and picked up his glasses to see the airplane as it headed directly for him. "I wonder if he's seen me," the grizzled seaman said aloud. Five minutes later, Culloch answered his call.

"Greetings, Captain. I've been awaiting your call," the British Intelligence agent called out. "Have you met our friend? Over."

"Hello Commander Culloch. Yes, I have just run into him by chance. I thought you'd like to know. Over."

"Indeed I do, Captain. Thank you for your report. Please share this news with our other friends, as we discussed," Culloch responded, signaling McGill to radio the Germans immediately with the news. The trap had been set. Now it was time to spring it.

"It will be my pleasure, Commander Culloch. I hope to see you very soon. Over and out," McGill signed off.

Moving to the other side of his cabin, he cranked up the German radio set that the stranger at Kerry's Ring had given him and called to repeat the news. "This is Captain Seamus McGill of *The Lovely Mary*. Come in, please."

There was an immediate response. McGill thought he picked up a slight German accent. "Yes, Captain. We have been waiting for your call. Over," a voice said crisply.

"I have seen the airplane. It is approximately one hundred miles due south of Dingle Bay. I am at anchor. Over," McGill reported.

"Thank you, Captain. Out," the voice curtly cut off the transmission.

Now, by God, all McGill could do was wait. He shifted in his chair uneasily. He wondered if he could attract the young pilot; perhaps warn him of the danger ahead. He picked up two flares and ran outside his cabin as the approaching airplane closed in on him, still several miles away. He lit the flares.

"He'll have to see these," McGill prayed, as the flares burst into flame, casting a brilliant red, reflective shadow on the gentle waves surrounding *The Lovely Mary*.

Thirty-Three

The radio crackled in the small Quonset hut that served as temporary headquarters for French Lt. Commander Laurent Marciél at the Dingle airfield. Having just completed a pre-mission briefing for the four hand-picked pilots who had been charged with the responsibility of protecting Lindbergh by intercepting the German fighters, the message from British Intelligence in London arrived at the perfect moment.

"Launch your planes immediately," was the order Marciél read from the hastily scribbled instructions handed to him by his adjutant and repeated them aloud to his pilots.

"Gentlemen, you are this young American pilot's only hope. He is lost without your protection. He will be murdered like Nungesser and Coli unless you are successful in destroying the Germans. Man your planes and leave immediately. Godspeed to you my brave friends. I am very proud to serve with you."

"*Oui*, Commander," the squadron leader replied immediately. "We shall not fail you or the lone eagle." Didier Michaud, at thirty-five the only member of the small squadron who had flown in the Great War, had become an ace in the skies over the French trenches in 1918, and he remembered well both the thrill and the terror of aerial combat. He also remembered the pain, having been severely wounded in the last month of the war. It had taken him nearly two years to recover, but now he was ready to taste German blood again.

"Come, my young colleagues, and I will teach you how to kill the Hun," he told the three pilots joining him, who together had never before flown in combat. "We will all return to the safety of this airfield and our families, I assure you."

Sprinting to their waiting SPAD XIIIs which had been warming up for the last twenty minutes, they immediately took the controls of their airplanes. Hurriedly strapping in, they saluted Commander Marciél, opening the throttles of their airplanes wide, then bore down the short grassy field two at a time. In minutes, all four were airborne. Dipping their wings in salute to their military colleagues, they veered to the right on a westerly course aiming for the last reported position of *The Lovely Mary* and its Irish Captain, Seamus McGill.

Less than ten miles away, hidden along the coast just north of Dingle, two German pilots received a similar message from an anonymous voice on their radio. "Hurry, he has been sighted approximately one hundred miles due south. Destroy the airplane, but first make sure the fishing boat is at the bottom of the sea. There must be no survivors."

Immediately, the German military pilots boarded their Heinkel 59 floatplanes, moored on the sandy shore and camouflaged by fir branches they had cut a hundred yards inland to cover them. The aircraft were virtually invisible from any aerial observers and far from the roads which would attract any of the farmers from Dingle Bay.

The Heinkel 59s started at the first try, and the two four-bladed, fixed-pitch propellers of each aircraft roared to life as the BMW VI V12 water-cooled engines reached optimum flight temperature within minutes. The airplanes were far more advanced than the French SPADS that had been assigned to engage the Germans, but neither of the Reich pilots had any combat experience, other than shooting down the helpless Nungesser and Coli in their unarmed *White Bird*.

With a range of over four hundred sixty miles, the Germans knew they could intercept the fishing boat and the targeted aircraft with plenty of time and fuel to make it back to their temporary landing base at the conclusion of their mission, where they would return to hiding and wait for the next hapless Orteig competitor.

The two planes taxied out into the ocean unseen and applied full throttle. They kicked up huge bursts of ocean spray as they gained speed on their unlimited ocean runways and took to the air. Capable of flying at one hundred sixty miles per hour, the two were out of sight within minutes, headed for *The Lovely Mary*. Unconcerned that they would be challenged, the two Germans flew less than one hundred feet off the sea surface at maximum speed.

They did not care whether the captain of the fishing boat saw them coming or not. He would simply be another helpless target, and the pilots would be heroes again.

Thirty-Four

Lindbergh was elated at the sight of the fishing boat. He was hoping to get the attention of one of its crewmen to check his navigation towards Ireland.

He aimed the *Spirit*, which continued to perform flawlessly, directly at the boat and dipped down to the sea surface, approaching *The Lovely Mary* at sixty feet.

"He's seen me, all right," Lindbergh yelled out loud as he spied the two glowing red flares that Seamus McGill had lit on the bow of his fishing trawler. The Captain waved the flares back and forth over his head to be sure he attracted the attention of the lone pilot. He was not disappointed.

Lindbergh took one slow pass over the boat and felt a surge of joy as he waved down at McGill. The sudden appearance of the boat and its captain completely refreshed him, and the chilling fatigue that had plagued him through the long night and into the early morning evaporated. He had been flying nonstop for more than twenty-six hours, but he could almost smell Paris, at least another seven to ten hours away by his calculations. Unaware that he was more than two and a half hours ahead of schedule and less than three miles off course, the *Spirit's* lone pilot soldiered on, his objective now closer than he knew.

McGill tossed the two spent flares overboard and waved back at the pilot with enthusiasm. He cupped his hands around his mouth and screamed at Lindbergh, who could not make out what he thought must be a greeting. He slowly banked the *Spirit* to the left and came around again. As he flew low over the boat he screamed, "Which way to Ireland?" even as McGill shouted back at him again. Lindbergh was puzzled.

I thought he told me to beware. Beware of what? Why won't he answer my question? He banked again and slowed his speed, attempting to pass over the boat at just over stall speed. Again he yelled, "Which way to Ireland?" but was disappointed to receive the same reply, which again seemed to be, "Beware." Confused, the pilot decided he was wasting precious time, waved to the solitary figure on the boat, and resumed his travel toward what he hoped was the coast of Ireland. Slowly he regained altitude, leveling off at five thousand feet, Seamus McGill waving all the while.

"I hope the young lad heard me," McGill prayed, wondering at the same time what he had been shouting down to him. He had not been able to make out the pilot's question.

Some forty minutes later, the German pilots, flying with wide-open throttles just above the white capped sea, spotted the single fishing boat, gently rocking in the midmorning sun. The lead aviator waved to his comrade, who veered off in search of Lindbergh, now seventy-five miles from the Irish coast, while he lined up his sights for a strafing run over *The Lovely Mary*.

Seamus McGill heard the Germans coming even before he saw them. Again he raced to his cabin, retrieved a flare, and lit it to ensure that they saw him. He watched as one of the fighters suddenly veered off and climbed high in the opposite direction, obviously in a chase toward Lindbergh. The lone German bore in on the boat.

McGill abruptly felt the hair on the back of his neck stand up. "Aye, Mary, I've a feeling this Hun bastard has an idea that I wasn't expecting," he thought out loud. He dropped the flare overboard and ran to his cabin to retrieve the only weapon he had on board, the military issue rifle he had carried through France a decade ago. He loaded it hastily, taking time only to insert three rounds. "There won't be time for much more," he thought.

From fifty yards away, the lead German pilot opened up his machine guns, and McGill watched as bullets rained down on the water aft of his boat, tracking toward him. He threw himself down on the deck as the German sped over *The Lovely Mary*. The Aryan pilot had missed completely. McGill stood up and watched as his assailant banked steeply a hundred yards away and took aim on a return pass, this time bow first.

McGill was unafraid. His anger at the unexpected challenge from the German pig was more than his Irish temper could bear. Running to the bow of his boat, he loaded a round into the chamber of his rifle and took careful aim at the pilot, now bearing down on him at a more leisurely speed. He fired his machine guns again, this time missing the fisherman by inches but blowing his cabin to shreds. McGill ducked as wooden debris rained down on him but stood his ground. As the German pilot passed over him again, he took careful aim and pulled the trigger of his ancient rifle. Only he heard the shot.

The oblivious pilot suddenly felt a jolt, as if he had been punched, then a wetness beneath his flying suit. He looked down to see a gaping hole in his uniform just above his heart. The bullet had passed through the right wing of his aircraft and hit him in the back as he gripped the joystick, preparing for another pass. At first he felt surprise, then horror to realize he was bleeding to death from the single bullet that had passed right through him.

Instinctively, he pulled back hard on his stick to gain altitude, aiming the airplane straight up into the sky directly over *The Lovely Mary*. But he had slowed to less than sixty miles per hour on his final pass; and as the Heinkel 59 reached fifteen hundred feet, it stalled from lack of power. The nose of the airplane slowly dropped, then fell over completely until the floatplane was in a vertical dive. The pilot, now almost unconscious and near death, was helpless to save himself. Without warning, his right wing burst into flames, its fuel tank having been pierced by McGill's perfectly aimed shot. In seconds, the airplane became a fireball, falling unimpeded directly over *The Lovely Mary* and its captain.

Seamus McGill saw what was happening, and in the twenty seconds it took for the German floatplane to crash into his treasured boat and explode, he did not throw himself overboard or attempt to save his life in any way. He had done his duty and was fully satisfied now with his time on earth, hard as it had been. His mind filled with memories of his adored wife, and as the airplane struck, he mouthed the words "I'm coming to you, my Mary."

The Lovely Mary broke in two from the impact and scuttled to the bottom of the Atlantic. McGill was incinerated in the blast. Within a few minutes, nothing remained of the airplane or the fishing boat and her captain, save for a few bits and pieces of floating wreckage.

Now some sixty miles from the coast of Ireland, Lindbergh was anticipating his first sight of landfall in over a day. He took a long pull of water from his canteen, unaware that less than five miles behind him, the other Heinkel 59 fighter pilot, oblivious to the demise of his partner, was racing at full throttle toward him. Flying at more than one hundred sixty miles per hour, the German closed the gap quickly on the much slower-moving *Spirit*, and within minutes he was behind Lindbergh, casually lining up his dual machine gun sights on him. The German pilot slowed his aircraft, enjoying the hunt, already savoring the taste of blood.

"I wonder if warfare is always this simple," the German pilot laughed to himself; but as he pulled the

cocking mechanism on his guns, the pilot became aware
of a presence to his left. Startled, he turned to find a
French airplane, a SPAD, he thought, at his side. He
looked directly into the eyes of Lieutenant Didier
Michaud, who waved and flashed a mischievous grin and
saluted the Hun in mock respect.

Caught completely off guard, the flustered German
pilot yanked his joystick forward into a desperate
spiraling dive in an attempt to gain the upper hand on the
interloper. *"Mein Gott,"* the German cursed, "where did
this swine come from?" He swung his aircraft into a wide
turn and climbed at full throttle, hoping to come up
behind the Frenchman.

Even as the terrorized pilot maneuvered to fire his
guns on the SPAD, Michaud turned, clearing an open shot
by his three comrades, who were blazing down from ten
thousand feet, the sun at their backs, to intercept the lone
German at full speed.

The German pilot suddenly saw the three SPADs
hurtling toward him. He was hopelessly outnumbered, he
knew. Even with his vastly superior airplane, there was
no hope of escape; but the young man, hardened by his
rigorous Luftstreitkräfte training, would not die without a
fight. He continued to climb, aiming his airplane directly
at the centermost SPAD, now less than four hundred
yards away, just as the three French pilots opened fire on
him. He pressed the trigger for his twin, synchronized
8mm Spandau machine guns and returned fire,
immediately scoring a direct hit on the center SPAD,
which began to smoke heavily. Bursts of fire rang out
from the remaining two French pilots, ripping into the
floatplane and setting it on fire. The German airplane was
riddled with gunfire, and its pilot was hit three times in
the chest and abdomen, but he continued his suicide
climb toward the enemy.

Realizing that a collision was unavoidable, twenty-one-year-old *Aviateur de Première* Classe Hénri Clavel, the pilot of the stricken SPAD, struggled to release his shoulder and lap harness as his airplane spiraled through the sky directly at the climbing German. With flames leaping into the cockpit, the young Frenchman stood up in his cockpit holding his parachute and tried desperately to jump over the side. But the force of the wind, as the screaming airplane continued to dive, was too much, and the pilot was thrown backward into the air. With a sickening thud they could not hear but felt in their bones, his colleagues saw Clavel's body bounce off the tail of his plane and ricochet off, his back broken. The French boy fell, paralyzed and unable to open his parachute. He soon disappeared from sight, falling seven thousand feet to his death in the calm waters below.

The SPAD and the Heinkel converged in a massive explosion, and the two remaining attackers watched as the wreckage, now a huge fireball which engulfed the two fused planes, simply fell from the sky, dropping more than sixty-five hundred feet into the ocean. There was no sight of the German pilot, who was too gravely wounded to jump from his plane.

Ahead, Lindbergh, too far away to hear the obscene chattering of machine guns firing or the ensuing carnage and explosion, was calmly checking navigation, completely unaware that his life hung in the balance of the battle being waged just hundreds of yards behind him. He thought for a moment that he had heard a thunder clap. "That's odd," he said aloud, leaning out the left window and scanning the horizon. "Not a cloud in the sky."

Michaud climbed to join his comrades, pulling into formation between them. He saluted the young pilots, who had engaged the enemy for the first time in their careers.

"Let us hope you will never have to meet the enemy again, my young friends," he said aloud but unheard. "The taste of blood and the loss of a comrade is something one never forgets. The longer one lives, the more vile the taste becomes."

The victorious French pilots, stunned by the loss of their friend and comrade, steered their SPADs to fifteen thousand feet, high above the unaware Lindbergh, and followed behind him in the event that there was another German fighter lurking in the skies somewhere near him. As the American pilot neared the coast of Ireland and satisfied that he was safe, they accelerated and left the silver-painted *Spirit of St. Louis*, glistening in the mid morning sun, to carry on its mission of completing the world's first transatlantic flight from New York to Paris. Michaud's orders were to leave Lindbergh as he traversed the Emerald Island to avoid being seen as his escort. He would once again pick up a flock of defenders, British military pilots in their ancient Sopwith Camel biplanes, as he flew over St. George's Channel and on over England.

After refueling at the Dingle Bay airstrip, Michaud and his squadron would once again engage the *Spirit of St. Louis*, albeit from a position far above and behind the silver plane, on the final leg across the English Channel and into France.

The American would never know how much danger he had been in, Michaud thought, or how the political leadership and best military minds of four nations had harnessed their collective willpower to protect him.

Nor would he ever know of the supreme sacrifice others had made to keep the wind beneath his wings.

Thirty-Five

At 11:00 a.m., Lindbergh looked down upon a small fleet of boats and noticed seagulls circling them. Land could not be far off. "It must be," the weary pilot thought.

Despite his near constant fatigue, he was wide awake from the surge of adrenalin that coursed through his body at the thought of being so much closer to his goal. He dipped the plane low over the choppy sea and steered the *Spirit of St. Louis* toward the nearest trawler. He passed over the ship's deck at fifty feet but saw no signs of life. Bringing the silver monoplane around again, he made another low pass, only to spot a man's head peering out a porthole window. It seemed as if he was afraid.

Lindbergh pulled up, irritated with himself for wasting time and fuel. He quickly rechecked his earth induction compass and his instruments. Pleased with the outcome, he guessed that he couldn't be more than ten miles off course. At noon by his watch, 5:00 p.m. local time, he proved himself wrong.

At first, it appeared to be nothing more than another dark cumulus cloud on the horizon; but as he gained on it, he was surprised to find it was a stationary object. For a moment, in the haze of his fatigue, he did not understand what it was and, finally, he knew.

At long last, it was land.

"Eureka, old girl!" he shouted to the *Spirit of St. Louis*, his home in the clouds for the last twenty-eight hours. "We made it," he said, patting his instrument panel as if congratulating a friend. His mind was a blur of freewheeling emotions, swinging wildly between elation, relief, pride and humility, all at once. A part of him wanted to laugh, but his eyes moistened. He caught himself quickly. "Wait a minute now, we've got a long way to go, don't we?" Paris was another six hundred long miles away.

Below, the Irish coastline loomed up out of the surf, and the *Spirit* passed over a rugged, rocky inlet that seemed to guide him toward grassy hills on the horizon. He reached for his map to get a bearing and stared at it in disbelief. Not only had he made landfall at the southernmost end of Ireland, but he was about to pass over the village of Dingle Bay, almost precisely where the line he had drawn on the chart in a hotel room in San Diego so many months ago intersected the island. His navigation was nearly perfect.

It was nothing short of a masterpiece. He had almost precisely navigated three thousand miles despite mind-numbing fatigue and foul weather that had sent him, again and again, in a frantic and desperate search for clear skies and respite from the turbulence that at times tossed him around the cockpit like a rag doll. He couldn't believe it himself.

Soaring with confidence, Lindbergh slowly increased his ground speed to one hundred ten miles per hour, determined now to make the French coastline before darkness descended again. At an altitude of four hundred feet, he passed over Dingle Bay and saw to his amazement that Irish villagers were pouring into the streets and waving up at him. He circled back around the small village again, passing even lower, and excitedly leaned out his right window to wave back.

"Well, I'll be. They've been waiting for us," he said to himself and chuckled inwardly at the unexpected warm reception. The country boy in him was somewhat flustered by the attention, but he lingered over the village and radiated in the revelry.

Flying low over the Irish Island, Lindbergh relished the beauty of the rolling green hills and was relieved that the endless monotony of the North Atlantic was behind him. Shepherds minding large flocks of sheep and farmers tending their fields waved to him as he sped over County Kerry on the eastern coastline at less than one hundred feet. At almost six o'clock local time, he flew out into St. George's Channel. He was actually somewhat disappointed to be leaving the friendly skies over Ireland, but the Channel's crystal clear waters were inviting, and the young pilot stayed low over its surface en route to the southwestern coast of England.

As he gazed down at the blue ocean beneath him, he saw great pods of bottlenose dolphins playfully breaching high out of the water, and he was mesmerized by their grace and powerful energy. He couldn't resist a closer inspection and circled around, flying within forty feet of the unruffled oceanic mammals. He was astounded to see one of the dolphins leap from the water and slap its tail on the surface, as if intentionally trying to get Lindbergh's attention.

With the demons of darkness and the monotony of the North Atlantic behind him, the young American pilot leaned out the window of the *Spirit* and filled his lungs with cool, crisp air. The wind on his stubbled face added to the relief he felt, and he was filled with a joy for life.

With his purpose renewed, Lindbergh once more pointed the nose of the *Spirit of St. Louis* toward the last leg of his epic flight and the "City of Lights."

Thirty-Six

At the corner of Wilhemstrasse and Leipzigerstrasse in Berlin, the formidable headquarters of the Luftstreitkräfte occupied an entire city block. The building's stark, yet colossal architecture gave it an air of invincibility, an attitude that the pilots of the Army Air Service shared as they fought in the skies over France during the Great War. Indeed, the building was designed to make visitors feel inconsequential in the presence of the extraordinary power of the Fatherland. On this overcast afternoon, dark storm clouds had gathered over the city, casting the white granite structure in sharp relief against the blackening sky.

"No, Gruppenführer Goering, I am sorry. We have not yet received any radio transmission from the pilots," Hermann Goering's aide reported in the huge, walnut-paneled office. The Luftstreitkräfte leader was alone in the cavernous room, sitting in front of a roaring fire in an oversized seventeenth century baroque chair that resembled a throne in its almost grotesque flamboyance. He was nursing a late afternoon cognac, anxiously awaiting the expected news of Lindbergh's untimely end.

The young blond, blue-eyed Lieutenant who served as his adjutant was somewhat tense, wary of his superior's unpredictable response. Goering was aware that his junior officer was increasingly nervous in dealing with him. He took great delight in terrorizing the young man, and what he had to say was not what Goering wanted to hear.

"Are you sure we have competent men at the radio?" the German Luftstreitkräfte general demanded, his reddened face giving away his barely controlled rage. "Have you tested these men, Oberleutnant?"

The twenty-six-year-old Lieutenant shifted uneasily at the sharp rebuke of his superior. "Yes, Sir, I have personally tested them. They are the best radio men in the Luftstreitkräfte, Herr Gruppenführer. I would trust them with my life." The wool collar at his neck chafed as he swallowed hard.

"Very good, Oberleutnant. Then you will have no problem in facing a firing squad with your subordinates if they have failed, yes?" Goering said quietly, a sadistic smirk curling his upper lip. He found great enjoyment in verbally assaulting his younger charges. Black clouds filled a floor-to-ceiling window behind him, and the eerie light cast dark shadows on his face. The effect was quite macabre.

The German Lieutenant's eyes could not hide his fear. He knew from experience that Goering was capable of administering his threat and would not give a second thought to watching him die. His mouth quivered.

"Yes, Gruppenführer, I will check the radio again at once," he said as he clicked the heels of his highly polished black riding boots together loudly and saluted the senior Luftstreitkräfte officer. Goering ignored the salute and dismissed him with a surly backhanded wave of his hand. The frightened officer hurried from the room.

The tall, handsome, but growingly overweight Goering enjoyed a bigger-than-life reputation among his Luftstreitkräfte subordinates. His brilliance as a pilot and military tactician was widely recognized, overshadowed only by his repute as a despicably cruel and sadistic brute capable of the most perverse violence. Only those closest to him were aware of his deepening dependence on morphine, the consequence of a severe leg wound inflicted in the air over France some ten years ago, which only fueled his savage mood swings.

He routinely terrorized junior officers who had failed or slighted him in any manner. Indeed, the slightest offense could bring the harshest of penalties. Consequently, Goering received little in the way of bad news from the advisors who surrounded him, leaving the Gruppenführer with a certain infallibility.

As he waited for word of the success of the two Luftstreitkräfte pilots on the Irish coast, Goering reveled in the thought that he had personally planned the murder of the American pilot. He absentmindedly toyed with the coveted blue enameled Blue Max medal hanging from his neck, which had been bestowed upon him for his twenty-two kills in the Great War. The Luftstreitkräfte officer delighted in the fact that American pilots had accounted for half of his victories.

He reached for his snifter of cognac and held it up to the light, staring into the bronze liquid in the crystal. *It seems we can add the blood of another American to our collection, yes, Hermann?* he thought to himself and ghoulishly laughed out loud.

The Lieutenant sheepishly re-entered Goering's office minutes later.

"Yes, Oberleutnant, you have news for me?" Goering demanded. The officer hesitated.

"Yes, Gruppenführer." The Lieutenant swallowed hard. "But not from the pilots, Sir, from our agent in southern Ireland."

Goering raised himself up in his chair, the hair on the back of his neck standing up.

"What is it?" the Luftstreitkräfte head demanded.

"The American has been seen in the skies over southern Ireland, Gruppenführer. It appears that he has escaped the trap, and we have not yet heard from the pilots." He flinched as he said the last words.

Goering stared at the young man for a long moment. Like an angry, wild cat, he lunged at him, wrapping his thick fingers around the officer's throat, strangling him.

"This cannot be, you swine! You are lying to me!" He released his grip and threw the helpless, choking boy to the hard floor. Goering's eyes were red with rage as the disciple of the devil pounced on the adjutant. The officer raised his arms to protect himself, but Goering was out of control. Mercilessly, he kicked the prone aide repeatedly in the head with his heavy, steel-toed boots until the boy's face was matted with blood.

Breathing heavily, Goering staggered back and fell into his chair. Still enraged, he stood again with a mind to kill the officer, but two sentries, drawn to his office by the commotion, entered before he could commit the murder. He picked up his cognac and drained the glass. His anger momentarily satiated, he screamed at the two guards to remove the bloody mess at his feet.

"Get rid of this coward and have his blood washed from my floor, it disgusts me," he growled.

As the sentries dragged the barely conscious officer from the room, Goering's thoughts had already turned to what he would tell General Udet. He had failed his commanding officer, who would have to inform the Chancellor. For a fleeting second, he thought of suicide as an honorable alternative.

He walked slowly to his desk and opened the top right hand drawer. A loaded Lugar P.08 stared back at him, always ready for whatever he had in mind. He picked the Army-issue pistol up and put it back in the drawer, closing it. *No*, he thought. *It cannot end this way. To have survived nearly two years on the western front, only to die in shame and humiliation?* He sat heavily in his desk chair, staring out the window on the south side of his corner office overlooking the Wilhemstrasse.

After long moments deep in thought, he whirled in his chair and slammed an open hand on his desk top.

Fuck Udet and von Hindenburg. It didn't matter if the American landed safely in Paris or not. The world would soon mock the heroics of Lindbergh or anyone else that successfully completed the one-way transatlantic crossing. The achievement would pale compared to what he was planning, and the world would know that a true genius sat at the controls of the German air force and had miraculously breathed life into its cold ashes. It was time to let Udet in on the progress at Lipetsk. Surely, the amazing developments he had to share with his commanding officer would take the sting out of the Lindbergh embarrassment.

When the cloak of secrecy finally came off *Amerike*, once again his countrymen would tremble with pride at the mere mention of the word Luftstreitkräfte. They would celebrate his name; but the Americans, smug in their victory and reveling in their continuous persecution of defeated Germany, would have a different reaction to the word -- terror.

Thirty-Seven

"The British Embassy in Ireland has just informed us that Lindbergh was spotted over Dingle Bay," Commander Culloch reported to British Prime Minister Stanley Baldwin at a hastily arranged meeting at #10 Downing Street.

"Our French friends were successful, Prime Minister, although unfortunately, they have suffered the loss of one pilot."

Baldwin winced. More needless bloodshed.

"I shall convey my regrets to Pierre-Paul-Henri-Gaston Doumergue at once," the Prime Minister said, motioning to an aide, who nodded in understanding. A telegram would be prepared immediately.

Culloch continued. "As we expected, a German fighter attempted to engage the unarmed American about seventy-five miles off the coast. The German was shot down before he could let loose a single shot."

"And Lindbergh?" the P.M. probed. "Is he out of danger?"

"To the best of our knowledge, he was not aware of either the German or his rescuers," Culloch responded. "As to being out of danger, perhaps, Prime Minister. We know that Nungesser and Coli were attacked off the Irish coast, and that has been our hunting ground."

"The Irish fisherman?"

Culloch shook his head. He had liked the old man and especially how he had not hesitated to do his duty.

"We have been unable to raise him by radio. It is not inconceivable that the German paid him a visit before giving chase to Lindbergh. Dead men tell no tales, Sir."

Baldwin shook his head. Was there no end to this madness? Culloch answered the question for him.

"Two things trouble me, Prime Minister," the British Intelligence Chief added without being asked. "The first is that it is odd that there was only one German. We expected at least two fighters or more. Pilots do not like to hunt their prey, even if it is unarmed, without a wingman. So we must continue to be vigilant until the American's landing gear touches down on French soil."

"I believe our fighters will take up a position to defend the lad all the way to Northern France, is that correct?"

"Yes, Sir, Lindbergh will be well protected," Culloch reassured him.

Baldwin waited for him to continue, but the Commander's eyes drifted away.

The P.M. was impatient. "Your second concern, Commander?"

The officer snapped to.

"Aye, Sir. I am also troubled by the description of the German airplane provided by the French pilots. Perhaps it is fortunate that there was only one enemy to deal with."

"What do you mean, Mr. Culloch?" the P.M. asked, intrigued.

"From the description, the German fighter is of an advanced design that we have not encountered before," Culloch answered. "It was exceptionally powerful and agile, and a floatplane of a design we have not seen before. German floaters were underpowered tubs during the war. The French overwhelmed them easily

Baldwin suddenly looked pained. "Why, that is not possible, Commander. The Germans cannot have enough resources to support their insane *Amerike* project and to develop new fighter aircraft simultaneously. It's preposterous, old boy. Why, it's a wonder they've been able to scrape enough people and materials together to build their bomber."

Culloch did not respond.

"I personally oversaw the disbanding of the Luftstreitkräfte and all their military engineering operations at the end of the war under the terms of the treaty," the P.M. continued, waiting for Culloch to agree with him.

The Intelligence agent said nothing but reached into his well-worn, black leather satchel and removed a large manila envelope. He opened it and carefully removed the contents, a thick sheaf of eight-by-ten-inch, black-and-white photographs. He began to spread them across the Prime Minister's conference table.

"With all due respect, Prime Minister, I believe these photographs, taken less than seventy-two hours ago at the Russian aviation facilities in Lipetsk, will enlighten you," Culloch said. "I have already dispatched one of my men to provide a duplicate set to Pipon Decker, head of French Intelligence. You can be sure he will share them with President Doumergue."

Baldwin rose to his feet and walked to the table. He picked up one of the photographs. The Prime Minister's face turned ashen as he reached for another. He didn't need to see more. It was the *Amerike* bomber on the runway at Lipetsk, either ready for, or perhaps already engaged in, full flight testing.

"My God," he said aloud.

Culloch's stare turned icy cold. He turned and faced Baldwin, all sense of rank etiquette momentarily suspended.

"I'm afraid it's out of God's hands, Prime Minister," he said. "Unless we descend upon these Hun bastards with the sword of the devil, the only use we'll have for God will be to appeal for his mercy."

Thirty-Eight

Unaware that a squadron of vintage British Sopwith Camel fighters was flying above and behind him as a protective escort, Lindbergh continued his epic flight low over St. George's Channel on a northeast track toward the southern tip of England. It was now nearly 7:00 p.m. local time, and the young American had been at the controls of the *Spirit of St. Louis* for nearly thirty hours.

The "Camels", so known for the fairing hump that surrounded the installation of two cowl-mounted Vickers 7.7 mm machine guns, had last been used for an actual mission in the final days of the Great War. Relegated to training maneuvers, they were up to the task of protecting the lone American, but barely.

In the economic depression years that followed the war, the British, like most of its allies, had made little investment in new armaments. The cost of new aircraft development, testing and manufacture was so high that Parliament would not even consider the urgent pleas of its admiralty to maintain at least a modicum of investment in military ships, airplanes and infantry weapons. Consequently, the British, as well as the French and Americans, were pitifully unprepared to defend their homelands, let alone take offensive measures.

Blissfully ignorant of his armed companions, Lindbergh listened with pleasure to the melodic roar of his single engine, which after so many hours in the cockpit had become no more than a steady hum to his ears. He was so attuned to the sound of his engine and its nonstop drone that should there be any change in its performance, he would catch it immediately. The fatigue that had terrorized him during the long night had evaporated, aided by a strong dose of adrenalin that surged through him from his growing excitement at the thought of reaching Paris. He had less than three hundred fifty miles to go.

Ahead on the horizon, Lindbergh saw the southwest coast of England begin to emerge. Flashing low over the surf, he soared over the rugged coastline that marked the county of Cornwall at the southern tip of the English Peninsula. Villagers waved up at him as he headed inland toward Plymouth, the harbor from which the Pilgrims had sailed to a new land in their quest for freedom. From there he flew to the north side of Britain from which he would head out over the English Channel, the last body of water to challenge him before France.

As he sailed over England and dozens of small villages, farms and fields, he fretted over the possibility of fog over the Channel or the northern coast of France and the possibility that he would have to turn back short of his goal of reaching Paris. He knew the Channel only by its reputation as particularly stormy; and now, in the last hours of his flight, unsettling images loomed large in his mind.

Although he felt wide awake alone in the cockpit that had become his home, Lindbergh unknowingly began to suffer the effects of sleep deprivation.

He dipped his left wing over Plymouth to get a clearer view of the last township he would see before heading out of the Channel. As he turned slightly, he caught a glimpse of a shadowy figure. He looked again.

There, leaning up against the cowl of his silver monoplane, he saw in his hallucinations the figure of his father, holding a straw hat in one hand while wiping perspiration from his brow with the other.

"Father," the younger Lindbergh exclaimed at the vision, "is it really you?"

"Yes, Charles. I've been with you for some time."

"You have? I didn't see you, Father. I've been quite busy up here, you know."

"So I've seen, Son. You're doing a good job. Your mother will be very proud of you."

"She worries so much, Father. Sometimes I have trouble talking with her."

"Yes, I'm afraid I had a similar difficulty with her, but that's not important right now. Do you know that you have just established a new world record for long-distance, nonstop flying?"

"No, Father. I was too busy to notice."

"I'm very proud of you, too, Son. It's been so nice to chat with you. We haven't been together in an awfully long time, have we?"

"I miss you, Father. I wish I had told you how much I loved you before you went away, but I couldn't find the words. Perhaps ..."

"Now, now, Charles. We Lindberghs have always had a difficult time with intimate words. I wish I had told you how much I loved you. For some reason, I could only say how proud I was of you. Pity I never told you."

"Father, stay with me. We have come so far and have so little distance to travel. I expect my photograph will be in the newspapers again if I make it to Paris. Wouldn't it be grand if we had our picture taken together? We could send it to Mother."

"I must go now, Charles, but be safe, my son. I'll be watching."

"No, Father, please stay a while longer. Please don't go father..."

The *Spirit of St. Louis* bucked from slight turbulence, startling its pilot back to consciousness. The young man felt a wetness on his face and realized he had been crying. The image of his father had been so lifelike, it took him several long moments to realize that the vision was not real. He choked up, agonizing over the ghostly conversation his mind had crafted, toying with his guilt at not being with his father when he died. His hand tightened again on the joystick, and he pulled back, willing the nose of the *Spirit* to climb higher into colder air to clear his mind. His throat was dry, and he drank long and deep from his canteen, no longer worried about running out of water.

Leveling off, he looked down only to realize that he had already left the shores of the English Channel behind. Ahead, the sea appeared cold and uninviting, as he had expected. Spread out before him as far as he could see, the Channel was the last major hurdle before Paris.

He suddenly felt bone tired again and wondered for a moment if he should turn back to Ireland. *Am I awake enough to stay on course?* To his relief, the skies ahead were clearer, and behind him, the setting sun broke through clouds and cast a golden light on the silver-painted wings of the *Spirit*. He knew that the French coast was now no more than an hour away. The four British fighters continued to fly cover above him. They would break away soon, leaving the unsuspecting Lindbergh in the hands of Didier Michaud's squadron of SPADs until the American crossed the shores of France.

His growling stomach told him he was hungry. Lindbergh tried to remember the last time he'd eaten. It was at dinner the night before he left New York. He reached for his small bag of sandwiches but changed his mind, deciding instead to wait until he cleared the Channel.

Some twelve thousand feet above him, the British fighter squadron commander gave a thumbs-up signal to his mates and pointed to the squadron of French SPADs, less than a kilometer away, which once again took up their protection of the American. The British pilots followed as their flight leader veered to the left and turned back to England, their mission to protect Lindbergh completed.

Less than sixty minutes later, Lindbergh stuck his head out the left side to see if he could make out land. His timing was perfect. The Cherbourg peninsula was just emerging on the horizon. The French pilots broke off their escort so they would not be seen.

"Good luck, my American friend. Godspeed," Michaud saluted the bravery of the Yank who had come so far.

In a few moments, Lindbergh was over Cherbourg, and he dipped the *Spirit* low over the village to get a closer look at the French peasants who were pouring into the streets and waving at him. It was nearly nine-thirty in the evening, and he had been flying now for more than thirty-two hours.

No longer worried about his navigation, Lindbergh followed a route he had memorized from the maps he had purchased in San Diego. He turned the *Spirit* slightly southward along the rugged cliffs of the French coast to the village of Deauville, where more Frenchmen were waiting to welcome him. He was elated as he flew low over the village, waving down at the cheering crowd, slightly in awe of the joyous reception. The young man from Minnesota thought he caught a glimpse of an American flag being waved at him.

Another hour, he thought, and then remembered his sandwiches. Nestling the joystick between his knees, he forced himself to eat one of the five sandwiches he had brought, but he found it tasteless and hard to swallow. He tossed the remainder of his food behind the wicker chair to which he had been virtually glued since leaving New York and tried to stretch his legs. It was hopeless, and he worried that he might not be able to walk immediately after he landed in Paris.

The twilight around him deepened, and the blackness of night once again began to surround the *Spirit of St. Louis*. Lindbergh shuddered slightly, an involuntary reaction to a chill that passed through him at the thought of being alone in the darkness again. He knew that if he could only hang on for a little longer, the lights of Paris would soon break through the blackness and guide him home.

He nudged the throttle slightly to one hundred twelve miles per hour. Anticipation was building, and he could feel his chest tightening. *I have to relax,* he thought. *We're almost …*

There! A glow ahead, shimmering beneath the night, and then, the lights! Lindbergh was so excited he yanked the joystick to the left as he peered out the window and dipped the *Spirit* hard on her side. An ocean of lights, like a sea of diamonds, glittered up at him. It was Paris, glowing for miles ahead on the horizon. Unlike New York City, the electric grid was flat and spread. He noticed almost at once that there were no skyscrapers. What he was looking for was the tallest structure in Paris.

He dipped lower to see the city close up, and the lights became distinctive entities, each attached to a building, a street or an automobile. In the distance he found what he was looking for, the Eiffel Tower.

Now he felt as if he was moving in slow motion. The pilot was numb with exhaustion; and as he contemplated landing now, he realized that he had little feel for his airplane. His mind was flooded with emotions, tossed between jubilation at his success and fear of trying to land his airplane without crashing. He was beginning to panic and felt his heart racing. *No, not now! We've come so far. I won't give in.*

He circled the Eiffel Tower several times, concentrating on working the controls of the *Spirit* to get back in touch with her. He climbed back up to three thousand feet, scanning the city for anything that looked like an airfield.

After long minutes, he spied a large, black rectangle northeast of the Eiffel Tower. There seemed to be lights evenly spaced out on two sides of the darkness. *It must be Le Bourget airfield,* he thought, wondering at the same time if it was a park or man-made lake or something else he had forgotten from his maps. No. It could only be the airfield. He circled what he thought was the airfield again and yet again, slowly descending, the *Spirit* banked on her right side so he could search the area for signs that it was indeed Le Bourget.

Suddenly, floodlights brought the area into perspective and what appeared to be hangers were bathed in the right lights. *Maybe they're looking for me,* he thought, but the space below him that was lit up seemed awfully small to land an airplane on. He felt lightheaded. *I've got to put her down soon,* he thought, aware now that he could black out at the controls.

He circled again, dropping to one thousand feet. Finally, he was certain. It was Le Bourget. Lindbergh brought the *Spirit* around one final time and lined up on the nearest edge of the runway. Lowering his flaps he flared the nose of the airplane up a bit and concentrated on his instruments. He was not confident enough in his depth perception to trust his feel for altitude and distance, so he abandoned the periscope and forced himself to concentrate on his altimeter, attitude and airspeed indicator. He would make an instrument landing.

He nudged the throttle up slightly to avoid stalling and pushed back into his wicker seat, watching the instruments as his altimeter gauge wound down the last hundred feet of space between the sky and earth. He eased back on the stick, flaring the *Spirit's* nose, and worked the rudder pedals back and forth. He closed his eyes at the last minute, for the first time in his career as a pilot uncertain of his landing situation.

With a gentle bump and a slight hop back into the air, the landing gear of the *Spirit of St. Louis* found its grip on the grass airstrip at Le Bourget Airfield and jealously held on to the earth. Lindbergh hesitated for a second to be sure, then killed his engine and let the airplane roll to a stop. As the propeller slowly wound down, Lindbergh found that he couldn't hear a thing. He quickly glanced at his watch. It was 4:22 p.m. in New York time; 10:22 p.m. in Paris. For the first time in thirty-three-and-a-half hours, the American pilot relaxed his grip on the stick, took a long, deep breath, and closed his eyes.

He had done it.

I'm here Father. Are you proud of me?

There was no response. Lindbergh opened his eyes and peered out into the darkness. He saw nothing and thought he must have landed well past the hangars he had seen on his final approach. Opening the single door, he swung his legs over the side of the fuselage and began rubbing his thighs vigorously, trying to get blood moving through them again. He had not been able to stretch out completely since takeoff at Roosevelt Field. "Guess I'd better wait for some help," he said aloud, hoping someone might hear him. "I don't think I can stand on my own."

Suddenly, he was bathed in a searchlight that someone had turned on the *Spirit*. Its brightness blinded him. Another searchlight turned on him from the other side of the field, now fully illuminating Lindbergh and *The Spirit*. The lights confused him, and he momentarily lost his bearings as to where he was on the field. His hearing was beginning to return and he turned sharply to a noise that sounded like an ocean wave breaking, disorienting him further. The ocean?

He peered into the darkness again, trying to pinpoint the source of the noise. His jaw dropped.

It was a wave. Emerging from the darkness on the north side of the runway, a sea of humanity, later estimated at more than one hundred thousand people, surged toward him yelling and screaming, "*Lan-dabairg! Lan-dabairg!*" It seemed all of Paris had come out to welcome him.

Finally, a mob of adoring Parisians did what no storm, darkness, loneliness, memory or hidden enemy had been able to accomplish. Lindbergh was completely terrified. He had not taken on the challenge of the vast North Atlantic to be a hero. The idea had never crossed his mind. His ego struggled to comprehend that others thought of him as one, and he was completely unprepared for the adulation suddenly foisted upon him.

As the screaming crowd besieged the *Spirit of St. Louis*, they pulled Lindbergh from his airplane and hoisted him up on their shoulders in joyous celebration, passing him over their heads for nearly thirty minutes before he actually touched French soil. Every man, woman and child among them wanted to touch him as their way of sharing in his triumph.

He was completely bewildered by the hysteria. The country boy who had flown so far would only allow himself the recognition that he had taken on the most daunting challenge of his profession and had been successful in the attempt.

But to the huge crowd this night at Le Bourget, and to millions more around the globe, Lindbergh was more than a man. He was a simple boy who personified simple men who dreamed of conquering the darkness and the unknown.

Thirty-Nine

They were invisible to all but the small animals and birds that lived along the river bank. Clad entirely in black canvas fatigues, their faces darkened with grease paint, only the whites of their eyes were left to give the intruders away. Pity the poor soul who got close enough to see them.

The dozen Royal Navy Marine Commandos of the British 63rd Division crouched low in the thick brush surrounding the supposed headquarters of the 4th squadron of the 40th wing of the Red Army at its Lipetsk, Russia, airfield. There were few Russians on this base, they knew, which was actually a secret German Luftstreitkräfte operation.

Major William Markham was the only one of his men who had been briefed on the full details of the work being conducted at the German base, and he had elected not to share all of what he knew with his troops. He did not want them distracted from their mission, which was to liberate safely the twenty-three prisoners of war of several nationalities who were still being held here some nine years after the Great War had ended. The thought of their enslavement made the thirty-three-year-old officer's blood boil, and his finger twitched on the trigger of his American-made, .45-caliber Thompson submachine gun.

Markham was the old man of his crack commando squad, having joined the Royal Navy Marines in early 1914 at the age of nineteen. The military was an attractive career path for a poor boy from Liverpool, but he had not counted on seeing action quite so quickly. Before the year was out, he had found himself in the ferocious fight to defend the Belgian city of Antwerp against the Germans and also took part in the Royal Marines' amphibious landing at Gallipoli in 1915. After evacuating Gallipoli, his division was sent to northern France to fight in the final days of the Somme Offensive. There British forces tried to force their way through German lines along a twelve-mile front bordering the River Somme. In one of the bloodiest battles in history, he remembered well being dug in on the banks of the River Ancre outside the tiny commune of Beaumont Hamel and witnessing the slaughter of hundreds of his fellow British "Diggers." He still had a taste for German blood all these years later.

The battle-hardened major extended two fingers and flicked them right, then left. Without a word, four men in teams of two silently moved out in opposite directions. Markham watched as they took up positions at the two corners of the barracks closest to them, a large, metal-roofed, Quonset-style hut where undercover British agents had indicated the POWs were located. On Markham's command, four more commandos moved out and took positions at the opposite two corners of the building.

Markham almost envied the exercise his eight men were getting. His legs were still cramped from the three-day trip hidden in a filthy boxcar on a train from Pärnu, a port city in southwestern Estonia on the Gulf of Riga in the Baltic Sea. His unit had made landfall there after a nearly week-long voyage from England aboard a nondescript freighter flying a Swedish flag. They had crept aboard the train well after midnight under a black, moonless sky on June 7th, 1927.

From there, they entered Russia at its northwestern border at the village of Pskov and traveled some seven hundred kilometers in the bumpy rail cars to Lipetsk. As luck would have it, the train stopped for the night on the outskirts of the city, and the twelve commandos waited in the relative safety of the boxcar until darkness.

On Markham's signal, the eight commandos poised at each corner of the barracks and threw open the single doors at each end. With silenced hand guns, they took out the single German guard at each, securing the building. After quietly rousing the POWs from their restless sleep and sweeping the barracks for more German troops, Markham's second in command, twenty-six-year-old Marine Sergeant Roy Evans, signaled to the major that it was safe to come forward. Markham and the three remaining commandos quickly moved out of the shadows and inside.

He found the POWs nervously waiting next to their bunks as ordered, not sure of what to make of the intruders. Having been enslaved by the Germans since the war, they had been numbed by their lives of deprivation, and the dream of freedom had long ago left their consciousness. Markham wasted no time.

"Good evening, I am Major William Markham of his Majesty's Royal Navy Marines, and these are my men. If you will come quickly, King George has kindly provided us with a boat on the Voronezh River which will take you to safety. If you will kindly cooperate, you will be in Britain in less than a fortnight and reunited with your loved ones shortly thereafter. Am I clear?" Markham finished, scanning the face of each man. He had to know if any of them had been corrupted by their captors. Two men began to sob. The others didn't flinch.

"Very well." He turned to Evans. "Sergeant, get these men dressed quickly, we have no time to waste." A commando came forward with a large duffel bag and began handing out black fatigues. In short order, the prisoners were ready to leave. Markham was painfully aware that not one of them had so much as asked a question of their liberators, such was the degree of the surrender of their minds. The Germans had virtually destroyed their free will. He wondered if they would ever recover.

"Ready, Sir," Evans reported, pulling a black mask over his head.

"Let's go then, Sergeant," Markham replied. "Each of you take two men under your wing. Evans, you take three. I will advance us on point."

The Marine used the muzzle of his gun to edge open the door closest to the outlying brush and carefully scanned the sixty feet of open space they would have to cover. From there, they would need to march quickly through heavy woods about a hundred yards to the closet bank of the Voronezh, where a forty-eight-foot barge was waiting to take them down river to tributaries that would lead them out of Russia and to the safety of the Black Sea. From there, they would intercept a waiting, neutral-flagged freighter which would take the commandos and their charges through the Bosporus Strait to the Mediterranean Sea, where the thirty-thousand-ton battleship *HMS Royal Oak* would be waiting to take them on the final leg to England.

Signaling to his men to wait, Markham sprinted across the open divide and hid in the brush. He again scanned the yard, searching for guards. Seeing no one, he motioned to Evans to send the first group toward him. In less than a minute, the three men were safely next to him. Another three started across.

Without warning, a lone German soldier turned the far corner of the building, casually walking toward their hiding place, out for a late smoke. Markham held up his hand to stop the commando and his two POWs from leaving the barracks, but it was too late. The German caught them in mid-stride.

"Oh, shit!" the soldier hollered. He turned to run. "Guards, guards!" he screamed again and again. He was too far away for Markham to stop him. The Major leveled his gun and was about to shoot the German when one of his men appeared from the end of the barracks and grabbed him. The commando silently stuck the soldier in the neck with a long knife and let him fall to the ground, but it was too late. The alarm had been sounded.

Almost immediately, the yard was a blaze of lights, and a klaxon blared into the night, alerting the base security force that they had been infiltrated. Troopers emerged from their own barracks and stormed toward the POW hut, searching for the source of the alarm. The Germans quickly spotted the prisoners running into the brush, and a dozen guns opened fire on them and their British rescuers as Markham led the group into the woods.

At the tail end, Evans knelt and made a stand, firing his Thompson nonstop at the advancing Germans. A half-dozen fell to the ground before he jumped to his feet again, chasing after his mates who were almost at the river.

"Hurry, hurry," Markham said coolly to his men as they reached the dilapidated barge. "Get them on board and start the engines. I'll cast off the lines. Where the bloody hell is Evans?" he hollered, suddenly realizing that his friend and comrade was missing from the group.

"He fell back, laying return fire," one of his men shouted back.

"Goddamn it," Markham muttered. "Cast off, now. I'll get him. Look for us in the water a half mile down river."

The Royal Navy Marine Major sprinted back into the woods, hoping he could reach Evans in time. The sound of rifle fire and the explosive burp of Evans' submachine gun broke the serenity of the thick forest. Markham saw the muzzle flash before he saw his man. Firing blindly at the enemy, he raced to Evans' side. The Sergeant was firing the Thompson with one hand. His left arm hung useless at his side. A bullet had torn through his elbow, smashing it.

"Get the fuck out of here, Major!" Evans shouted at his commanding officer. "I got these motherfucking sod bastards," he yelled just as another bullet hit him in the right shoulder. He fell to the ground.

"Fall back, goddamn it," Markham screamed at him. "Get on your feet, Mate. We can still make the boat!" He laid down a long stream of fire that forced the Germans to stop and fall to the forest floor. Markham grabbed the Sergeant and pulled him to his feet, forcing him ahead of him on the dark path back toward the river's edge. The Germans were up quickly, and Markham fired at them even as he ran behind Evans.

Somehow reaching the river bank, Markham yelled for his first officer to follow him. They sprinted along the river bank in a desperate bid to catch up to the barge, which had already passed the half-mile mark. The commando at the helm, with little ship's training, was struggling to bring the boat close up to the river bank so the Major and Evans could jump aboard. He suddenly heard scraping along the underside and realized that he might run aground. The young commando quickly spun the wheel to the right and headed back to the middle of the channel. They'd have to swim for it. Frustration brought tears to his eyes.

With the POWs safely aboard and below deck, the remaining commandos took positions topside and began laying down fire behind Markham and the Sergeant, who they could now see racing along the river bank. Too late, several Germans chasing them realized they were caught in the open and fell in a barrage of machine gun fire from the barge.

Markham, out of ammunition, stopped and tossed his weapon, pushed Evans into the water and dove in himself. He wrapped his arm around the badly wounded

Sergeant's neck and began towing him to the slow-moving barge. A German rifleman, waiting behind the cover of a large oak tree fifty yards away where he could avoid the British fire, calmly took careful aim with his Mauser 98 rifle and squeezed off two rounds in rapid succession. Both found their mark.

Markham, swimming for his life in the muddy water in a hopeless bid to reach the barge, took the first shot in the center of his back, almost certainly severing his spinal cord. The second smashed into the back of his skull, nearly decapitating him. He died instantly. Evans, suddenly without the Major to keep him afloat, desperately tried to keep his head above the water, now red with blood and bits of brain matter. With both arms all but useless, he sank beneath the surface just as a bevy of gunshots rang out from the Germans, now huddled on the river bank. He drowned before they could murder him.

Aboard the barge, Markham's troops watched helplessly as the two men fell dead in the river, just meters from safety. They returned fire on the Germans but within a few minutes were out of range as the ship moved out into the middle of the shipping lane. They watched as two German soldiers waded out into the river and dragged out Markham's body. It would give them an idea of the identity of the intruders who had stolen their prized POWs.

At the base, Colonel Janzig had been awakened by the gunfire and hurried to take command. Markham's body was brought to him. The Major had carried no papers, but the bayonet he kept in a black leather leg scabbard was a dead giveaway with its Remington mallard's head engraving. Janzig was certain beyond a doubt that he been a victim of the British.

Aboard the barge, Corporal Riley Jordan gathered the remaining commandos and barked orders.

"Stay sharp, Mates. Given the Major and Evans, shit, it'll be a bloody fucking sin if we don't get these poor bastards back to England," the twenty-two-year-old corporal, next in the line of command, summed up their feelings.

"Something tells me the Krauts won't be after us, not with what's coming at them in the next hour," he continued. "By now they've probably figured out it was the Brits who popped their cherry, all right, and you can imagine they'll be scurrying around like the vermin they are to save whatever the fuck it is that's so bloody important to the frigging Admiralty."

He hung his head, tired, and pulled a pack of cigarettes out of his fatigue jacket, lighting one. The boy inhaled deeply, blowing the smoke out towards the stern. Looking out over the horizon, he realized that the sun would be up soon, and with it, the large target they had just left would be fully illuminated.

"They were good men. I hope the bloody flyboys knock the living shit out of those bleedin' bastards," he finished. The men nodded silently, the fight gone out of them for the moment.

"We've a bloody job to do, too, Mates. Let's get these boys home to their mothers."

Forty

Janzig hurried back to the communications center near his office. "Get me Gruppenführer Goering, immediately," he barked at a radioman.

"Herr Goering is not available, Colonel," Berlin responded. He is entertaining the head of the Red Cross in Berlin, a Mrs. Heidelman. They are behind closed doors."

"I demand to speak with him. It is most urgent!" Janzig replied curtly, trying to keep his temper.

"I am sorry, Herr Colonel, but he has left orders not to be inter ..."

"Goddamn it, you idiot! We have just been attacked by British Commandos. Put fucking Goering on the radio immediately, or I will see to it that your balls are cut off and burned as you watch. Do you hear me?" The base commander could feel his heart pounding in his chest.

"Yes, Sir, at once," came the weak reply. Goering was on the line a few minutes later.

"What has happened Janzig, quickly," Goering demanded.

"I fear we have been found out, Herr Gruppenführer. British commandos have attacked the base and escaped with the POWs," Janzig reported. He could imagine Goering frothing at the mouth at the other end. "We have suffered many casualties, as well, but we killed their leader and another."

"Goddamn it!" Goering screamed. "Are you sure they were British?" he demanded.

"I am certain. Their weapons were American. Herr Goering, I fear ..."

Goering cut him off in mid sentence. "They took the POWs? That means there is another attack coming, Janzig. We have had a security breach. They are after the bomber."

"*Amerike*? How is this possible?" Janzig responded incredulously. "We have taken every precaution." His voice trailed off as he began to consider the possibilities.

"That is not important now, you idiot!" Goering screamed into the radio. "What is vital is that we save *Amerike*. You must get the bomber airborne immediately. If I am correct, they will probably attack at daybreak, and you will be caught with no hope of escape. Get *Amerike* in the air now!" he demanded.

"Yes, Herr Goering, at once," Janzig responded, realizing that his career was now in tatters. The only thing that could save him was to prevent the bomber from being destroyed.

"What of the commandos, Herr Goering? Should we give chase?"

"Forget the fucking commandos, you idiot. Get *Amerike* airborne now!" Goering was screaming into the radio so loudly that his voice was distorted by feedback. "I will have your head if you fail me, do you understand?"

"Yes, Gruppenführer Goering," Janzig replied, hardly recognizing the voice of his longtime friend. It struck the base commander that he was as expendable as any of Goering's subordinates. He dropped the microphone and turned away from the radio.

He hollered for his adjutant. "Fuel *Amerike* immediately and load her with the new bombs simultaneously. Have the crew report to the airplane and taxi out onto the runway as soon as possible. I will take command as the pilot. Make sure there is water and stores aboard. We may be in the air for some time." A plan was already taking shape in his mind. "Sound the alarm for all men to man their guns. See to it that the anti-aircraft guns are at the ready."

"At once, Colonel," the adjutant responded and raced out the door of Janzig's office, already barking orders.

Less than two hundred kilometers away, Wing Commander Tony Haselton of the Royal Air Force was at the controls of a Handley Page V/1500 super long-range heavy bomber, eleven thousand feet over a barren Russian landscape. Behind him, fourteen more of the dual-winged, fifteen-ton behemoths, bristling with Lewis automatic machine guns, were in a tight V-formation. Their crews were on high alert scanning the surrounding skies for German or Russian fighters. They had been flying for nearly six hours following takeoff from a small military airfield in Tallinn, the capital city of Estonia, and were closing in on their target, the Lipetsk Russian military air base.

The British bomber group had been hastily assembled at the order of Prime Minister Stanley Baldwin just days before. After seeing photographs acquired by British Naval Intelligence operatives that clearly showed the enormous German buildup of aviation resources in Lipetsk in direct violation of the Treaty of Versailles, there was no choice. The Prime Minister had ordered the immediate destruction of the facility after first conferring with American President Calvin Coolidge and French President Pierre-Paul-Henri-Gaston Doumergue. The triumvirate had agreed that the probable damage to Allied relations with the Russian Empire was worth the risk, given the lethality of the German weapons program. President Coolidge, in particular, had been insistent on bombing Lipetsk, knowing in his heart that the German military would not hesitate to bomb a major American city if it had the capability. Prime Minister Baldwin had similar concerns. Neither knew how close they were to the truth.

"Let us bite the head off this snake once and for all, Gentlemen," Baldwin had pleaded, "for all our peoples." There had been no dissent.

Coolidge wanted desperately to use American forces to carry out the raid, but he had been convinced that the U.S. simply did not have the airplanes or trained pilots to carry out the mission. He was quick to berate his Generals for the poor state of the U.S. Army Air Corps readiness, but politically was reminded that he had savaged the War Department's budget for new aircraft development in the fight to revitalize the economy following the economic depression of 1919. Baldwin volunteered British forces for the mission.

"It just so happens that the R.A.F. developed a long-range bomber in 1918 for the sole purpose of raiding Berlin," he said. "Pity the Armistice interrupted the plan, but my military command informs me that we have the capability of striking Lipetsk, if we can secure a base of operation within seven hundred fifty miles of the city.

"I know just the place, Gentlemen. The small nation of Estonia, situated right on Russia's northwest border, owes us one," Baldwin had concluded.

Indeed, the Estonian government did owe the British Empire a debt of gratitude. Following the German occupation of the country during the Great War, the Russians had invaded the tiny country again just days after the Armistice had been signed. Shocked by the premeditated treachery of the Bolsheviks, the small and poorly armed Estonians fought back in a war of independence. The British had rushed arms and military advisors to the grateful people's army known as the "Rahvavägi," which subsequently pushed the Russian Red Army out of the country. The Estonian government's approval for the R.A.F. to use the military air strip at

Tallinn as the stage for the Lipetsk bombing mission came without hesitation.

The airplanes had arrived on the same steamer as Major Markham's commandos in the port city of Pärnu three days earlier after sailing from England the previous week. The R.A.F.'s long-range, heavy bombers, which had been based at the military airbase at Bircham Newton in Norfolk, had been tied to the decks of the freighter and covered with heavy canvas for the voyage. With its unique folding wing design, the airplane could fit on the deck in roughly half the space of a normal fix-winged aircraft of the same dimensions and allowed the R.A.F. to commit fifteen of the bombers for the mission. Wing Commander Tony Haselton was grateful for the additional planes.

"Intelligence indicates we can expect a rough ride over Lipetsk," Haselton briefed his pilots shortly before the fifteen, seven-man crews manned their bombers for the early morning raid. "We will leave at 0230 hours and fly at eleven thousand feet. The darkness and our altitude should hide us through the night. We should be over target at first light, before Reveille."

The one hundred five R.A.F. pilots, co-pilots, navigators, bombers and gunners were gathered on the steaming tarmac of the Tallinn airfield on the banks of the Gulf of Finland in the early evening of June 10th, hours before they were to man their planes. Among them, only Haselton, one of Britain's leading aces in the Great War with thirty-four German kills, had any combat experience.

Almost a father figure among the lads under his command, the thirty-year-old pilot from Lancashire was determined to bring each of them back in one piece. He would not give in to what he knew were enormous odds against them, relying instead on his own dogfight-hardened battle skills.

During the war, Haselton's fellow pilots had thought he was a madman in the skies over the blood-soaked battlefields of France. He seemed to be intent on getting himself killed as time and again he dove in to attack whole squadrons of German fighters all alone with seemingly reckless abandon for his own safety.

It was not unusual for the British pilot to be seen battling four, five or even eight Fokkers at a time, inflicting numerous casualties or kills while taking heavy fire himself. Eventually and inevitably, the German survivors would tuck their bruised tails between their legs and scurry for safe air, fully believing that the Brit who had engaged them was insanely superhuman. In fact, Haselton barely made it back alive from these encounters, his Sopwith Camel often being torn to shreds. Although he had more than tempted the Devil himself and had been badly wounded three times, the courageous pilot had managed to stay alive to the war's end. He had been decorated with both the Distinguished Service Order and the Victoria Cross for his gallantry, the latter having been pinned on his uniform by King George V.

Today, the British Wing Commander, who had been singled out for command of this critical mission by the Admiralty, was relying on the same strategy. He would convince the Germans that although their numbers were few, the R.A.F. pilots were suicidal in their intent to destroy the Lipetsk air base. Haselton planned to scare the Germans into defeat.

"The Krauts have erected heavy anti-aircraft fortifications, so we will have only one choice when we get over the target, Boys. We're going to have to go in very low, below their bloody guns, at roughly one hundred fifty meters."

A low murmur of anxiety erupted among the pilots, most in their early twenties, some fresh out of flight school. Hazelton's proposed tactic was uncharted territory for all of them.

"My intention is to go in low, so low that we'll scare the bloody hell out of the bastards. We want them to think we're bleedin' starkers. Pilots, you follow my lead. We will approach the objective two abreast and then fan out for our individual targets," Haselton instructed. "Those of you following the lead aircraft must not steer off the tail in front of you. Slip to either side as you approach and avoid the upward concussion of the bombs already dropped and that you will surely encounter at such a low altitude."

"Also, there is a strong possibility that we may meet resistance from fighter aircraft known to be based at Lipetsk. Intelligence has indicated the Krauts have some experimental designs that are operational and highly lethal. Again, we won't know what to expect until we get over the target. Gunners, keep your eyes open and your guns cocked. You may get a bleedin' workout before this is over."

"Once we have spent the package, we will head due west for Tallinn. We'll have the Camel boys to look out after us on the last leg, about one hundred fifty miles out; but until then, we're on our own," Haselton said, referring to the R.A.F.'s small fleet of vintage Sopwith Camel fighters that had arrived with them on a separate freighter. Only six fighters could be made operational, including the four that had flown cover for Lindbergh as he had approached Cherbourg on the French coast several weeks before.

"Look, boys, this'll be no fucking picnic," Haselton concluded, looking out over a sea of concerned faces. He lapsed into the jargon of the British working class, from which most of them hailed. "But don't get your knickers in a twist. As the Lord is my witness, we're going to kick the bloody piss out of these heathen sod and live to tell our ankle-biters about it. The Germans are all mouth and no trousers, Mates. If it weren't true, how do you suppose I'd be bleedin' well standing here?"

"So keep your peckers up, and climb into the rack for a while, or write your missus," he said trying to be lighthearted. "On your bikes at 0200 sharp."

He hesitated, looking out over them, trying to fit as many faces into his memory as possible. "Any questions?" he grinned.

It took a moment of silence before the first pilot snickered. Then came a cautious wave of quiet laughter. Finally one of them yelled, "Fuck the bloody Krauts if they can't take a joke," and the airfield was filled with tumultuous laughter.

Now, less than two hundred kilometers from the target, the sound of their laughter reverberated in Haselton's mind. The hair on the back of his neck was standing at attention, a sure sign that trouble was near.

"God help us," he prayed, knowing full well that God didn't pick sides in the lunacy that was war.

Forty-One

The Handley Page V/1500 long-range heavy bomber was first produced in 1918 at the behest of the British Admiralty, which required the company founded by aviation genius Frederick Hanley Page to produce a "bloody paralyser of an aeroplane."

The four-engine bomber was built expressly to bomb the city of Berlin in the Allied efforts to bring the Great War to a conclusion as quickly as possible. Ironically, on the very day that four of the huge airplanes were scheduled to fly their first mission over the German capital and drop some thirty thousand pounds of explosives, the enemy capitulated to the western Allied forces. The war had ended, and in all probability, the need for the Handley Page V/1500 had ended, as well. But with fortuitous foresight, the British Admiralty mothballed fifteen of the eighteen airplanes that had been produced by the war's end, using the remaining three for training.

Designed at the gigantic Handley Page factory in the Cricklewood district of North London, the huge V/1500 biplane had employed leading-edge technology and was the first British bomber aircraft to use four engines. The Rolls-Royce Eagle VIIIs developed a massive three hundred seventy-five horsepower each and were mounted in a revolutionary configuration. Two engines were mounted back-to-back in a single nacelle, one acting as a pusher, the other as a tractor. The bomber was nearly twenty meters long with a wingspan of thirty-nine meters, and it stood seven meters high at its upper wing.

While its maximum speed was only one hundred fifty-nine kilometers per hour, the airplane could carry its crew of seven an astonishing range of more than fifteen hundred kilometers.

As a war machine, it was exceptionally lethal, carrying American-designed .303 Lewis automatic drum-pan, magazine-fed machine guns in the nose, dorsal, tail and on both sides of the fuselage. It was capable of carrying up to thirty-five hundred kilograms, or thirty-one hundred kilogram bombs, internally and mounted on two hardpoints under the fuselage. Fully loaded, it weighed fifteen tons. The world had never seen so much killing power in one package.

At the controls of the lead bomber, Hazelton scanned the horizon trying to discern cloud cover over Lipetsk. Heavy, cotton-like cumulus blanketed the sky at five hundred meters, profiled by the slowly rising sun at daybreak. Below the clouds the air would be crystal clear not only for their bombing runs but also for the anti-aircraft gun crews who would be trying to blow holes in the squadron of R.A.F. bombers.

Each of the planes had been assigned a specific target. Haselton, in the lead aircraft, would bring the group over the target but would not drop his bombs immediately, instead turning wide around the airfield and lining up for his own run at the tail end of the pack. This would give him the opportunity to assess the damage and drop his load wherever it was needed to complete the mission. The number one target had been described to him as a huge, all-metal black bomber which was believed to be on the runway waiting further flight testing. Haselton didn't know the particulars, but the Admiralty had briefed him that this airplane was to be taken out at all costs. *At all costs*, he mused, knowing what that really meant.

The next three aircraft were assigned to take out the base headquarters, barracks and design facilities. Three more were to eliminate the factory. The next four would take out the giant hangar and as many aircraft on the field as possible, and four more were specifically assigned to destroy the German bomber. Finally, Haselton was to fix on a target, drop his load, and then head for home with throttles to the firewall. On paper it worked out perfectly. *It always does,* the well-read Haselton thought, knowing full well that the Greek philosopher Plato was right when he wrote, "Necessity, who is the mother of invention."

While each of the bombers was equipped with air-to-air radios, Haselton had elected not to use them so as not to risk discovery by potential eavesdroppers at the Lipetsk air base communications center. Instead, the pilots would follow a do-as-I-do rule. Haselton pushed the yoke of his flight controls forward to dive low over the Russian countryside as the R.A.F. bombers approached their targets, and fourteen more aircraft dove behind him.

At Lipetsk the situation was chaotic. Crews had urgently pulled the *Amerike* bomber from its hangar and were just finishing fueling. A full complement of thirty, one-hundred-kilogram super bombs, the lethal fuel-air explosive for which base commander Colonel Rainer Janzig had overseen the development for exclusive use in his frightening new bomber, had been loaded into *Amerike*'s internal bomb bay. Its four engines were running, and the sleek black bomber was ready for takeoff. A vehicle raced up to the airplane, and Janzig, already wearing his Luftstreitkräfte flight suit, immediately boarded the airplane and took his seat at the controls. Without hesitation, he swung the nose of the giant bomber around and taxied to the end of the runway for takeoff.

Janzig had already logged nearly a hundred hours in the black bomber and had found it to be amazingly agile for such a large aircraft; but like all new airplanes, it had idiosyncrasies. *Amerike* displayed her growing pains only on takeoff, requiring a vast amount of runway despite the enormous power of her four, twelve-cylinder B.M.W. engines, before she had enough air under her wings to fly. The extra long runway at Lipetsk could just handle *Amerike*'s appetite for tarmac. Janzig had already devised a plan to add four small, liquid rocket boosters adjacent to each of her engines, which would significantly increase the bomber's takeoff speed and eliminate the problem; but there had not been time to test the plan.

Poised at the end of the runway, Janzig stomped hard on *Amerike*'s massive disc brakes and forced the throttle to its maximum. The four B.M.W. engines roared in protest as rpms built toward red line in each engine. Janzig was beginning to panic. At any moment, he expected to see Allied bombers dropping through the clouds. Tony Haselton didn't disappoint him.

Just as the base commander lifted off the brakes, releasing his hold on *Amerike,* and the giant bomber lurched forward, Janzig spied Haselton's R.A.F. bomber low on the horizon. He could see additional planes behind him but couldn't tell how many. *Amerike* began to lumber down the runway as the first explosions from the thirty anti-aircraft units began to spit into the sky. The eighty-eight millimeter guns could fire as many as ten rounds per minute, and the Lipetsk gun crews had been well trained, but the British bombers had achieved nearly complete surprise as they began to attack.

As Wing Commander Haselton led his squadron over the edge of the airbase, he could feel the turbulence caused by the exploding shells above him. *It's working,* he thought. *The gunners will have the devil of it trying to hit our bombers flying so low.*

Haselton flew his lead Handley Page bomber directly over the long runway. Behind him, the aircraft of his squadron were peeling out all over the airfield searching for their assigned targets. The sky was full of bursting artillery shells as the German anti-aircraft gunners desperately tried to zero in on the British intruders but couldn't find the mark. A thick haze of smoke wafted across the runway even before the first R.A.F. bomber dropped its payload.

Just as Haselton reached the end of the runway and began to climb and bank around, the first bombs exploded directly on top of the large, metal-roofed barracks building. The explosions were deafening, rolling all the way into Haselton's cockpit. He grinned with delight.

Just as he made the turn, he saw the bomber, huge, black and bristling with machine guns, beginning its long run down the air strip in a desperate gamble to escape. "Damn!" Haselton swore, knowing the primary target of the raid was now making a run for it. He picked up the microphone of his radio and barked for the aircraft assigned to taking out the German bomber. "Flight leader to …" he began before remembering that he had ordered all radios turned off to avoid an accidental broadcast which might give the location of the squadron away.

"Bloody hell," he yelled to his co-pilot, Allen Brighton. "Bring this motherfucker around with me, Al. Hurry, we don't have much time!" The two pilots forced the controls right in a sharp, full-throttle, banked turn, hoping to line up behind the menacing black German bomber. But Janzig's tail gunner had already seen the Handley Page turning toward *Amerike* and swung his guns around toward the huge, hideously fragile-looking biplane. Before he could shoot, the British nose gunner lit up the runway with incendiary tracer bullets, chasing the behemoth's tail as it attempted to escape. As the British bomber picked up speed toward *Amerike*, the R.A.F. gunner's spread found its mark, and the German gunner was silenced before he could get off a single burst of his machine gun.

All around him, Haselton saw his squadron laying waste to the enormous Lipetsk air base. From what he could tell, every target had been hit and was burning, save the most important one of all, the one he was chasing. Huge cauldrons of flame and black smoke were leaping into the air, and the Wing Commander saw fighter aircraft neatly parked on the tarmac systematically being butchered by his squadron's bombs and Lewis machine guns. The anti-aircraft fire was relentless, filling the air with red explosions that continually missed the mark. *It's a scene from Dante's Inferno,* Haselton thought, happy that for the moment he was on this side of hell.

The Wing commander's bomber continued to gain on the huge German warplane, still struggling to lift off. Haselton could see that the giant bird was getting lift and watched as the tires of its massive landing gear finally lifted off the runway. He couldn't coax more speed out of the Handley Page, and the German bomber was already moving faster than he could fly the ancient V/1500. He yelled to his gunners to fire at the black bomber's engines. It was the only hope of either knocking it out of the sky or at least slowing it down. Haselton knew that if the enemy airplane made it to altitude, it would be all but impossible to stop it, such was its speed, heavy armaments and twenty-six-thousand-foot ceiling.

Out of the corner of his eye, the Wing Commander saw one of the starboard engines of a V/1500 explode into flames. Helplessly, he watched as the young R.A.F. pilot at its controls tried vainly to gain altitude out of the way of the anti-aircraft shelling but instead flew his airplane directly into the line of fire. Four more shells hit the airplane instantly, and the British bomber exploded in midair. Haselton could only scream at the enemy in rage.

Ahead of him, *Amerike* was gaining altitude and speed and was pulling away from the British bomber, despite the R.A.F. gunner's continuous fire. Haselton thought frantically, searching for another way to stop the giant bomber. At the controls of *Amerike*, Colonel Janzig was gaining confidence that he could outrun the British intruders.

"The bastards will pay for this," he screamed into a microphone to his crew spread out through the plane. "We will make our way to London, do you hear? I will annihilate it with our super bombs," he snarled, his appetite for blood building as he looked over his shoulder at the blazing ruins of the extraordinary facility he had carved out of Russian soil.

"The pigs! I will piss on them, do you hear me?" His voice bellowed through the black bomber even as his gunners frantically searched the skies around them for R.A.F. targets.

"The tail is knocked out, Herr Janzing," *Amerike*'s navigator yelled to his superior.

"Take his gun, you buffoon," the besieged Colonel roared back. "Shoot that son of a bitch behind us, or I will have your neck, do you hear me?"

"Yes, Colonel, at once," the navigator replied and strapped himself into the tail gunner's turret. Almost at once, Haselton's nose gunner ripped into *Amerike*'s tail again, killing the German before he could fire a shot. Janzig felt the bullets rip into the bomber's tail and smelled smoke.

"Goddamn it," he screamed, "get this bastard off of us!"

The words were hardly out of his mouth when the left gunner on Haselton's airplane finally found *Amerike*'s left wing, spraying both its portside engines with incendiary bullets. The inboard engine caught fire immediately, whipping flames against the fuselage. It was only a matter of seconds before the outboard engine was engulfed as well.

Robbed of half his propulsion and fighting terrific asymmetrical thrust that threatened to turn the bomber upside down, Janzig struggled desperately to regain control of his airplane. With black smoke now pouring out his portside wing, he pulled back on the control yoke, frantically urging *Amerike* higher. "We can still make it!" he screamed into the microphone. "Return fire! I demand it!"

Despite Janzig's efforts, the giant bomber was slow to gain altitude with half its power gone. Haselton suddenly saw the black beast rear up in front of him, presenting a perfect target. Without hesitation, all its guns blasting, Haselton's V/1500 bore down upon the doomed German masterpiece, looking for the kill. Incendiary rounds flew toward the bomber so thickly that they appeared to form a blazing path right up to the airplane. Without warning, *Amerike* exploded in a massive fireball that spread out a hundred yards in every direction.

The blast caught Haselton and Allen Brighton directly, exploding through the cockpit windshield of their straining Handley Page. Neither one of them had a second to consider what they had done, that their sacrifice had insured the success of their daring mission. The lead V/1500 exploded a second later in another great fireball that lit up the morning sky over Lipetsk even as the smoldering remains of *Amerike* littered the banks and the surface of the Voronezh River with burning debris. It was not far from where the lives of Major William Markham and Sergeant Roy Evans had been extinguished earlier that morning.

Their mission complete, the thirteen surviving R.A.F. bombers turned for home, flying low over the wreckage of their Wing Commander's V/1500. Every man among them, God-loving or God-fearing, felt compelled to utter a prayer for their souls and to wonder if what they had accomplished today was worth the blood it had required.

Epilogue
June 13, 1927

Sitting beside New York City Mayor James J. Walker atop the back seat of Official Car No. 1, a large, open, black Cadillac touring car flanked by uniformed policemen on horseback, Charles A. Lindbergh forced a smile. The car moved slowly through a blizzard of cheers, paper scraps, and tickertape raining down on him from adoring spectators in lower Manhattan office buildings and brokerages. He looked out over a sea of New Yorkers who lined the city streets. They had come to celebrate his triumphal return to the United States. As the car stopped momentarily at City Hall, some ten thousand school children, gathered from the public schools, sang "Hail the Conquering Hero Comes" to the dazed and embarrassed pilot.

Lindbergh was astonished by the outpouring of emotion he saw on every street corner on the faces of more than four million people who had turned out for the wildest ticker tape parade the world's biggest city had ever witnessed. Actually, he was a bit frightened by the reception, which served to remind him that his life would never again be the same. The relative obscurity that had protected his cherished privacy was gone. He was now a figure that had been saluted by European royalty, heads of state and a million Frenchmen who had lined a parade route along the Champs-Élysées. In America he had become a national hero who was the recipient of a U.S. Congressional Medal of Honor, joyful parades and testimonials. TIME Magazine described him as the most cherished citizen since Theodore Roosevelt when it named him its first Man of the Year.

The Mayor turned to the reluctant hero and nudged his side. "Charles, do you realize how few people have ever been honored this way by the great people of New York?" he asked. "None other than Admiral Dewey, Black Jack Pershing, Teddy Roosevelt, Bobby Jones ... hell, kings, queens, princes and dukes. You're in mighty fine company, Son. What do you have to say for yourself?"

Lindbergh stared back at the smiling Mayor. He had no idea how to respond.

From the instant the landing gear of his beloved *Spirit of St. Louis* touched down at the Le Bourget Aerodrome in Paris on the night of May 21, 1927, he had quite literally become the most famous man on the planet. The quiet, shy and unassuming country boy from Little Falls, Minnesota, who had previously aspired to be a country's best air mail pilot, had become the entire world's greatest living hero.

Unbeknownst to Lindbergh, a different kind of salute occurred on the same day as the euphoric celebration in New York in three nations a continent away. There weren't crowds of people at these ceremonies. Indeed, few people even knew they were taking place.

In the small Irish port village of Dingle Bay, a quiet service was held at St. Mary's Catholic Church, overlooking the tip of the Dingle Peninsula, for the fisherman, Seamus McGill. Many of the villagers attended, wanting to say goodbye to the lonely man they had known either by name or face. They had all known him as their fellow parishioner, the late Mary Elizabeth McGill's husband. There was no body to consecrate or mourn. The man simply never returned from the sea and was presumed lost.

There were few tears for the grizzled seaman, whom the dedicated Catholics all assumed was happy to join his

Mary in everlasting peace, save for his three children, who were devastated by his loss.

In the back of the church, a lone man dressed crisply in the blue uniform of an Officer in His Majesty's Royal Navy stood in homage, silently praying for a man he barely knew but for whom his respect ran deep and eternal. For British Commander David Culloch, McGill's loss was a bitter pill, for he felt a personal responsibility for the old man's death. *If only he'd known what his sacrifice would mean to so many,* he thought, regretting that he had not shared with the humble fisherman more about the importance of his courage to the nations of Europe and America. He left the church silently, hat in hand, with the secret of Seamus McGill's courage intact.

At the French military airfield on the Normandy coast in Caen, France, the entire base complement turned out for a memorial service for twenty-one-year-old *Aviateur de Première Classe* pilot Hénri Clavel, who had died defending Lindbergh from the Germans near the Irish coast.

The bells of Saint-Pierre Church in the center of Caen pealed as the base commander ordered a minute of silence for the fallen warrior, whose body had not been recovered from the Atlantic Ocean. Lieutenant Didier Michaud, commander of the squadron that had intercepted the Germans and flown cover for the American pilot, gave the eulogy. Of those present, only he, the surviving pilots of his squadron, and the base commander were aware of the circumstances of Clavel's death.

As Michaud spoke before the long rows of standing soldiers in their dress uniforms, a long, black, closed limousine pulled up near the ceremony. From it emerged French President Doumergue, who had made the long drive from Paris to attend the service.

Michaud stopped at the sight of Gaston Doumerge. "Monsieur President," Michaud said in genuine surprise, "it would be my honor, if you wish to speak."

Gaston Doumerge looked over the French soldiers and shook his head. Removing his hat, he replied, "Thank you, Lieutenant. But Hénri Clavel was a soldier who paid the supreme sacrifice for France and deserves the praise of his colleagues and his nation. He deserves better than the hollow words of a politician. Please, carry on."

In Britain, at Portsmouth City, Hampshire, at the headquarters of the Royal Naval Marines and the south coast's Royal Air Force contingent, more than five hundred officers and enlisted men from the two military units gathered to pay homage to their sixteen brethren who had given their lives in the battle of Lipetsk.

Among the mourners were the twenty-three prisoners of war who had been liberated by Major William Markham, Sergeant Roy Evans and a small squad of commandos, British Prime Minister Stanley Baldwin, and United States Secretary of State Frank B. Kellogg, representing President Calvin Coolidge.

"...Wing Commander Tony Haselton ... Lieutenant Allen Brighton ... Sergeant Robert ..." The silence was deafening as the name of each man, including the crews of the two R.A.F. bombers lost during the Lipetsk raid, was read aloud by Prime Minister Baldwin. The air was filled moments later by a sole bugler who played the funereal "Last Post," which had been written for a soldier's funeral during the Great War, and "The Rouse," signaling the end of the day. Three wooden-wheeled, iron cannons were fired seven times each in a twenty-one-gun salute.

The aging Prime Minister, who himself had served only briefly as a Second Lieutenant in the Malvern, Worcestershire Artillery Volunteers and hated guns, flinched at each explosion. So did civilians all over the

United Kingdom when simultaneously, twenty-one-gun salutes were inexplicably fired at Hyde Park, the Tower of London, York, Edinburgh and Stirling Castles in Scotland, Cardiff in Wales and at Hillsborough Castle in Northern Ireland. When the British press clamored for a reason for the display, Baldwin's spokesman offered only that "it was a military exercise in timed precision," an official statement that sounded good while meaning nothing. The matter was dropped.

For his part, Charles Lindbergh, the world's hero and newsreel idol, never knew of the efforts of so many to protect him from an enemy he had not offended. Indeed, his only crime against the German Republic was the fact that he was not a German. Protected from the secret of the supreme sacrifice that others had made so that he might live, he struggled only with the demise of his freedom from celebrity.

As well, the humble country boy could not have guessed that he was the unwitting instigator of a plan crafted by evil men to use mass murder as a weapon to secure their dream of a global empire.

The fires over Lipetsk burned for two days before the ashes of Germany's latest attempt at human supremacy cooled at last. In the days that followed, winds off the Voronezh River grabbed hold of the delicate gray matter that was once bricks and mortar, metal and flesh, and thrust it up into mountains of soft white clouds, where it was absorbed into the jet stream.

Weeks later, having ridden heavenly winds around the earth, microscopic particles of the battle carefully hidden from the world rained gently down over fields and forests and cities, continents away.

In New York, some of the dust landed on the head of a small boy who was licking the top of an ice cream cone his dad had bought him as they strolled down Broadway, father and son exulting in the fleeting but exquisite relief of a day without care, in a world without war.

About The Author

 **F. Mark Granato's** thirty year career as a corporate executive in a Fortune 50 company brought with it extensive international experience in the aerospace and commercial engineering and building fields. Now that he has served his time, he is finally fulfilling a lifetime desire to write and especially to explore the "What if?" questions of history. In addition to "Beneath His Wings: The Plot to Murder Lindbergh", he has published "Of Winds and Rage" and "Titanic: The Final Voyage". He writes from Wethersfield, Connecticut, with the help of a large German Shepard named "Groban", who occasionally asks probing questions.